I0788531

Ship's Champion

Feb 7 , 2024

by

Brian P. Emerick

Table of Contents

Chapter 1
Challenging the Master

Eyes squinting, Choundry stood reveling in the breeze blowing the tatters of his travel-worn shirt. The sense of all-consuming fatigue lifted for a brief moment as he took in the scent of land, his land, his home. Turning briefly to the sound of rapid footsteps approaching him across the deck of the small brigantine that had been his home for more than three long years, Choundry felt a shiver run up his neck. He turned to face the small man that he had come to detest: Captain Johnston, the ship's master and one of the most purely evil men that Choundry had ever encountered in all his wanderings.

"What do you think yer doin?" the Captain said, with a tone of underlying disgust. "Ain't you supposed to be workin?"

Choundry looked into the man's eyes and answered with every ounce of contempt he could muster, "I've filled my obligations to you," he bluntly stated, "Our deal was for three years of honest labor. What you've tried to get me to do hasn't always been honest, but I've given you your three years and more, and today's the day I take my leave of you and this ship. Beyond this coast lies my home, and I'm for shore as soon as you put into port."

His hand cocked, rigidly gripping a thick rope starter that he had used on Choundry mercilessly over the past three years, Johnston stood his ground, his face betraying a deadly intensity. He was sweating, and Choundry could hear the faint sounds of teeth grinding as the Captain tensed in that all too familiar way that preceded his lashing out with the hated whip.

Choundry voiced, "And I'll not idly take a beating from you anymore either. I've taken it from you all these years as it is the law of the sea. I've needed to endure your cruelty so that I could get back home, but know now that I'll not tolerate it any longer. Hit me with that starter, and I'll break your back, you scum."

Johnston leaned forward, his body swayed as he strained against his anger and something he hadn't felt in a long while: fear. He looked into the eyes of the man that he had bullied for so long. He realized that he'd grown to fear Choundry's physical strength, a lithe, powerful frame that had grown and filled out over the past three years of hard and grueling labor. Years in which Johnston had been able to gradually make do with fewer crew working his ship as he forced this young man and his friends to greater efforts.

The seconds ticked past. Choundry could feel the wrath of the little man building and almost overflowing into brute violence. Abruptly, the moment passed. Johnston seemed to shrink in on himself as he glanced sideways at two other crew members who'd been listening intently to the confrontation. The cracks and weaknesses in the ship's master had been revealed. It wouldn't be forgotten that he could be backed down. Johnston's tyranny of his crew had ended. The rules of these rough men were simple; they would follow anyone they believed in, but they demanded their leaders be as strong as the oak that was used to build their ships. They would face any storm in a ship that they believed to be strong, but a weak leader, like a ship that had proved to be flawed or weakened at a critical juncture, couldn't be trusted. A captain who showed fear was not to be trusted or obeyed. Johnston knew that he had made a mistake. He faltered and appeared to reconsider confronting Choundry again, but the moment had passed. In a fury of frustration, the Captain turned and cursed at the other seamen to return to their duties.

Choundry turned again toward the distant outline of the shore. After a second's hesitation, he heard those same footsteps receding back along the deck of the ship. The sound of the footfalls grew slower and fainter. Choundry looked ahead again and began to notice details of the oncoming coastline. Small hills, the tops of individual trees outlined against the morning light. He couldn't see anything familiar as yet but he could sense the pieces of vague memories starting to stir and come together. The smell of the land was faint, but he could clearly detect the musty fumes coming from the lowland swamps that dotted this part of the coast. He couldn't be sure, but the hill to the north of where they were heading had a familiar angle to it, one that made him remember days of scrambling among rocks along with his brother and cousins. His thoughts touched on those long-ago days when they would yell in excitement, each competing to find the greatest discoveries: caves, special shells, or interesting bits of flotsam washed up by the waves. The simple joy of good friends and a day free to explore a vastly exciting world. He felt a sudden pang of loss as it struck him that life would never be that simple and carefree again, that joy would never be so pure again or so easy to feel. Even coming home after so long an absence, he knew that any joy of homecoming would be less than what he'd dreamed of during his ordeals.

A melancholy descended on him for a moment as he fell again into the same worries that had surfaced again and again as to what he might find upon his return. He returned to an awareness of his surroundings with a small jerk of his head. He would not fear the future that he had dreamed of: let whatever happen that might happen, he would deal with it when it came.

It was time to gather his belongings and prepare for his leave-taking from the ship. He had several friends among the crew, the kind of friendships that were forged through sharing hardships and dangers. Three years of voyaging throughout the world, constantly traveling from port to port carrying whatever someone would pay to have transported or whatever could be stolen or cheated from the unwary. Facing the screaming mid-ocean storms where the waves would knock men overboard in the briefest of moments. Choundry took a moment to remember one such storm where he had to stand at the aft railing, looking back at a face that he'd known well and counted as a good friend as the ship moved forward and away, unable to turn or attempt a rescue. Seeing the look in his friend's eyes, he realized that the relative safety and security of the ship had been traded for a sure and lingering death. These were the same men who he had stood shoulder to shoulder with to repel pirates and to battle other ship's crews. They faced not only the dangers of the sea but also the ports of call where men could go missing, and no one would bother to search for them. Places where, if you didn't have your friends along, you might end up floating face down in the morning tide.

He and these men had shared many an adventure together, but they had also shared the back-breaking work and the cruel treatment aboard ship. The eyes of those he passed showed a mixture of emotions. Faces were sad, eyes misty, but some showed anger at one of their own leaving. Some faces showed something else, too: a yearning to have what he had, a place to return to, a place to call home. These were the men who had lived so long on the sea that they no longer knew of anyone who cared for them or who cherished their memory. It was from listening to these men that he had resolved to return home and put his back to the sea. He had promised himself that he would return to those he loved before he had been forgotten or given up totally for dead. He yearned for the strength of roots, of knowing that someone cared whether he made it home at night. He would see a friendly face upon walking into a taproom or pass someone in the street and enjoy the warm feeling of unexpected friendship resumed.

He felt the thrill of excitement long suppressed. He had been afraid to think of a homecoming because of the pain that the memories and worry would bring. He had learned to push it to the back of his mind and go about his duties. But now, with home in sight, he allowed his thoughts to run free. If anyone that he loved were still in this town, they would certainly be surprised to see him return from what must surely have seemed to be certain death. Although he had tried to write several times, the thought of the pain that such a letter would bring had stayed his hand. Yes, they would have long ago accepted his loss.

Chapter 2
Foul Beginnings

He thought again of the fight that he had gotten into three years earlier: his last day in this land. Choundry had thrashed a man for some crude remark that he had made to his sister, Catherine. The man had seemed vaguely familiar as Choundry passed him on the street. When Choundry heard him voice several words low and to Catherine, he turned to see Catherine blushing furiously as she pressed herself to him for protection. Choundry asked the man what he had said, and he replied, "I only offered to pay her more than you." Sensing Choundry's seething silence, the man said, "Come now, the girl could obviously do with a little more coin."

Choundry glanced at his sister to see that this barb regarding the state of her clothing had sunk deep as well. In a fury that included his sense of frustration at how unfair life had been for his family since his father died, he struck out and felt his fist make solid contact with the man's chin. The man crumpled to the street, but he quickly regained his feet and rushed towards Choundry with his fists raised. It was as if he were engaged in one of those prize-fighting contests that Choundry had seen at the local fairs. Catherine yelled her alarm, but Choundry had been in too many street brawls to think that fighting had any rules. He shot his foot out, connecting with the man's knee, and he heard a loud popping sound that was immediately followed by a howl of pain from his opponent. He followed that up with a quick jab to his nose that soon started a stream of blood flowing down his chin. The man fell to the ground and curled into a ball, all the while emitting a small whining noise. Choundry took a moment to look to the faces of those in the crowd that had formed to watch the confrontation. Although he saw a few familiar faces of those he counted as friends, he saw that most of the onlookers wore expressions of shock or disgust.

Realizing that he had better get Catherine home before anything else happened, he turned and started pushing through the crowd. As he did, he saw his friend Patrick move to his side. With a backward glance that betrayed a nervousness, Patrick said, "You'd better move a lot faster. Do you know who that man is that you just crippled?." With a glance to his right, Patrick said, "Why, he's none other than Jason Burke, the son of Robert Burke, who owns the biggest plantation in the region."

Choundry remembered now where he'd seen the man before, and the memory included several people sitting in a carriage as it was pulled by four fine white horses. He could see the townspeople doffing their hats or nodding their heads in mute respect and homage to the occupants of the carriage as it slowly rolled past. With a sinking feeling, he realized that this time, his temper may have really been his undoing. Cursing to himself, he continued on his way to his family home, Catherine following closely.

Rounding the corner a block from his home, he chanced to glance back and caught a glimpse of a man who attempted to duck behind a side building. Choundry's nervousness mounted. He decided that, to be safe, he would make sure that he didn't lead trouble directly back to his family. He pulled Catherine beside him and instructed her to go into the apothecary on the corner and ask Mr. Milner, the owner if she could use the back door to exit. He stressed to her that she must make it home as quickly as possible and warn his brother Kyle as to what had happened and to beware.

Upon leaving Catherine, Choundry moved slowly for another block to ensure that the fellow following him had ample opportunity to stay with him rather than turn back to follow Catherine. Choundry led him several blocks in a wandering course through the old town until finally, he ducked down a side street, crab-walked under the boardwalk across the square, and emerged in the alley that he and his brother had used so often in their adventures through town. After but a quick several minutes of rapid walking, he reached the rear of his family home. Ducking in, he glanced down both directions of the street and was sure that he hadn't been followed. Feeling slightly better about his prospects, he grinned in relief as he stepped into the parlor. His brother Kyle was waiting for him. The grim expression on Kyle's face warned him to silence as he moved into the room and then spotted his friend Patrick seated in the corner sedan. With a sense of alarm, he realized that should Patrick not have taken care, then his efforts at evading his followers may have been for naught. Rushing to the window, he pushed aside the curtain enough to glance out onto the street only to see several people moving about and talking, several of whom he did not recognize. With a sigh, he let the curtain go and turned back to the room. His brother's accusing stare met him along with the even more disturbing sight of his mother sobbing quietly into a cloth.

"What have you done now, brother?" Kyle stood and paced forward to within a hand's reach of Choundry. At first, he looked as if he would continue forward but stopped and waited for a reply. Choundry looked to those within the room and stated.

"Patrick and Catherine will have told you what happened," he said defiantly. "I acted to preserve the honor of our sister."

His brother's look changed slightly to include a touch of sadness. "Will you never grow up?" he said with a sigh. "We aren't little boys playing at games. Your actions will bring ruin down upon this family just as we were finally repairing the misfortunes that befell us following Father's passing."

Choundry knew how hard his brother had worked to rebuild the family fortunes. When his father passed, he took with him the silversmith skills that his family's income had relied upon. His brother, barely an apprentice at the time, had worked hard to do his best, but his fledgling skill was not up to the standards of those who had come to expect the artistry that his father had produced. As a result, business had fallen away until they could barely find the means to fill the table with the evening meal. Choundry had tried his best to seek work, but nothing consistent could be found. It had been a rough several years, but gradually, the natural skills that his father had passed to Kyle had begun to emerge, and his services were more frequently sought out for more than crude repairs. Choundry now realized that his actions might end in enraging the very social class that his brother relied upon for his business.

Further arguments regarding the reasons for his behavior died on his lips. Choundry looked from his brother to his mother. Upon seeing her tears, his resolve weakened. Standing before his mother, as he had so often in the past when he had done some childish wrong, Choundry looked down, unable to meet her eyes. He said, his defiance melting away, "I'm sorry, Mother, I didn't think what consequences my actions might have. I acted in anger. It seemed so unfair…… I couldn't stand to see Catherine shamed in public…… since father passed away. These people have been smirking behind their hands at our misfortunes. I …"

Whatever else he might have said was left off as his sense of failure was replaced by a need to make things right. What could he do? How could he protect those he loved?

"I must go to Mr. Burke before he does anything to this family," he said. "I must place myself before him and explain what happened, and I will face whatever punishment is fit, and if the man has any heart, he will be satisfied with his pound of flesh."

He turned to Patrick and motioned for him to follow. As he moved to the door, he could hear Catherine's pleading voice trying to persuade Kyle to stop Choundry from leaving. With a sense of bitterness, he noticed that he heard no words from his brother as he stepped through the front door and out onto the street. Little did he know that those brief moments would be the last that he would spend with his family for several years.

Striding down the street, moving back in the direction toward where the earlier altercation had occurred, Choundry turned to Patrick," Where do you think that I might be able to meet Mr. Burke?."

After a moment's pause, Patrick offered, "I wouldn't think it would be a good idea to see him at this moment, and he will still be full of anger. It might be best to wait a bit and make a formal request to see him to explain what happened."

Choundry could see the wisdom in allowing the initial shock of the moment to pass and allow cooler heads to prevail. He said, "Here, Patrick, I will write a note to Mr. Burke requesting a meeting with him at a public place so that everyone can see that I have faced up to my actions. If you would be so kind as to carry it to his lodgings and present it to one of his staff, I will find a place to wait until the time is right."

Patrick agreed to carry the message. Choundry took paper from his pocket and, stopping at the neighbor's dry goods store to borrow the use of a pen, he wrote a quick message in as formal a tone as he could manage. Patrick hurried off, paper gripped tightly in his hand. Choundry took a moment to be thankful for the support of his friend. Patrick had always been a strong ally over the years in the various adventures they had shared. His friend had a natural sense of flair when sticking up for those he felt were wronged.

Moving to a small tavern on the outskirts of town, Choundry sat in the back and ordered a small beer. He placed his hands around the flagon to stop them from fidgeting. As the time passed slowly, he ran over in his mind what he would say to Mr. Burke. His thoughts ranged from begging for mercy to implausible stirring speeches whereby Mr. Burke would surely be swayed by the cheering of the crowds. Finally, as the time drew near, he ended his musings still mystified as to what he could say other than to explain to the great man exactly what had happened and hope that he was a man of honor.

As he left the tavern, Choundry noticed that it was getting to evening, and the sky was overcast. Light was fast disappearing as he moved along the streets towards the inn where he suspected Mr. Burke would have his lodgings. The walk took a matter of a quarter of an hour but by the time he reached a point a few blocks from his destination, it was full dark. Looking ahead, he could just begin to make out the lights of the inn when he heard light steps rushing up behind him. Without thinking, Choundry turned and twisted, bringing his arm up instinctively. It was the slight bending of his right knee that saved him from a much more severe injury; as it was, he sensed a large bulky form moving quickly down on him, as well as felt a slamming blow to the left side of his forehead. At first, all he could see was a blackness that was shot through with flashes of brightness. He staggered and felt himself gradually falling to his knees. He raised his arms in an instinctive attempt to prevent further injury, but that only served to allow whoever it was to kick forward into his stomach, forcing him to double over in pain and gasp for air. Voices came from his right….hushed but with a tone of urgency. Some of the words could be heard …….:"be quick and finish him"……."pay for my pain"…."dead"….. Dread filled him then; he didn't want to die ….he lashed out with his fist and felt it hit something solid, followed by a grunt. His vision began to clear, and he could start to see outlines, but just as he started to raise himself to his feet, he felt a massive pain on the back of his head, and then he fell into blackness.

Chapter 3
More Painful Memories

His memories of the next several days were confused, with vague sensations of being dropped, his head hitting something hard, and the taste of blood in his mouth. At one point, he remembered hearing someone yelling close to his face, and then much later, he woke briefly to find himself lying with his face partially immersed in wretched-smelling water. All of these memories were mixed with the sensation of having his arms pinned to his sides and the sounds of cursing and laughing. Gradually, awareness began to return, and he started to recognize shapes as faces that drifted in and out during his brief, pain-filled moments of lucidness. He could remember someone thrusting their face close to his and staring into his eyes as if evaluating him…as if trying to come to some decision.

At last, he was able to drift away into a blessed, undisturbed sleep, a sleep that was deeper than any he had known before. A sleep that, when he finally began to awaken, he tried desperately to regain, if for no other reason than to escape the pounding in his skull. As his consciousness began to return, he started to notice other things: discomfort from something gouging into his back, horrid smells, a gentle rocking sensation, and the sounds of angry sea gulls. Moving his back to ease away from the offending object, he let out an involuntary groan. Soon, he heard the sound of footsteps approaching, and then something poked roughly into his side. A voice said, "It looks like he'll live after all."

He felt rough hands grab him and lift him bodily to his feet. At first, his legs refused to hold him upright, but a raspy voice ordered him to stand, and when he continued to wobble, he felt a slap across his face that made his head feel as if it were about to explode. He steeled himself and pushed up with his legs, and finally, he was able to hold his weight. He still couldn't move his arms, and as awareness started to return, he felt himself being pushed back against something solid. Moments later, someone, using a thick, worn rope, bound him upright in place. Blinking the crust from his eyes, he tilted his head up and began to scan his surroundings.

His first realization was that he was on a ship. With a start, he looked further and then swung his head, first to the right and then to the left…looking for anything that might be familiar, but as far as his eyes could see, all that was visible was water: rolling waves and white crests. All around him was activity, men scurrying about with their eyes focused forward. Occasionally, he would see one man strike another with what looked like a small whip. Often, these strikes would be accompanied by cursing and threats. He struggled against the ropes and then realized that he was tied to a mast, one of three on the ship. After a few minutes of looking around, he heard a voice behind him say, "Well, look what we have here, the gentleman has finally decided to grace us with his presence."

Emerging into view from his right, a scraggly-looking man of medium build strode past him and turned to stand with his face looking up into Choundry's. The man sported several days growth of beard, and he had the greasiest hair Choundry had ever seen. He stood for a moment glaring into Choundry's eyes, and gradually, a smile formed on his lips, a smile that bodes nothing but ill. The smile revealed a mouth full of uneven, stained teeth with at least one broken off and jagged.

The man pulled himself up to his full height and said, "Now listen to me and hear me well, as I'll not say it again. My name is Johnston, but if I ever hear you call me anything but Captain Johnston or Sir, you'll be swallowing your teeth or strung up for a lashing, do ye understand?" When Choundry nodded wearily, he continued: "I took a chance on ye lad, by rights ye should be laying at the bottom of Fulton's Bay right now, and if you're not careful,

I'll change my mind and throw ye overboard with nothing but a cannonball sewn into your jacket. If anyone back there ever finds that I didn't do fer ye, why I'll be facing charges and worse. So, ye see, ye owe me, lad. Ye owe me yer life and more. I saved yer life, and by rights, I can take it any time that I wants to."

Choundry's face must have reflected the questions racing through his mind because Captain Johnston continued, "After yer little crimes ashore, ye rightly should have been taken to the edge of town and hung from the nearest tree. Instead, in order to keep the peace and to save the squire's son the embarrassment of everyone knowing how you'd bested him, it was decided to just make you disappear. That's where good old Captain Johnston comes in. They paid me fair to get rid of your body during the night. I was to take you out with my small boat, weigh you down, and slip you over the edge to find your just desserts, as it were. Lucky fer you, me ship has been running short-handed for a while due to some unfortunate accidents. I decided to take a chance on you and save your worthless skin. Ye owe me, ye see; ye owe me yer life."

After a pause, he continued, "I'm a generous man." The last remark was accompanied by a rattling sound that could have been a chuckle. He went on: "Look around you, ask anyone of these low-life scum; ask em if Captain Johnston ain't a generous, kind-hearted soul."

Choundry looked at the nearest man who was busy half running from the front of the ship, and in passing, the man averted his glance and looked down to the deck as he passed Captain Johnston.

"As I said, I'm a generous man. When I make a bargain, ye can bet yer soul on it. Here is the bargain that I am offering.": at that point, Johnston pulled a rusted blade from the rope belt at his waist and held it in front of Choundry's stomach, the point just touching the skin and bringing a crawling sensation, "I will give you two choices, ye can accept me as your rightful Captain and work off the debt that ye owe me, or ye can refuse. I have to warn ye, though, that if ye refuse, I'll have no use for a useless mouth to feed. In which case, you'll be getting what I should have given ye and as what was promised to the Squire."

Choundry worked his mouth and tried to moisten his lips. He haltingly found his voice and asked, "What debt do I owe you?."

Captain Johnston's eyes started to harden, and he inched forward, the tip of the blade just beginning to pierce Choundry's skin. Choundry added, "Captain Johnston, sir."

This seemed to mollify the man, and he smiled briefly. "Three years of hard work at half wages ought to be fair. In exchange I'll feed ye more than you'll deserve, let you purchase slop trousers and jackets whenever yours wear out, and I'll teach ye discipline and how to be a proper seaman. At the end of three years, you'll be a free man. What do ye say? Do we have a deal?"

Choundry's head was spinning, everything had happened so fast. It seemed that one moment he was walking the streets of his town, and now he was strapped to a ship and being told to choose between death or years of servitude! How had this happened? Captain Johnston leaned forward and, with a foul breath and a hard edge to his voice, continued: "Usually when I take a man into servitude, I brand him to seal the bargain so's he won't soon forget, ye seem to be of better stock than most, I will allow that. If you give me your sworn word to serve the agreed term, I'll forgo the branding, but if I think for a minute that you are planning to run on me, I'll gut you for the worthless cur you'd be…now, as I said; do we have a bargain?"

Choundry knew that he had no choice, and it grated his very being to say the words, but he finally blurted out, "Yes, as I see that I have no real choice, you have my word to serve you for three years. Know, though, that when that time is over, I will be free, and if I choose to return to my home, that will be my choice to make." Captain Johnston breathed in and, for the span of several heartbeats, seemed to hold his breath. The point of the blade pressed slightly harder into Choundry's stomach, starting a trickle of blood trailing down. After a moment's hesitation in which Choundry began to worry that his hard-headedness had finally been his downfall, the Captain breathed out and pulled the blade back and replaced it into his belt. He said, "Yer in no condition to work today, but I'll have no one laying in bed while others work, you'll hang here until it's dinner time. Be ready to work tomorrow, or you'll feel the whip. There is much to learn and ye had better learn it quick."

With that, the Captain turned and walked forward, seemingly forgetting all about Choundry for the next several hours. Choundry could tell by the position of the sun that it was close to midday, and as the hours progressed, he had to endure the sun, a growing thirst, and the gradual onset of nausea from his weakness and the constant motion of the ship. Choundry thought back to his early childhood when he had worked many hours on his uncle's ship as it plied trade along the coast of his homeland and to the surrounding shores. He had enjoyed the hard work and the close friendships that he'd found during those months, times where he learned what he could of the sea life. He knew that there was much that he never had the time or opportunity to learn. Realizing now that his future would depend to a large extent on his ability to fit in and find a place here, he'd started to study the movements of the crew and watched how they interacted so that he could discover what would be expected of him. He watched the men who toiled at the tasks on the deck and were constantly under the eye and the ever-darting, short whips of what must be the Captain's senior men. He also noted that some of the sailors were able to move away and gain what seemed to be the most privacy possible on the small confines of a wooden ship. These men swung up and quickly climbed the ropes, moving nimbly up without seeming to pause as they reached the first set of sails. He watched these men and promised himself that he would learn whatever it took to survive here, that he would make it through his "debt" and live to return to his family. His rash behavior had gotten him into this mess, but at least his family would be freed from any reprisals from the Squire's men if they thought him dead.

Later that day, one of the men came forward and started to untie Choundry. "Cap'n doesn't allow us any knives, so this may take a while. He said. After a few minutes of the man's fumbling, Choundry felt the ropes loosen. He was able to catch himself from pitching forward as his legs started to buckle once his full weight was released. Standing up fully, he stretched his back and could feel some of the soreness starting to loosen. The sailor waved for him to follow as he shuffled onward. Choundry could smell food somewhere in the ship, and his stomach reminded him that he hadn't eaten in what must have been at least a full day. Other men in the crew seemed to be working their way to the rear of the ship, so he moved in that direction, merging into the small crowd as it moved slowly forward. At one point, someone shoved a small wooden bowl into his hands along with what appeared to be an ancient, battered spoon. As he neared a man who stood ladling some greyish matter from a large pot, he heard, "Move along, move along, there's others waiting." As his turn came, he thrust forward the bowl to have it filled only partway. When he looked into the man's eyes, he received a sneer and response that "full meals only goes to those who give a full day's work; be happy with what ye have." Choundry stepped to his right and followed the back of the next sailor as he moved forward. Each man seemed to be moving about to find some spot on the ship to sit. Choundry remembered that, on his uncle's ship, the men had been allotted a bench that could be erected at mealtimes and would allow them to sit in small groups or "messes." These men surrounding him now didn't seem to have the energy to talk and even seemed to lack the will to group together except in twos or threes. Choundry found what appeared to be a spot that no one else was planning to use, and he sat to eat his meal. As he started to eat, his gorge rose several times on the greasy mess that he found in his bowl. Since his father's death, Choundry had gotten used to eating meals that most others would turn their noses up to, especially when he wanted to leave what was there for his mother and sister. He forced himself to eat every bit of the food to make sure that he had sufficient strength for what was to come.

The next several days were worse than Choundry had expected, but he was able to eventually stay slightly ahead of the small whip or "starter," as he learned it was called. He learned to run when a task was ordered and to not be the last man to get there. He learned the names of several of his fellow crew members and what might be expected of him throughout the day. Captain Johnston kept to himself, watching his crew and the workings of the ship. He would often be looking out to sea or scanning the sails. Occasionally, he would call an order, either forwarding it or sending it to someone up in the rigging. The ship's routine seemed to have been established long ago, and Choundry found that his life was tolerable as long as he worked hard and stayed one step ahead of the men with the starters.

Several weeks had passed, and the routine was settled and somewhat predictable. Choundry was losing weight and becoming even leaner than he had been, even though he'd never had much extra weight to him. His shoulders were broadening, and he could just begin to match some of the men in the performance of some of the more demanding tasks. Two of the crew he could now deem to be his "friends," although the life aboard the "*Merlin*" did not lead one to be too friendly. Darcy was a man of medium build and a dark complexion. He'd been with the ship for three seasons and told Choundry that he planned to try and find another ship whenever a chance presented itself. "This ain't no happy ship, but trying to get yer pay from Captain Johnston is nye on impossible, so I guess I'll have to leave empty-handed," he said.

Darcy was a "topman" who enjoyed his freedom in the upper regions of the ship. Andy was a small man who said that he was originally from Cornwall. He seemed reluctant to talk of his home, and whenever others brought up the subject of their families, he would get a far-off look in his eyes and would often get up and move away. Choundry sensed a sadness in the man that seemed to fill his eyes and deaden the tone of his voice. Andy was often on the receiving end of the "starter," and the senior crew seemed to take delight in cursing Andy in their attempts to get him to move about his work a bit quicker. Andy had been with the ship for five years, and he seemed to have accepted his fate and his position on the ship. Choundry was on the same watch as both of these men and, as a result, they started to eat their meals together. Choundry was invited to move his cloth hammock closer to his new friends.

Chapter 4
Life Aboard the *Merlin* and Banti-Town

The *Merlin* was a small three-masted ship that seemed to make a living with trade along whatever route might take them to their next cargo. So far, the ship had made two ports, one in Lisbon and the other along some dark coast where they put in for water and supplies. At the second stop, the Captain had gone ashore overnight, but the crew were not allowed off the boat, not that anyone was interested in going ashore with the scarred savages who seemed to be watching and waiting for something to happen. At one point, the Captain emerged from the trees and was seen to be walking rapidly down to the ship's boat. He wasted no time in shoving off, making swift passage back to the ship. As Captain Johnston boarded the ship, he seemed to be very excited. Once he'd taken a moment to swallow down a glass of wine, he started calling orders to get the ship underway. Choundry was surprised when the Captain ordered the ship to sail southward instead of heading out to sea to make their way back along their previous course. For several days, the ship hugged the shore, moving slightly out to sea as nightfall would come, almost as if the Captain were afraid of what might be hidden in the dark, forbidding jungles that covered the coastline.

At the end of the eighth day of travel, a small sail was seen just on the horizon and along the same general course as the *Merlin*. The Captain ordered that the sails be shortened, and the boat slowed as they went into the early evening. On this night the *Merlin* did not move out to sea as was her usual practice but rather continued on her course. A few hours after dark, the Captain ordered all lights extinguished and threatened a lashing to anyone who raised their voice above a whisper. As the night progressed, he ordered his senior crew forward to his cabin. All other crew were ordered to stay on deck and be ready for duty. At one point, as the night progressed, Choundry was sitting with Andy as the Captain and his picked men emerged from his cabin. They moved forward and stood together, whispering to one another. Eventually, Choundry noticed a distant light along the coast. The Captain noticed the light as well and passed the word for silence among the crew. Several men loosened the ship's boat and lowered it to the water to trail by a rope. As the light neared, Choundry could start to make out several buildings and what appeared to be a series of docks. At that point, all sails were taken in, and the ship began to wallow as it lost headway.

The Captain and six of his crew then moved aft and, pulling the boat close to the ship, they clambered aboard and began slowly rowing in toward the distant shore. After that, it was just blackness and the steady rhythm of the waves. The crew lolled on the deck, waiting and wondering what was happening ashore. Just when Choundry thought that he could discern gradual lightening on the horizon, he heard distant shouts and what sounded like several gunshots being fired, followed by a period of quiet that lasted approximately half an hour. A small fire sprung up ashore, and shortly after that, Choundry could hear orders being passed; silence seemed to no longer be an issue. They began to move forward again and coasted slowly along until the ship was roughly directly out from the bonfire ashore. As the light continued to grow, Choundry could make out several huts and one large central building with a pier attached. Tied to the pier, Choundry could make out two small ships; one had two masts and was roughly half the size of the *Merlin,* and the other was a much smaller single-masted vessel. There was activity occurring on the pier, and several individuals could be seen carrying objects and boxes down to the larger of the two ships. Shortly after that, both ships began moving out from shore.

The *Merlin* got underway and quickly added sails until it cut through the swells at a rapid pace. The other two ships fell in behind the *Merlin*. They continued on for the rest of the day and on into the night. Midway through the next day, a lookout called down that smoke could be seen along the shore and back beyond the sheltering jungle. As they drew near to the source of the smoke, Choundry saw the mouth of a small river emerging. At first, it seemed much too small for a ship of the *Merlin's* size to enter, but as the ship turned toward this opening, it became apparent that Captain Johnston planned to enter. These must be very familiar waters to the Captain as he didn't even bother to place a man in the front to call out depth soundings. The ship had to maintain a good bit of headway as it entered the mouth of the river in order to counteract the force of the oncoming current. Once inside the mouth of the river, the waterway opened up, and a large cove could be seen to the left. Captain Johnston steered the *Merlin* into this cove. Once out of the direct flow of the river, the waters calmed, and the *Merlin* moved quickly on, making room for the other two vessels following immediately behind. After a few minutes, Captain Johnston called for a shortening of sails and eventually ordered the anchor to be dropped. A small cheer went up from the crew, the first sign of enthusiasm Choundry'd seen from the majority of them since he'd joined the ship.

Andy moved up to stand beside Choundry and whispered, "This Banti-town, ye be careful here, Choundry. Stick close to Darcy and me, and you will be fine. This is a rough port. We've lost more than one shipmate here."

The Captain strode to the middle of the ship and looked around at his crew. Leaning back with his hands on his hips and with a raised voice, he said, "Listen up, lads, this is as close to home as we have. I have some business transactions to complete, and when I do, I will be giving ye a measure of the pay that ye have comin to ya.

Bear in mind, for those who might be interested in leaving this ship and not returnin, that this port is surrounded by a land filled with savages who'll eat the meat from yer bones and fierce creatures who would have ye dead in less than a hunderd steps into the jungle. I'm a generous man, so I'll make sure that ye all get a chance to enjoy the delights of Banti-town, but ye all best remember that yer the crew of the *Merlin,* and when I say to get back aboard ship ye better jump to it or I'll make ye wish ye had."

The Captain then strode to the ladder and was soon on his way to the shore with several of his men. Those who stayed behind were sorted into three groups, and each would go ashore for eight hours and then come back to the ship to relieve the next group so they could take their turns ashore. Choundry stood with Darcy and Andy during the sorting, and they were chosen to stay aboard the ship as part of the third and last group to go ashore. All the time that they were sorting out the groups and assigning duties, Choundry could hear a variety of noises coming from the town. Occasionally, there would be a yell or the sound of a woman's laugh or scream. Shots would sound at various points, and he could hear the sound of what seemed to be a large group of men yelling and arguing. As the afternoon wore on, the ship's boat made a return trip to the ship. As it neared, Choundry could see two men lying in the bottom of the boat between the rowers. As they drew close to the ship, the rowers yelled for a hand from nearby crew members. As they handed up the inert forms, Andy came up to him and said, "That's Darcy's mate, and it looks like he's been stabbed good, and the other fella has a bump on his noggin as big as a beef joint. It's like that here, and these won't be that last of em we'll see today."

A few hours later, the first shift of shore goers returned to the ship. The Captain had made good on his word to pay them their wages, and they had obviously spent a good share of it on rum. Several had to be hauled bodily up and rolled onto the deck. The next group to go ashore had to step over the drunken forms in order to get into the boats. Within a few minutes, Choundry and his friends were left standing amidst a mass of drunken men, most of whom hadn't the ability to stand, and some who could only roll to their sides to retch into the scuppers or stand at the railings casting their freshly bought rum into the waters. Choundry could now see the wisdom of the three shifts: one to go ashore, one to recover, and one to watch over the ship.

Several hours later, the ship's boat again made a trip back to the ship bearing an inert form. This time, the crew seemed somewhat subdued, and as they neared, they called, "It's Smitty. They done for him in the pit." As they raised Smitty's form to the ship, Choundry could see that the man had several wounds, some of them gaping and ragged. Smitty's face was bruised, and it looked as if his mouth was stove in. One of the Captain's men ordered that Smitty be wrapped in canvas and stowed aft in the cable locker "Until we can row him out of the cove and bury him decent."

Andy stood to the side and leaned forward to whisper to Choundry, "Mind what I say and stay with Darcy and me when we go ashore. Smitty thought he was a tough man, but theys more tougher men in that town then ye have ever met in the towns of home."

When the second group returned to the boat, and Choundry and his friends were being rowed ashore, he could feel an excitement building at the prospect of his first steps on solid ground since he'd left his home. Much had happened during the past several weeks, but Choundry had a feeling that he was going to be stepping into a world that he might not be prepared for and that he'd better heed the warnings from his friends. As they stepped ashore, the group seemed to be instinctively holding together as they started walking into town. To their left, a naked woman came running out from a doorway, only to be grabbed around the waist by a wild-haired man and pulled back into the building. The woman's screams changed after a moment into peals of laughter that could be heard echoing from the doorway. There were several men lying in the dirt or propped against buildings, one man snoring loudly as a small boy searched through his pockets. The smells that greeted them as they walked further into the "town" ranged from roasting meat to the near-gagging smell of human waste rising from the ditches and pools of water flowing between buildings and lining the path they followed.

Before they had left the ship, each man was given several coins. Choundry had placed his in his pocket, but some of the others had them clutched tightly in their hands or jingled the coins nervously as they continued on through the town, exploring their options. One of the men who had been with the ship a number of years suggested that they look for "Clara's" for "a bit of a something." After looking further, it seemed that they must have found the drink house that they were looking for, and the group entered. The interior was dimly lit from several windows, although most of those had thatch screens, which were either a sad attempt at making the place presentable or, more likely, a means to keep even a few of the ever-prevalent flies at bay. One man asked if this was "Clara's," and that was met with several titters and open laughs. A woman approached. It was difficult to discern what her age might be as she was probably the dirtiest individual Choundry had ever seen, and her hair was left in wild tangles that hung down in clumps.

"Clara's been dead from the pox fer many a month. I'm Angela, or "Angel," as the lads like to call me. What be yer pleasure…a cup of the finest rum in town, or woulds ya like to spend some time with me or me girls behind the curtains?"

Scanning the room, Choundry was able to see three other individuals who looked vaguely like females. Thinking back to his home and his mother and sister and their carefully brushed hair, their manner of dress, and even their clean smell, he found it hard to imagine that any man would be willing to spend time with these women, even after being aboard ship for months at a time. Several of the men ordered a cup of rum and pushed one of their meager hoard of coins forward. One of *Merlin's* crew grabbed a woman at the back of the room and proceeded back into the curtained area to the calls and laughs of his mates.

Choundry ordered a cup of rum and sipped that slowly, barely tolerating the rawness of the liquor. He was standing next to Darcy and taking in the sights when he heard two men at a nearby table talking about something called "The Pit." One man was bemoaning the loss of his money and asking his fellow to buy him a last drink before they returned to the ship. The other fellow laughed and said, "Tis your own fault fer betting at the Pit. Maybe ye should offer to play, and then maybe ye'll earn your moneys back." he followed this with a raspy laugh and then downed what remained in his cup and stood to leave.

Choundry looked to Darcy and asked, "What is this "Pit" I've been hearing about?" Darcy looked to his side before turning to Choundry, saying, "It is a place where men do battle for money. Bets are made, and at times, the coins involved can be staggering. Ye could buy a manor for what is won or lost in that room."

"The Captain is mad to play and bet at the Pit," he continued. Whenever he gets his hands on any money, we ship down here to Banti-town so the Captain can try his luck. He always loses, and what's more, we always have a number of our crew show up dead the next morning. You stay away from that place and away from the Captain's eye while yer here. Mind me, don't go near the building at the end of this street, as that's where the Pit is located. Ye can't miss it as there's yelling and cursing from that building all day long, as I'm sure ye've heard now and again since we've been here."

Indeed, Choundry had heard the noise, and even now, he could hear a distant sound of discord rising and falling in waves of intensity.

Choundry was no stranger to barroom brawls, and he occasionally participated in wrestling matches when they were set up back home, winning more than his share. During the time that he'd spent with his uncle, some of the crew had played at the new-fangled "boxing" and even practiced with cutlasses "Just in case pirates show up."

Choundry knew that it had been quite a few years since anything resembling a pirate had been seen in his home waters and that the crew was just trying to scare a young man new to the sea, but he participated in these practices, trying his best to soak in what the crew could teach him. Choundry felt that he could hold his own against most men, and the extra bulk that he'd put on since he'd joined the ship made him feel especially fit. After he'd finished his drink, Choundry looked at the few remaining coins in his stash and thought of what he could do with such a meager pittance. It would buy him a few more drinks; he didn't even consider taking one of these girls or any other if they were an example of what could be found in this wretched town.

Choundry gave this some quick thought and decided that he would see if he could purchase another set of trousers to replace the ones that he'd worn since he'd come to the ship. Choundry did not want to eventually be forced by modesty or the elements to have to purchase a pair of trousers from the Captain's locker, especially since the choices all seemed to be worn paper-thin and were mostly from men who'd died in service to the ship. Seeing that Darcy and Andy were both deep in their cups and starting to lean against one another, Choundry figured he wouldn't get much enthusiasm from either of them if he were to suggest looking for a place to purchase clothing.

Choundry asked a man standing to his left where he might find a place to purchase good, strong clothing. The man gave Choundry directions, and a few minutes later, after slipping away from the bar, Choundry found himself standing in front of a hut that had its front wall open to allow passers-by to glance in at the tables of wares set up along each wall and piled in the center of the room. Noticing Choundry's interest, a small man with thinning wisps of hair seemingly plastered to his scalp came scrambling out from behind a low counter. "What'll it be? A pocket knife for fixing yer rigging? Maybe a pair of shoes that would fit you just right? How about a telescope? I gots one of those real cheap, and a man of yer upstanding stature is sure to need one of those."

Choundry told the man that he was merely looking for a pair of strong trousers, and the gleam left the man's eyes, and his smile quickly evaporated. "Looks in the pile yonder on the floor," he said with little enthusiasm. "Find what ye want, and we'll talk."

Choundry searched through the pile and eventually found a serviceable pair of trousers that should last him for quite some time. After bringing it to the store owner, they eventually settled on two of the copper coins that Choundry carried and the trade of the trousers that he currently wore. Choundry had been hoping to have a spare set of trousers, but he couldn't afford much more than the two coppers. As there didn't seem to be any choice or reason for modesty, Choundry paid the man and changed into the new pair of trousers while standing in the middle of his store. As he was starting to leave, he decided to ask the man what the cost of a good clasp knife might be. As it turned out, it was several times what Choundry had left to him.

Upon leaving the store, Choundry stood contemplating what he should do with what remained of his time ashore. He still had several coppers left, but he was not interested in drinking more than his fill, and there didn't seem to be much left to do in this town except patronize other places that might offer the same limited choices. Thinking of a clasp knife, Choundry began to walk the town in search of other stores that might have knives for sale at a price that he could afford. There were only two other buildings in town that sold various articles, and when Choundry inquired, he found that the price asked at the first store had actually been the lowest price that he was able to find. If he wanted the knife, he could try to borrow from Darcy or Andy, but he was loath to owe money to any man.

At this point, he had walked most of the town, and he had unthinkingly wandered close to the building that Darcy and Andy had warned him about. He could still hear the yelling and uproar from those inside. The noise seemed to be building in intensity until it finally reached a fevered pitch and then crashed down into loud cursing and laughing. Clearly, there was some form of betting going on. Previously in his life, Choundry had experienced reasonably good luck betting at the county fairs and the backroad fights and had often walked away with more coin than he'd started with. Choundry hesitated for a moment and then decided to take a look inside the building, thinking, "A quick bet or two, and then I'll either have my knife or be broke. Either way, I can still be back on the ship in time."

As Choundry entered the building, he could see a circular area that was walled off in a small depression in the middle of the floor. Men were sitting in clumps all around the outside of the building. Across the room, he could see Captain Johnston sitting with his men. The Captain was sitting with his head held forward and clasped in his hands. He was rocking back and forth. At that point, Choundry also saw, in the central area, a man almost directly in front of him but mostly hidden behind the short wall. Choundry walked forward and peered down into the ring and was able to see that a second man was lying motionless on the floor. The man was obviously dead. As he looked further, Choundry was able to see that the dead man had suffered several bloody wounds, and where one of his eyes had been, there was nothing but a bloody hole. As he peered at the ruined face, Choundry suddenly realized that the man was familiar to him and, in fact, had been one of his crewmates who had been among the first group to leave the ship. Choundry began to slowly inch back from the edge of the ring and thought to make his way quietly to the door.

As he turned to leave, he saw that he'd been noticed by one of the Captain's men. Choundry made his way to the door and quickly exited. He was several yards down the road when he heard his name being called behind him. He turned to see the Captain's man shouldering his way through the crowd and looking intently at him. "Choundry, the Captain says that he needs you right now," the man said. "You had better get moving now, or he'll not be happy."

Choundry turned and, after a brief hesitation, went back into the building.

Moving his way through the crowd, he eventually made his way over to where the Captain was sitting. As he drew near, the Captain looked up and gave him a long gaze, seemingly trying to decide something. Finally, he said, "Choundry, yer mine for three years, and you'll do as I tells ye, now answer me this; have ye done much fightin where yer from?"

Choundry thought for a moment and replied, "Nothing formal, but I've done my share with the lads in the county."

"Aye, I'll warrant ye have," the Captain replied. "I'll tell ye what I'm going to do; as I'm a generous man, I'm going to teach ye a new skill, and you're likely to make a little coin in the process. Are ye game?"

When Choundry hesitated, the Captain went on, "It don't matter what yer say cause I'm ordering ye to anyway. Here's what yer gonna do. Ya see the man standing in the ring across the way? That be Captain Mason's champion. Now, I really don't like Captain Mason, and he don't like me, so it really boils me blood that the Captain's champion has bested the best men among the *Merlins*. He has also won most of the money from the prizes we brought in today, money that rightly belongs to me and the crew and to you too! In a way, that man has stolen from us all, and I need a brave man to challenge their champion to get it back. Are ye for it?"

Choundry definitely did not want to get into the ring with a man who had beaten his shipmate to death with just his bare hands, but he couldn't see how he could refuse a direct order from the Captain.

Seeing no way out of the dilemma, Choundry responded, "I didn't agree to hire on to fight in a ring. I agreed to work your ship. I'll not do it."

The Captain appeared to be thinking for a minute and then looked to one of his men and said, "Go about the town and find me another one of my crew by the name of Andy. I think that he'll make a good second choice to Choundry here." Knowing that the slow and plodding Andy wouldn't last two minutes in the ring, Choundry reached out to hold the man's arm before he left. The Captain looked over at him with a shrewd look in his eyes and the traces of a smile touching his lips, and Choundry finally said, "I'll do the fighting if those are choices that you lay before me."

As the Captain went off toward another group of men across the room, one of the captain's men pulled Choundry aside and told him, "This be a fight for men of the sea, there are no rules, and it's not over until one man is either dead or out of the fight for certain, no one cries foul, and if you don't win you'll either be dead or crippled. The Captain is going to bet a lot of tin on you, lad, so you'd better fight well for him, or you won't leave this land alive, even as a cripple, most like."

Realizing now just how bad a mess he'd gotten himself into, Choundry started to move toward the ring only to be stopped again by the Captain's man, "Beware this man, he likes to bite ears, and he goes for your eyes if he can, and mind that I saw him close to losing one time, and he pulled a knife and kilt the man he was fighting, knives is against the rules so he lost the round, but he was the one to walk away just the same."

Choundry stepped over the side of the wooden wall and dropped lightly down to the dirt floor of the ring. Looking across the ring, he noticed the familiar face of Darcy peering from the crowd. Choundry tried to smile and then shrugged his shoulders to show his chagrin at the mistake that he'd made. He began to walk to the middle of the ring. His opponent was a big man, scarred about his face and naked torso. The man moved with confidence as he approached in a half crouch, staring intently with an angry glare. The man then stood totally still except for the flexing and opening of his right hand as if he ached to grab something and throttle it. Choundry wasn't sure how the round would begin and was unsure what to do when a voice from the side of the ring called out, "We have a new landsman who just joined the *Merlin*. See the purser if ye'd like to place a bet. The odds are really very good, and ye could win a king's ransom if ye gets lucky, all bets in, all bets in."

With a roar, the crowd surged over to one side of the ring, where several men were standing atop barrels taking bets. The yelling began again and started to build. After a few minutes, when the scene seemed to have frozen in time, the noise from the crowd subsided. Finally, silence descended over the crowd, and the same man who called to the crowd before now yelled, "Attention, all bets are closed. These fine champions are ready to do battle. Let's have the crowd count down."

He raised his arm and then brought it down just as quickly. When he brought his arm down, the crowd yelled in unison, "Ten," then "Nine" and at five, his opponent crouched down and began to circle to his right. At "two," he feinted forward, and Choundry took an involuntary step backward, which brought a smile to his opponent's face. After "one," there came a roar from the crowd that signified the fight was on.

Captain Mason's man rushed forward, obviously hoping to grapple and make it a quick fight. Choundry did a quick sidestep and tripped him as he passed. His opponent fell forward and curled, only to spring up and rush back in. Choundry knew enough not to let this man get a grip on him since he was obviously an experienced brawler, and he could do Choundry serious damage in a short time. Choundry felt that he needed to stay out of this man's grasp and give himself some time to study his opponent to see if there might be any openings or weak points. With a rush, the man came at Choundry with his arms widespread, hoping to grab him and make it a close-in fight. Choundry back-pedaled at which the crowd began to rumble its disappointment. Choundry moved back and to his left just as his opponent reached for his arm. He grabbed the man's right wrist, pulled forward, and twisted, sending the man forward and tumbling into the side wall of the ring. This only served to infuriate the man, who came up with a snarl. He rushed in again in an attempt to force Choundry back into the wall and limit his options for movement.

Choundry knew that he was losing ground and that he would need to do something quick, or he'd be forced into the type of fight he most likely could not win. As the man moved forward, Choundry reversed his direction and stepped forward to swing his right arm in a club-like movement that slammed into the man's left ear. As he connected and tried to step back, the man grabbed his arm and held tight. Choundry felt himself being pulled closer to the man and knew that he was in trouble. He stepped forward and tromped down hard on the man's foot, but this didn't seem to have any effect. He then swung his arm back and brought his elbow slamming back and connected hard with the side of the brute's head. The effect was immediate as the man let go of Choundry's arm and stepped back to shake his head, spraying droplets out from a bloody cut below his left eye. After this, the man was a bit more wary of Choundry, and the sound of the crowd changed as well, as though hushed in disbelief.

Choundry was feeling pretty good; he had connected strongly against his opponent several times and had yet to have any serious damage inflicted, and despite being slightly winded, he felt as if he had a good chance to win. At this point, his opponent started to move in a pattern that prodded Choundry backwards, again trying to limit his options for movement and bring him to grips. Just as Choundry had fallen into the pattern of movement and was slightly lulled, the man rushed forward and kicked into Choundry's left knee. Choundry heard a crack and felt an intense pain in the back of his knee. He jumped back and hopped on his right leg just in time to evade another onrush. He twisted and tried to place his left leg down. At first, the leg would not take his weight, almost buckling under the load. In a moment, he was able to place some of his weight down on the leg, but he knew that he couldn't trust it. His opponent stopped for a moment, spread his arms high and wide, and circled in an attempt to show the crowd that he had Choundry right where he wanted him. The crowd rewarded him with a roar of approval.

Choundry knew that his options, and probably his future, were very limited now. He now could not outmaneuver his opponent, and he couldn't allow him to come to grips. With that realization, Choundry knew he needed to take control of the fight from his opponent by going on the attack. If he had any chance at all, it would be to weaken his opponent enough to offset the advantage Choundry's injured knee had given him. Choundry stepped forward and stood solidly on his sound leg, and brought his right arm up in a solid swing that landed squarely on his opponent's broad grin. He felt the cracking of teeth, and as he stepped back, he could see that he had mashed the man's lips even further. His opponent reeled back and stood bent forward while he spit out blood and bits of teeth. Choundry limped forward and swung again, only to have his blow glance weakly off the side of the man's head as he lurched to the side. The man grabbed out, and before Choundry knew what was happening, he was engulfed in the man's arms and being lifted off his feet.

The crowd roared as if they knew that the fight was close to an end while Choundry arched his back and twisted, trying to break the crushing grip. He could hear a deep rattle coming from his opponent and realized that it was the twisted laugh of a man who enjoyed inflicting pain. Choundry knew he only had moments before he would be unable to break free. He quickly snapped forward again, except this time he led with his forehead and brought it down, crashing on the nose of his opponent, resulting in an instant spraying of blood from his opponent's nose all over both of them. Then Choundry reversed and twisted, moving his lower body back away from contact with the man, and then he slammed his right knee forward and up, making contact directly and ferociously with his opponent's groin. With a scream, the man let go of Choundry and stepped back to cup his ruined nose with one hand and his crotch with the other. Choundry knew that he had been lucky so far and that he should follow up quickly on his temporary advantage, but he stood for a moment to catch his breath and see if his opponent might ask for an end to the fight. Choundry looked to the man and asked, "Do you yield?" to which the man replied in a voice distorted by his pain and his crushed mouth, "Ye don't know this, but we have to fight to the death, or both of us will be kilt. I have to do fer ye, or I'm dead as well."

Choundry had never killed another man in his life, and he had no wish to do so now. He tried to find some way out of this but couldn't. He realized that if he ever wanted to see his family again, he needed to do whatever it took to stay alive; he needed to be a whole man if he ever hoped to avenge the deed that had been done to him.

Choundry crouched down and started stepping forward. His opponent now had a different look in his eyes, and it was no longer Choundry who began to give ground. His opponent was obviously attempting to avoid Choundry's punishing fists. Choundry could feel the man's fear, and he thought that it would be a mercy if he were to end the bout quickly and possibly save the man's life by causing him to become incapacitated enough to end the fight but not kill or severely cripple him. Choundry set himself to move forward and deliver a quick series of hits to the man's head and face, which, hopefully, would send him down. As Choundry moved forward to deliver a quick jab with his left arm, the look in his opponent's eye changed; he could see it go from wariness to a quick look of excitement. Choundry had allowed his attention to be diverted to the man's eyes, and he only realized that something was wrong when he saw the man turn and bring his right arm up from where it had been twisted behind his back. Choundry felt an instantaneous sharp pain in the back of his left arm, and as he pulled back, the pain began to build. He looked down to see his own blood seeping through the sleeve of his shirt and starting to drip down his side. Before he could react to this rapid change in circumstances, he saw his opponent step forward; Choundry instinctively raised his left hand as far as he could to ward off what might be coming. His entire attention shrunk to a small area on the back of his left hand where, all of a sudden, a blade sprouted out with a spray of accompanying blood. Once again, he felt that same sharp pain.

The shouting of the crowd took on a different tone as there was a clear uproar of anger. Choundry tried to push back, but the blade, with his left hand impaled on it, was pushed relentlessly back towards his chest. At this point, as the man lifted up and pushed forward and down, Choundry's left knee buckled, and he went down on his back. His opponent came with him and used the momentum of the fall along with the weight of his body to force the knife down toward Choundry. It all happened so quickly that Choundry barely had time to react, and even when he did, it was too late. He felt the bite of the knife as it entered his chest. The man obviously knew where he wanted the blade as he placed it so that it entered Choundry's chest right above his heart! Choundry could feel the sickening sensation of the blade piercing his flesh and the grating of the blade as it slipped between two of his ribs. The man above him grunted with effort and pushed even harder as Choundry felt blackness rushing in and then knew no more. Blackness engulfed him, and his last thoughts were of his mother and his wish to see her even just one more time.

Chapter 5
The Training Begins

The first thing that Choundry was conscious of was dreaming. In the dream, he struggled with shadowy figures who kept darting in and inflicting pain. Each time, he would try to react, but only to be caught unprepared by the next attack. As the dream started to fade, his thoughts began to coalesce, and Choundry experienced a sensation of surprise that he was unable to think at all. As the dream faded and Choundry's senses began to return, he once again felt the familiar rhythm of the ocean rocking him. The smells and sounds were familiar, as well as the voices that he could hear in the distance; he was back on board the *Merlin*.

How? How does a man survive a blade being sunk into his heart? He could distinctly remember the sensation of being slowly impaled with the knife. He had other injuries as well. As he moved his left hand, he could feel that it was swathed in cloth, and he stopped when he felt an intense pain with the attempt. He shifted his shoulders to a slightly more comfortable position,, but the pain that this brought caused him to release an involuntary moan. He tried to open his eyes, but they were crusted shut, and, at first, he couldn't force them open. He remembered the fight and the blood from his opponent's nose spraying his face. This must be that same blood and grime from the fight. He tried again and was rewarded with first one eye and then the other breaking free and opening. He was in a dark room, but there was light shining from a partially opened door. It took him a moment to realize that he was in the Captain's own cabin. He was having trouble breathing and felt that something was compressing his chest. He moved his right hand up to his chest only to find that his chest, too, was swathed in a bandage. He lay still and tried to collect his thoughts.

Before too long, he heard approaching steps, and Andy stepped into the room carrying a bucket. He laid it next to Choundry and was about to turn and leave when he realized that Choundry was awake.

"Well, bless me, miracles do happen," he said, crouching down and placing his hand on Choundry's shoulder as if to assure himself he really was alive. "I thought ye were dead and gone. Thank the Lord that the Captain decided to wait."

Choundry tried to speak and, after a few strained noises, found his voice; " How did I come here? I thought I was dead for sure."

Andy looked down at him and smiled.

"Mate, I know it was for me that ye stood into that ring. I'll never forget that, ye can be sure." After a pause, Andy said, "Twas, your hand that saved ye." When he saw the puzzlement in Choundry's eyes, he went on, "When that bastard slit ya with that knife and then stabbed ye in the hand with his blade, he pushed into ye trying to carve out yer heart. When we saw you fall as ye did, we thought fer sure that ye was a goner, especially as the blackguard twisted and turned the knife in yer chest like he was carving a Christmas goose. Blood was everywhere. It wasn't until we pulled him from ye and wiped aside some of the blood that we realized that ye were still breathing. The bladé was a killin' blade fer sure, but it was only so long. With yer hand pinned on the blade, it had only a couple of inches showin' to do ye harm with, and I guess that weren't enough to reach all the way down to yer heart. Twas a miracle. I says so then, and I says so now. Ye were meant to live as a reward for yer good deeds."

Choundry lay still for a while after Andy had left, finally drifting back into a fitful sleep until, at some point that must have been around the evening meal, he awoke to the sound of footsteps. Looking up, he saw the Captain enter the cabin. Captain Johnston glanced around and noticed that Choundry was awake.

"Well, it's about time ye were awake. At least now ye will be out of me cabin," he said.

Choundry started to try to sit up, but the Captain told him to lay still.

"Ye've earned a rest, and I need ya to get good and strong for our next meeting with Captain Mason."

The look on Choundry's face must have shown his confusion as the Captain began to explain. "Ye made me a great deal of money by winning yer match like ye did."

When Choundry continued with a puzzled look, the Captain explained, "That cheating slime that was Captain Mason's champion lost the fight the minute that he pulled his pig sticker, he knew that be the case but he also knew that it was his only chance of walking out of that ring on his own two feet. Well, it ended up not mattering anyway as Captain Mason's men was so mad they gutted him on the spot."

Captain Johnston had a distant look on his face as if remembering and reliving some pleasant memory. "Yep, it about kilt Captain Mason to pay up. I'll cherish the memory of the look on his face all year until we meet again for the next fights. That means that we got a whole year to get you better and to train you to beat Mason's next champion. You can bet the next one won't be so easy for ye. So's get yerself better and we'll be setting up your training schedule as soon as yer fit."

Choundry felt a deep sense of despair as he realized that he hadn't escaped his fate, he'd probably just postponed it.

Over the next several weeks, Choundry's strength returned, and he gradually resumed his duties. He started to think that the Captain had forgotten their discussion when one day he was approached by one of the Captain's senior men: a man called Trevan. As Trevan drew near, it was obvious that he was angling toward Choundry.

Choundry sensed something amiss. When Trevan was within a foot of Choundry, he pulled out a knife and made a quick swing towards Choundry's open right side. Choundry twisted in time to have the blade only make a shallow gash along his ribs, and he followed through with a slam to the back of Trevan's head that pushed him forward into a stumble that led to careening off of the forward mast. Trevan stood slowly with a smile and a laugh, "That's good, that's real good, but you'll have to do better if I'm going to bet me money on you. Starten after this noon meal, you and I are going to start practicing the use of the blade. You will need to get a lot better than you are if you hope to stand against some of the real jack tars the other boats will be sending yer way."

Choundry responded, "Where is my blade if we're going to be practicing?." Trevan said, "You can use that there belaying pin as yer blade until I'm sure ye won't be sticking me with anything. The worst kind of dangerous man is one who doesn't know what he's doing; ya never know what he'll do cause he don't know hisself until he does it."

Later that day, Choundry began the first in a series of training sessions that started with knives and then went to a variety of weapons that could be found on the *Merlin's* deck. As his strength fully returned and there was no longer any danger of his wounds reopening, the Captain started to send men against Choundry to test him and teach him the various fighting skills they each had from their home countries and had mastered over their lives as seaman; skills that grew from experiencing the dangers in an endless number of ports of call, barroom brawls, and sea battles. Choundry endured several humiliating defeats at the hands of more than a few of these men, but his natural athletic ability and his eagerness to learn soon encouraged each of these men to share their secrets of staying alive; the dirty tricks and the fighting techniques they had relied on to survive in the harsh and pitiless world where they traveled.

Choundry learned to be always aware and to react with lightning speed to unexpected attacks. The crew all started to enjoy the "game" of testing and challenging Choundry. Each knew that even though there was an enjoyment that could be shared when these spontaneous battles erupted somewhere on deck, there was a seriousness to the sparring, too. Choundry needed to learn and improve. Each skill learned, and each victory meant an even better chance in the ring. For this reason, the men did not hold back in their attacks, and as a result, Choundry would usually sport numerous visible bruises and several new scars to match the ones that he'd gained in his first visit to the ring. Truth be told, Choundry came to enjoy the game because it stopped him from thinking of home. He enjoyed the sense of mastery over his movements and actions that he was developing, and he saw that the men no longer went about their duties with a sense of drudgery. Choundry was fairly certain that this was as close to a "happy ship" as Captain Johnston would ever have.

During this time, the Merlin had traveled along some of the previous trade routes that Choundry had seen before. At one point, Choundry thought that he recognized a point of land, but then the ship veered off and continued on its journey. He suspected that the Captain had chosen to skip Choundry's home port in order to ensure that he wouldn't have to explain his newest crewmember to those in port who would not be too happy to see Choundry back from the dead.

Two months after his fight, the *Merlin* was cruising down towards one of the spots where the Captain liked to "hunt" for "easy pickins" to supplement *Merlin's* earnings from its trade route. When a two-masted ship was spotted approaching, the Captain went part way up the ladder and, using his eyeglass, fixed his gaze on the approaching vessel. The crew was ready to grab lines and wear ship to run from this vessel; each knew that the Captain would never take a chance on attacking a ship that was roughly the size of the *Merlin;* he would often say that "He never saw the profit of takin one ship and losing half yer crew doing it when, if yer has patience, ye can take half a dozen lesser ships without a scratch." So, it was with some surprise that the Captain ordered the *Merlin* to turn toward the oncoming vessel. He ordered a special flag to be raised. As the captain stomped to the front of the ship, he called orders to "Move close to that ship and heave to."

The oncoming ship made a similar move towards the *Merlin.* As the two ships neared, they both pulled in their sails and lost speed until they were lying within two cables of one another. The Captain used his speaking trumpet to call across to the other ship, "Do ye accept?." Evidently, he must have received some form of reply that Choundry couldn't hear because the Captain followed up with "Which will host?." After a pause, the Captain turned and yelled at his crew, "Ready the ship for guests!"

What followed was to be repeated periodically over the next several months; the *Merlin* would either be the host ship or a contingent would row across to the other ship. In any case, once greetings had been made and spirits passed to the crew, a clearing would be made in the center of the deck amidst a ring of seamen from both ships. Choundry would be brought forward, and the other ship would produce their champion and a fight would ensue. There were rules for these fights and a winner would be called if an opponent were thrown to the deck at least three times or one champion were bloodied sufficient to have the Captains agree to call the match. Both Captains were very careful to give the appearance of fairness as both ship's crews were usually armed or could quickly reach weapons if an argument were to flare up.

With Choundry's recent training, he was able to defeat his opponents without receiving too many beatings or open wounds in the process. There were at least two men that he fought who were about as good as his opponent had been in the ring. In both cases, he was able to win the match by using a series of throws and tripping techniques that he'd learned from several of his shipmates during his training. Choundry did suffer a broken nose during one match, and he picked up two new scars, one above his right eyebrow and another on his left shoulder where a large wooden splinter had been driven into his left shoulder and needed to be cut out. In preparing for one of these fights, the other ship's Captain told Captain Johnston, "I been hearing about your Champion. They say that he has yet to be defeated unless you count that first fight in the ring at Banti-town. I'm thinkin that you'd best give me better odds if we are gonna have a match."

Choundry was able to win this match as well, and, truth be told, the match was not much of a challenge.

Following that fight, and after the other ship's crew had left the *Merlin*, the Captain called Choundry to his cabin. When Choundry entered, the Captain was seated in his canvas-back chair and eating his evening meal. Between bites, the Captain looked up and said, "Now look here, Choundry, yer gettin good, real good. Too good for the lot that we've been meeting out here in this part of the seas, and word is getting around, so the pickins won't be so easy from now on. We're gonna change our cruise to a different area and start including some ports that have bigger tournaments. I have a place that I want to go to first, where you'll meet the best brawler that I have ever known. He can teach you a few things that the lot on this ship can't. I can't afford to stay too long anywhere, but maybe we'll drop anchor for a week or two to give you a chance to try yer luck with Dan Fletcher. I imagine that he would relish getting back into the fights, even if it is to work with a pup like you."

At first, Choundry didn't reply, but risking the Captain's wrath, he voiced, "Captain, I signed on to work your ship, I had to accept what you pay your crew as I had no choice. I'm making you a lot of money with these fights, and you stand to make a great deal more in the future if I continue, I think that I deserve to have something as well, some portion of the winnings."

The Captain's face reddened, and at first, Choundry thought that he was choking on a piece of meat from his meal. The Captain's jaw clenched and the muscles on the side of his jaw were working back and forth grinding his teeth down. After a moment the Captain seemed to gain control of himself and, after giving himself several breaths, he looked at Choundry and said, "Any other time that one of me crew were to talk to me like that I'd have them gutted and thrown overboard. Just this once I am going to overlook your sass. I do see that you has a point and with me being a generous man, I am going to allow that you deserve something as well. I's not going to increase yer pay aboard this ship as all me crew gets paid the same. I will take a silver coin and bet it on yer next fight, if ye win that fight then the coins ye earn will be yours and ye can bet that and all yer winnins on each fight going forward. I holds the money as I don't want that kind of tin being loose on this ship. I do have one stipulatin though….as I said, I holds all the money and if you lose a fight then I take what I bet on you out of what moneys that you have in my holdin, tis only right as I am investing so much time and money in you like I am. Why, if you never loses a fight you could walk off the *Merlin* a wealthy man! There's nothing fairer or more generous as that."

Choundry thought for a moment and told the Captain, "I agree to what you've said with only one change, I want my winnings to be kept separate from the ship's money and your money and I want a reckoning after each fight with the total written on a paper that shows what I am owed."

Again the Captain's eyes took on an angry glare but that quickly passed. Choundry knew that the Captain never planned to pay him whatever he would earn, but he would deal with that later.

Over the next several weeks, the ship had three encounters and Choundry fought three bouts. In each he won his match. After the first match, Choundry had his silver coin free and clear from the Captain. Choundry chose to bet all that he had on each of the next two matches, knowing that if he left any as a reserve that the Captain, in the event of a lost match, would claim it all to cover his losses. After the second and third match, he went to the Captain's cabin and sat with him to see the four silver coins placed in a small leather bag and stored in the ship's chest. Each time the Captain would take an odd piece of paper or scrap of cloth and pen the total and then make his personal mark. Then he would give it to Choundry with a gruff remark.

After one of these matches the Captain relented for a moment and even seemed friendly to Choundry. He chuckled a moment and then said, "I has to admit, you be making me a lot of money, Choundry, tis only fittin that ye get a taste of it too. I can afford real wine now and there's money enough in the chest that I may even pay the lads some of the moneys they got coming at the next port. We be getting near the place where me old mate Dan Fletcher lives, get yerself ready Choundry cause ye haven't fought a real fighter yet but that'll change soon. Ol Dan is the best I seen in dirty fightin and brawlin. If ye can learn to match him you'll be makin us both piles of tin."

Choundry continued to practice as well as perform his duties on board the ship. He was learning the names of the various sails and now that he'd managed to have several of the crew work with him on fighting practice, they were more than willing to show him the various skills that a sailor learns over years at sea. He learned knot tying and splicing ropes, how to adjust sails to catch the wind just right. He also began to take turns learning how to steer the ship. His skills grew and he started to feel a true affinity with the ship; how it moved and what it needed to become the almost living thing that would spring from one wave to another; blasting spray high and surging on to grab and thrust through the next oncoming wave. He enjoyed the feeling of taking on the force of nature and battling through to not only survive but to bend the winds and waves to his command; driving the ship forward or turning with the wind to ease and use even the smallest breath of a gust. He still had much to learn but the crew and the Captain were willing to allow him to volunteer to learn and master new tasks.

A score more days followed where the *Merlin* did not meet any other ships so there were no opportunities for ship-to-ship bouts. During that time, they stopped at two ports briefly to exchange cargos but quickly moved on without the Captain allowing the crew any shore leave. Eventually the *Merlin* came in sight of a shore which appeared wildly rugged and on which only small and stunted trees grew. In the distance, the men could make out what looked to be a mountain peak with two matching points. There were no houses or signs of life along the stretch of coast that they could see and after a brief conference with one of his crew, the Captain ordered the ship to turn and follow the coast north. Gradually, as the ship moved along the coast, small cottages could be seen on the cliffs overlooking the sea. Then, gradually, larger buildings and barns could be seen until a fairly large town was visible in the distance. The port, located where the town met the sea, was not overly large and the piers that jutted into the waves were in a degree of disrepair. No other ships were seen in the port; only small skiffs and single-masted coastal crafts. It took the rest of the afternoon to make their way into the small harbor and find a place that provided the *Merlin* a degree of protection from the winds.

The Captain called the crew together and told them, "We be stayin here fer a while, I've business to do. I want ye all to remember this: yer *Merlin* crew and ye better be ready to leave when I says, remember that we will be here fer a while so don't waste all yer pay the first day cause I'll not give ye more no matter what ya says I owes ya, and finally, if bad weather comes and I call fer ye I better not see any laggards cause the ol *Merlin* will need to be shifted or she'll run to ruin on these shores, this be the most miserable harbor in all this area and there is a reason we has no other big ships to keep us company. If ye don't heed the call, if it be made, then you'll taste the cat or my name ain' Captain."

Shortly thereafter, Choundry found himself seated behind the Captain in the ship's boat being rowed ashore. Once they'd tied to the pier, they moved quickly on into the town. The Captain clearly knew where he was going as they wound their way quickly through the streets and eventually stopped outside a large barn on the outskirts of town. There wasn't any sign to mark the building but it was obviously a busy place. People were moving about engaged in various tasks and the sound of hammering could be heard coming from behind the building. The Captain entered the building while Choundry and the other two members of the *Merlin's* crew waited outside. The Captain came walking back out of the building accompanied by a hulking man who was wearing a thick leather apron.

As they drew closer, the Captain turned to the man and said, "This here be the lad that I want ye to work with."

The man seemed to be carved in stone, with forearms and shoulders that were truly impressive. His face was lined, and soot was smeared on the right side of his face. The grime was not the first thing that one noticed, though, as once he moved close enough to see, Choundry was able to make out a mass of scars that crossed his face. His nose was thick and had a twist to it that gave him a curiously friendly look when matched with his wide smile. "Pleased to meet ya, lad," he said. "I hope that you won't mind me saying that I hope you know what yer getting into. Fighting ain't a place with a future. Most men who enter the ring end up begging for their bread somewhere as a cripple or lying in some shallow grave. Are ye sure this is what ye want?" At this point Captain Johnston stepped forward and said, "He has promised me years of honest work and I've his word on it. If he don't honor that word, I gets to send him home to where he'll get a quick blade and a watery grave. I've already invested a great deal of money in this lad and he owes me for the training that he's been getting. He'll take to the training honest-like or I'll have the hide off of him."

Choundry stepped forward and said, "Enough of this talk. I would welcome any training that you could give me, I want to live through my years of service to the Captain and then go home to settle some debts. I would be in your debt if you could help me to survive the ring and be able to walk away."

Dan looked to Captain Johnston and said, "It's not Choundry here that'll be in my debt if I teaches him, it'll be this tight-fisted scoundrel" pointing to the Captain.

Captain Johnston thought for a moment and then said, "All right, I'll pay ya up front what we agreed for the next 10 days of training. Looking at Choundry, he went on "but I'll have ye know that I'll be takin the price of this trainin from yer winnins if ye have any."

Choundry thought for a moment and then said, "Agreed, if I have winnings it will be because I've survived and that would make this training well worth the money paid."

The next several days were some of the most physically demanding Choundry had ever endured. Dan set up work bags and weights that he made Choundry hit into, carry, and thrash around. He would then take breaks from his stable work to instruct Choundry in various holds, hitting techniques, and throws. Once he'd explained what he wanted, Dan would run Choundry through a slow-motion walk through of the technique and then stand back and say, "Have at it, do your best."

Choundry would then proceed to step in and work through the techniques, but Dan would shift slightly and, with seemingly effortless ease, throw Choundry over his hip or flip him onto his back. Dan's hands seemed to move faster than the eye could follow. Choundry realized that he was in the presence of a master and the thought of ever facing someone like Dan in the ring was shocking. Choundry now realized that he hadn't learned as much as he'd thought: that he was still easy prey if he were to ever meet someone as skilled as Dan. Five days into the training, Captain Johnston showed up and watched the practice. Dan went to him and the Captain asked if Choundry was any good and if they'd be ready in another five days. Dan replied, "He's a great natural talent but he has much to learn if he's to survive with some of the lads he'll meet on the southern coast run."

When the captain showed his disappointment, Dan told him, "I'll tell ya what I'll do, and understand this isn't for you, it's for Choundry here as I've taken a liking to him. I'll train him as he should be, but it will take me a month or two and I'll do it for the price that was agreed to." Captain Johnston thought for a moment and said, looking at Choundry, "If I leave ye here for a while I want yer sworn word that ye'll be here when I gets back and that ye'll come back aboard the *Merlin* willingly. And I wants ye to know that ye'll not be getting paid during this time as I'll not be getting honest labor. Agreed? And I wants yer word." Choundry thought for a moment and then held his hand out to shake the Captain's, "Agreed, I'll be here when you get back," he said.

Since there was no longer any reason for the *Merlin* to stay in port, the ship weighed anchored and sailed on to the rest of its trade route along the coast. Captain Johnston said that he expected to be able to swing back again in approximately two months' time.

Choundry felt an odd sense of loss in seeing the *Merlin* sail out of the harbor without him. As much as he'd endured during the past several months, he had learned a great deal and experienced adventures that he would have only dreamed of at home. He had made several good friends and, although he didn't recognize it, his relationship with Captain Johnston was gradually changing. If he had taken a moment to think of it, he would realize that it was quite a leap from his early days on the *Merlin* where he endured abuse and humiliation to a point now where he is striking bargains and negotiating with the Captain. If he had taken a moment, he would have recognized that there were no other members of the *Merlin's* crew who would be allowed to talk with the Captain as he was now becoming accustomed to doing.

Training resumed later on the day that the *Merlin* sailed. Choundry had begun his routine of bag work when Dan walked in and said, "Choundry, I know Captain Johnston enough to know that you most likely have not had a moment of enjoyment or relaxation since you entered his ship. I am giving you the rest of today and tomorrow off, you need to prepare your mind as well as your body for what the next couple of months are going to bring. If you are willing, I am going to work you in the smithy between the times yer training, if you're in agreement I'll pay you a fair wage for your labor and advance you some now so you can go in town." At first Choundry didn't know what to say, unexpected emotion welled up and he almost unmanned himself by tearing up at this first sign of kindness that he'd experienced in many a day.

"Aye, working in your smithy would be welcome break and I've always been interested in the trade," he said. "Whatever you can show me would be appreciated and I'll try to give you my best labor for all your kindness."

After Dan gave him several coins, he said, "You will be sleeping in the barn in yonder loft so come back whenever you'd like and just be careful not to trip over anything coming in and I only have one rule..no fire."

Choundry thanked him again and turned to walk down into town but before he could take more than a few steps, Dan called, "Mind, if you hear the church bell ringing get back here as fast as you can, we have trouble with bandits raiding the town and the town calls all men of fighting age in for service to fend off any raids, they're a scurvy lot, and would as soon stick ya than give you the time of day. They steal food, women, and anything they can carry away. It's been a while since they've been here but beware if you hear the bell." Choundry nodded his understanding and resumed his walk into town.

The thought of having the rest of the day and the next all to himself was like having too much wine…he felt light-headed and giddy. Brushing his clothes clean the best that he could to be even slightly more presentable, Choundry walked on through the closest portion of the town. He eventually stopped at an inn and had an ale and some of the soup they had boiling over the fire in the common place. The barkeep was a hairy short man who moved like a barrel between the tables and guests with a certain grace and ease that could only come from many years of plying his trade. The barmaid was a woman whose smile came quickly and who had a pleasant soft voice. The woman reminded him of his own mother far away and he turned to his ale with a tinge of sadness. He thought for a moment of seeing if he could send a letter home telling them of what had happened to him but he realized that, with the very real chance that he would never live to see his home again, it would be a cruelty to get their hopes up only to never lay eyes on him again; they would always be wondering and never know for sure what had happened to him. Better to survive what was to come and then return home if he could.

Choundry spent the rest of the evening wandering throughout the town, just enjoying the feeling of not having to be running anywhere or answer to anyone's orders. As night began to fall, he made his way back to the barn and ascended the ladder into the loft. The straw upon which he laid down seemed to be the equal of any rich man's bed; it felt and smelled of a remembered cleanliness that brought such good memories that he fell asleep in moments with a smile on his lips.

The morning saw a meal brought to the barn by Dan's wife and their smallest child. It seemed a feast compared to what he'd been used to recently. He tried to remember the manners that he'd had no call to use these past months. The little child; no more than three or four, watched him shyly from the protection of her mother's skirts. Choundry finished quickly although he couldn't help but relish the last few bites of biscuit that seemed heavenly after the rock-hard ships biscuits that he'd had on the *Merlin*. Dan's wife, Mildred, was a comely woman who had a warm and caring disposition that seemed to include all those around her. Choundry found himself thinking that Dan was a lucky man to have found such a caring and loving wife and mother to his children. It was no wonder that Dan seemed a happy man; he had all that any sane man could wish for; a wife and family to be proud of and a skill that kept them all warm and fed. Choundry promised himself that he too would one day have such as this, he would first learn to be successful, build a life and some security and then find such a woman as this.

Chapter 6
A Brief Glimpse of Happiness

Later that day found Choundry wandering the nearby hills and exploring the outskirts of the village. As he passed through some of the outlying buildings it became apparent the town had experienced better times in its past. Several buildings were burnt and at least two small farms were lying empty. The town had attempted to build a small stone wall for protection but less than half of the wall was completed, and it looked as if no one had been working on it for quite some time. Choundry walked into town and stopped at the same tavern where he'd eaten at the previous evening. He enjoyed a wonderful meat pie and a small pitcher of milk. Afterwards, he sat close to the fire just enjoying the sense of well-being that a good meal and good company will bring. As he sat talking occasionally with the barkeep, he suddenly saw the man lift his head and cock it to the side. His manner changed and Choundry could feel the sense of alarm building in the man.

"Clara," the barkeep yelled, "Grab the grankids and get to the cellar." Then he moved quickly to grab various items from under the counter and fled to a back room. Choundry, suddenly sitting alone, was left puzzled by what had happened. After a moment, he noticed the faint sound of a church bell ringing frantically. Choundry jumped to his feet and ran as quickly as he could up the street to Dan's barn. When he arrived, he found Dan organizing a group of men who quickly started to move onto the road towards the upper part of town. Choundry joined them and hurried past the majority of the group until he was abreast of Dan.

When Dan saw Choundry he gave a twisted smile and said, "It's good to have another man to answer the call, especially one with some fighting skills. I am afraid that most of the men behind me have stout enough hearts but little in the way of skill with a blade or their fists."

Occasional shots and screams could now be heard from the direction where they were hurriedly heading. As they drew closer, several townsfolk raced past them, some clutching their children or some treasured belongings. Coming to a corner, they were able to see down the adjoining street and they caught their first glimpses of the attackers. Running from one open building to the next, several men could be seen, one carrying a torch. Dan shouted to the men behind him and several broke from the group and headed to deal with the men they'd just seen, while Dan continued down the road with the remainder of the townsmen, which numbered about 25, including Choundry.

At the next corner the defenders ran straight into a large group of marauders. Dan saw them break from the nearest cluster of buildings and called for his men to attack. The marauders were weighted down with plunder and one or two were dragging women toward several nearby horses. Choundry saw a man directly in front of him pull a horse pistol and fire into a townsman, bringing the man down in a pile. Choundry raced forward and grabbed the pistol and, yanking it free from the man's hand, he quickly swung it up and brought it crashing down on the side of the bandit's head. He could feel the man's skull caving in as the bandit dropped like a sack of flour. Choundry had a moment to think that this was the first time in his life that he'd ever killed another human being. As this thought quickly entered his consciousness, he had to thrust it away just as quickly as another brigand followed after the first; this one was holding what appeared to be a ship's cutlass. Choundry still held the empty handgun and used this to deflect the blade as it came whistling down in a wicked overhand swing. Choundry stepped in and grabbed the man by the throat and lifted him bodily off the ground as his continued with his forward momentum. He continued to lift and then brought the man down, breaking his body over the edge of a wooden trough. Choundry reached down and pulled the man's cutlass free and, gripping the cutlass in one hand and the handgun reversed and held as a club in the other, he moved on, looking to help where he could. Several of the townsmen were lying in heaps or pulling themselves away from the fight but there were more than an equal number of marauders who lay still in the road. The remaining bandits dropped their plunder and ran for the safety of their horses with townsmen following quickly behind.

Dan pulled Choundry to a halt as they surveyed the scene. "Twas good work you did here today," he said. You saved more than one of these men from misery."

As the pursuit of the remaining bandits continued down the street, a degree of quiet fell in which a new and ominous noise could be heard from the other side of town. Choundry and Dan turned quickly and, as one, they started to race back along the road they had just arrived on. Dan called to any of his remaining men to join them as they raced back to meet this new attack. They now realized that the first attack was designed to draw away the defenders and allow for a second attack to strike while the town was unprepared to resist.

Dan raced ahead, obviously fearing for his wife and children. As they rounded the corner and his barn came into sight, there did not seem to be any activity in the streets, all seemed calm. Dan took a moment to run inside his house to check on his family. When he came back out it was obvious from the look on his face that his family was safe and unharmed. The noises they had heard were close now but were coming from the center of town. Dan obviously struggled with his need to stay and make sure that his family was safe, now that the attack was so close to his home. He quickly came to a decision. He entered his barn and came out with two horse pistols, one he kept in his hand while the other he thrust into his belt. Although there were only six men now with Dan, including

Choundry, they turned and began to run towards where the attack seemed to be occurring.

Because of Dan's delay in getting his weapons, Choundry had been able to move further down the road and was therefore in the lead as the small group sped down into the town. Coming to the small tavern where he had just enjoyed his most recent meal, he saw the figure of a man, with the familiar broad shoulders and portly body of the tavern keeper, sprawled in the doorway. Blood covered his head and he lay as if dead. Hearing a screaming echoing from just down the street, Choundry put on a burst of speed that brought him to the next intersection of streets. Directly in front of him, he saw a familiar piece of clothing that turned out to belong to the tavern keeper's wife; she was being hauled bodily aboard a horse and as she resisted the man slammed the hilt of his sword down on the top of her head causing her to go limp.

Choundry felt a rage explode in him, his sense of honor was outraged at how this fine woman was being treated. All of the pent-up anger and frustration of the past several months made him momentarily fog his vision with a red anger that drove him forward toward the horseman. He heard himself voice a yell as he moved forward that caused the man to look up in alarm, he saw Choundry's onrushing figure and dropped the woman as he reached for his sword. Choundry's anger was so extreme that he raised the cutlass high and leapt at the man. His opponent tried to raise his blade into a defensive position but Choundry, in his anger, moved with such brute force that his blade was knocked aside as Choundry's cutlass swung in to catch the man in the side. The force of Choundry's blade brought it halfway through the man's body before it wedged itself in the man's spine. Choundry tried to pull the blade free but succeeded in only pulling the dying man from his horse. Once he realized that he could not free his cutlass, Choundry quickly looked for the blade that his recent opponent had dropped. He saw the blade and retrieved it quickly. Stepping to the side of the fallen woman, he assured himself that she was still breathing. He pulled her inert form into a nearby doorway to protect her from further harm and then he stood and looked about him.

The fight seemed to have initially gone poorly for the townsmen but, with the recent arrival of several new defenders, the tide was turning in their favor. Choundry could see Dan standing toe to toe with a smaller man who had long knives held in each of his hands. Dan had only his two pistols which were obviously discharged, as he was now holding them by the barrels and using them as clubs to fend off the shorter man's slashes. Dan stepped back in what turned out to be a feint and the shorter brigand took the bait; stepping forward and making a wide slashing move with one of his blades. At just the time that the blade passed inches from his belly, Dan started his move inward in what looked to be almost a graceful dance move. He brought one pistol up in a movement designed to cause the smaller man to flinch to one side and then he followed this up with a crushing downswing from the other side.

Even from the distance that Choundry was standing he could clearly hear the sodden impact of the ball at the end of the pistol grip as it caved in the man's skull. Turning towards another group of fighters, Choundry joined in the conflict but the brigands' will to fight was lost. They started to break off in ones and twos and run towards the outskirts of town. As the fight slowed, Dan called Choundry to his side and said, "Once again, we are in your debt, you fought well and I am thinking that it was a fine day for us all when I struck a bargain to train you. I underestimated you when I talked with the Captain, you have a rare natural talent for the fight, I promise you I'll do my best to show you what I can before you go, you'll be needing it where you're going, I'm thinking."

A little later, Choundry worked his way back into town and found several women kneeling next to the tavern keeper's wife. She sat up and looked about her. Seeing the man that attacked her lying nearby; with the blade still wedged in his body and the hideous wound gaping in his side, the woman's eyes swung to Choundry's, and tears began to stream down her face.

"Thank you young man for what you did, I owe you my life and more."

At that moment, a sudden memory must have come back to her as she mouthed the words, "Pete, oh my Pete" and then she tried to stand while saying, "I have to see to me husband. That bastard may have done for him, I needs to see to me Pete."

Choundry helped steady her and then supported her as they moved up the street. Fearing what they'd see as he remembered the body of the tavern keeper lying in his doorway, Choundry and the woman made their way back to her home. As they neared the house, Choundry could see that the body of the man was no longer in the doorway. As they entered the dimly lit tavern, he could see the form of a man slumped over one of the tables sobbing and rolling his head from side to side. The woman rushed to his side and clutched him close to her breast. "Pete, you wonderful man, I thought they'd kilt you." The tavern keeper rose to his feet and held his wife in his arms, burying his face in her hair and sobbing. Once emotions had begun to settle, the woman pulled away from her husband's arms and pointed to Choundry, "This be the man who saved me from death and worse. He came to save me like an angel from heaven."

The man pulled from away his wife and stumbled over the Choundry, "Tis my whole life and more that I owe ye lad. I don't know how I'll ever repay ye for what ye done."

Choundry wanted to give the couple some time to be together to quiet the terrors of almost losing their dearest treasure, so after a few moments he told them that he needed to check on how others in the town were doing and he quickly left. He spent the rest of the day helping to clean up the mess made by the raiders and tending to the wounded, finally finishing his day with the solemn task of helping with the digging of graves for those lost that day.

As night fell, Choundry made his way back to Dan's barn where he found his mentor and his family talking with their neighbors and sharing a meal in the yard under a sprawling tree. They asked Choundry to join them. Dan looked to Choundry and said, "Well, it looks like you've picked up a splendid blade and a decent pistol."

Choundry had forgotten both weapons that he had stashed in his belt. When he pulled the blade free, he saw that it was indeed what appeared to be a finely crafted sword. The horse pistol was a rough cousin of the matched set that Dan possessed but it seemed serviceable. Dan went on "We'll see what else we can find from the men that you killed today. It's only fair that you have the spoils, and since you seem to have arrived with no belongings of your own, maybe we can make up your kit for when you return to the sea. By the way, you had better eat up good, tomorrow we start the training and I'll not have you giving half measure, especially as you've just had a full day off!" The two men laughed together as they moved to the table where a full meal was laid out.

Chapter 7
A Tempting Offer

The next two months passed quickly and Choundry found himself challenged on many levels. He developed a quick friendship with Dan, and they would often work from sun up to well into the evening. Dan's training on fighting techniques was grueling and he occasionally brought in some of his friends in town to challenge Choundry. One local man had spent many years in the east among the Asians and had learned several different fighting techniques. He was able to show Choundry two new throws and some defensive maneuvers that he'd never seen before. When he and Dan were not working on his fighting skills, they would take time to work in the smithy.

Choundry was fascinated by the magic that Dan seemed to be able to work on the iron. It never failed to amaze him when Dan would take a seemingly useless blob of ore and work it into an implement, a hasp, or some beautiful metalwork. One day Choundry helped Dan finish an ornate gate for one of the wealthier merchants in town. When they went to install the gate, Choundry was the object of many glances and whispers among the merchant's three daughters. Thinking of the girls later, he grew melancholy as he realized that the type of life that a "good girl" from a "good family" would want was beyond his means. The skills that he was learning were valuable for him at this point in his life but would not provide him with any means of earning a living and raising a family as his father had done.

Eventually the morning came when the *Merlin* was sighted entering the harbor. Choundry packed his belongings into a chest that he and Dan had fashioned and joined with nails and hinges that Choundry had fashioned himself. Contained in the chest were several sets of clothing, and two pairs of shoes that he had been able to trade for. The chest was fashioned in such a way that there was a compartment in which Choudry was able to store his sword and pistol. Dan had also shown him how to make a false bottom in the chest that would allow for smaller items to be stored with little chance of being discovered.

His leave taking with Dan and his family was difficult as he'd come to feel almost as if he'd become one of the family. After talking briefly with Captain Johnston, Dan came to Choundry and said, "I've returned the money that the Captain paid me for your training. What you did for us in our time of need as well as your work on the forge paid me well for the time that we spent practicing; and truth be told, I enjoyed seeing you learn, you have some great skills and I hope to see you return to our town some day to tell me tales of your adventures." With that he and Dan shook hands and Choundry started walking down to the harbor.

As he passed the tavern on his way through town, Pete and his wife were waiting for him. Pete pressed a wrapped bundle of food into Choundry's hands and also gave him a small book, saying, "From our talks I know that yer a man of letters and I'm thinkin that ye might enjoy something to read on yer journeys. It's small payment for what ye done. If ye ever come back this way there'll be a tankard of ale waiting for ye on the house, and welcome."

All through this time Captain Johnston remained strangely quiet. As they moved down to the dock, the Captain walking ahead and Choundry carrying his sea chest on his shoulder, various townsfolk came up to Choundry and wished him Godspeed and good luck. Once they had climbed into the ship's boat and were most of the way out to the *Merlin*, the Captain said in a distracted tone, "Choundry, ye be a strange man that be true."

That was all he said. When they boarded the ship no word was said regarding Choundry's chest. He was allowed to carry it below and place it beneath his hammock. His friends greeted him and there seemed a genuine happiness in most of the crew to see that he had returned. Darcy grasped his hand and said, "The old *Merlin* just wasn't the same ship without ye, we're glad to see ye back, lad."

Chapter 8
New Challenges

Things gradually settled back to their old routine. The one change that did occur was that the Captain's men no longer pushed Choundry or used the starter on him. The tale of the fight that had occurred with the bandits at the town must have been told and retold among the crew and no man aboard wanted to test Choundry's new fighting skills.

The Captain continued his practice of stopping small craft to confiscate whatever he wished. One time there seemed to be an argument, and then a scuffle, on one of the smaller boats. Afterwards the Captain's men returned to the ship and were unusually quiet. Looking back at the craft they had just plundered, Choundry thought that he saw the vessel was slightly lower in the water than he'd remembered. There was little that he could do regarding the Captain and his senior men as they kept most of their actions to themselves and they never discussed what occurred aboard the vessels they visited.

The first major port they came to, as they continued their travels, was the largest Choundry had seen since joining the ship. The Captain ordered the crew to stay on board while he went ashore. A barge eventually came to the ship's side and their cargo was shifted from the boat to the waiting barge. Later, another barge came up to the *Merlin's* side and they brought aboard fresh stores and supplies. As the sun was setting, another barge was poled from the shore, this one had a cargo of barrels of pork and bags of charcoal. It took the crew well into the evening to lift the cargo from the barge and place it into the ship's hold. By the time that Choundry and the other men had finished carrying the bags of charcoal, they were covered with such a black coating that those who could swim opted to jump from the ship's side and wash the grime from their bodies. Those who could not swim took turns working the pumps and spraying each other with sea water until they had cleared themselves of the soot.

Later that evening the Captain returned long enough to order Choundry to make ready to go back ashore with him. After the Captain had made a brief visit to his cabin, they both went down into the ship's boat and were rowed ashore. The Captain looked to Choundry and told him, "This be yer test to see if all the sweat and coin that I put into ye was worth the effort. The man that yer gonna face tonight is a past champion of the ring. Now mind ye, these folks want a civilized fight, as if there is any such thing, so they don't abide by killin. They do allow some crippling but it can't be too obvious. I don't care whats ye need to do to win, ya just do it. I'm getting good odds on ye, Choundry, and I'll bet yer coins as well; two to one! If ye wins you'll be having some real coin to yer name, if ye don't win, just remember you'll end up all the poorer, just as poor as ye was the first day I laid eyes on ye."

With that, the boat touched the stone jetty and the Captain stepped quickly up onto the walkway with Choundry close behind. They made their way up through a busy crowd of sailors and workmen unloading two ships that were tied to the dock and threaded their way into a crowded bazaar that seemed to go on forever. Choundry couldn't remember ever seeing so many people together at one time in his life. The only thing coming close to this was the county fair back home. Many of the people in the crowd were dressed in rich and foreign-looking clothing. Many had swords belted to their waist and some even had pistols. The vendors had stalls and pushcarts loaded with wares of an amazing variety. If Choundry hadn't been following the Captain, he would have dearly loved to wander and explore.

As they moved further into the town, the number of vendors and salesmen began to decrease until they were striding virtually alone down a broad avenue. Being familiar with the types of places that Captain Johnston usually frequented, Choundry was expecting to turn down a side street to find some dingy building that held the usual fights hidden from the view of the local authorities. Instead, they crossed the street and headed for an immense stone structure, in front of which a small crowd was gathered.

As Choundy neared the building, several young men stepped clear of the crowd and eyed him closely as he approached. One turned to his companions and could be heard to say, "Ah, here we have the mysterious challenger! Why, he looks barely old enough to be a bucket boy at the fights let alone someone's champion!"

With that, the small group standing with the young man all laughed and patted him on the back. Choundry felt his face redden as he passed the young man, but he couldn't stop himself from responding "If you think that I'm such a youngster, then place your bets accordingly or shut your trap."

As Choundry moved on into the building he could hear the young man and his friends sputtering and cursing him. As he strode further into the building, he now saw that there were some women scattered in the crowd. The Captain stopped to talk with another man and Choundry was forced to bide quietly. One woman stepped closer and looked intently at his face. With a bold look to her eye, she reached out and ran her hand over Choundry's shoulder and arm. "My what a fit and fine specimen of a man you are! You are perfectedly beautiful! It's a shame that you will be putting this fine body and face in danger. I wish I'd found you sooner, ah well, let's see how you do and maybe we can have some fun anyway."

She turned and walked back to a group of individuals all dressed richly, some waving feathered fans to cool themselves in the heat. Several of these individuals had been watching the interplay between Choundry and the woman and now they were obviously talking about him and laughing occasionally.

The Captain seemed to have finished his business. He looked around and, finding Choundry, he motioned for him to follow as he worked his way forward and started down a set of steps. When they reached a floor that seemed to be well below the level of the street, Choundry could make out a hallway with a series of doorways to the left side. The hallway and the rooms that they passed were all dimly lit with torches and candles. The Captain found a room to his liking several doors down and upon entering turned to Choundry. "The fights start in about an hour. I want ye to rest. Mind ye, don't accept any food or drink from anyone here, these high caste people are even worse than the lowliest pirate in the ways they'll cheat. Ye only drinks what I gives ye meself and ye don't need to eat anything whiles yer here. And one other thing: one of their favorite tricks is to send a woman to a young fighter just before a fight to sap his strength. I'll be close at hand so don't be doin anything stupid." With that the Captain turned and made his way down the hall, leaving Choundry alone.

Choundry spent a quiet hour seated in the near dark trying to remember all of the things that Dan and his friends had taught him. He visualized the various fighting techniques that he'd learned and tried to think through how he should react should he be attacked in various ways. No one approached him during this time, perhaps thinking him not worth the effort to sabotage. Eventually Captain Johnston came back into the room and told Choundry, "Tis time, I tried to get ye one of the top players but they won't let me place ye at that level until ye've proven yerself. Yer fighting a new man. A crewman from one of the ships down at the port, he's some type of champion along the eastern route and they says he has beat every man easily who has come against him. I hates to see ye fightin someone we don't know hows he fights but I just heard that he has already fought twice today and the men he fought each didn't last more than two rounds, one man he knocked cold before he could draw a good breath. I don't like it, I don't likes it a bit." After pausing, the Captain went on, "Well, I guess we got no choice, if we backs out now, we lose our bets anyways, might as well give it a go."

A few minutes later, the Captain and Choundry were standing in the entryway to what was the biggest room that Choundry had ever seen. He couldn't imagine the skill that it would have taken to build such an immense structure! Crowds were already moving toward their seats; row upon row of stone and wooden benches built in such a cunning manner that the ones to the rear gradually rose up to allow for a clear view of the fights. The middle of the room had essentially the same type of ring that Choundry had become familiar with in the past, although slightly more elevated and the wall was topped with a single strand of rope. There were also two gates to enter the ring, one immediately in front of him and the other directly across the ring.

To Choundry's right he saw the young man that he'd taunted earlier as he and his friends entered the room and moved to be seated in one of the front rows. Choundry stepped forward and walked through the gate. He heard the gate being closed behind him. As he stood there, unsure of what to do, he could hear various comments from the crowd. The young man yelled down to Choundry, "I've bet enough on your loss that my friends I will be dining well tonight while you're looking for your teeth in the ring." This elicited several nervous laughs from people scattered in the crowd.

After several minutes, Choundry saw what must be, his opponent stride through an archway across the room. Several cheers could be heard from the crowd as this man grabbed the top rope and leaped over it and into the ring. Once in the ring the man started to strut around in a circle with his arms raised, waving to the crowd and encouraging cheers. He was a squat, compact man with a thick torso and arms that were bulging with muscles. His complexion was dark, and he had thick black hair that reached down to his shoulders. Exuding confidence, he walked forward and stood with his hands on his hips examining Choundry. With a smirk and a look to the crowd, he yelled at Choundry, "Two minutes, you down in twooo minutes" and then he started into a series of almost acrobatic leaps and twists that were clearly designed to impress the crowd and intimidate Choundry. Watching the man, he recognized some of the maneuvers as those used by one of Dan's friends; a man who had spent the better part of a day teaching him some simple defensive techniques.

Choundry had a moment to think about what was to come. He realized that this man displayed a much higher level of skill with this unique type of fighting. If Choundry allowed himself to be drawn into trying to compete with him using the other man's fighting style he knew that he was bound to lose. That meant that he had to find some way to counter the man's fighting style and bring the fight to a quick end. Choundry felt that he had two advantages: the first being that the man was overconfident after his two earlier wins and the second was that the man had no idea that he was facing someone with training, albeit minimal, in methods to defend against the types of attacks he was likely to launch. The second advantage would only last until the first time that Choundry used one of the blocking techniques, after that the advantage would be gone because the fighter would certainly sense that there was something different about this foe. Again, this meant that, once the fight started, Choundry had only moments until any chance that he had would quickly go away.

As Choundry studied his opponent's moves, he noticed that he tended to return several times to a series of kicks. He obviously had practiced these kicks and had the routine down to one fluid set of movements. Choundry began to believe that it was the use of this specific kick that had likely been used to bring down the man's previous opponent who had gone down "before he'd drawn more than a couple of breaths:" Although it was a gamble, Choundry felt that he should stake his initial strategy on the counter move for just such a kick. Eventually, a man came to stand on a raised platform close to the ring, and Choundry knew that the bout was moments from starting. He saw his opponent tense and move into a stance with his body turned at an angle and his right foot pointed forward toward Choundry. This was the same stance that the man had used earlier as he was showing off his fighting skills. The call to start the bout was a simple "Fighters, begin."

As his opponent started his initial rush forward, Choundry stood totally still. When the man began the series of steps that would lead to his devastating kick, Choundry waited a split second until the man had committed to the movements and then Choundry dropped into a one-legged squat while twisting and using his extended right leg to make a broad sweeping motion. If Choundry had guessed wrong he would be wide open for a period of several heartbeats, certainly enough of an opening that this man would finish the fight quickly. As it turned out, Choudry's guess had been correct, and the man's foot shot into the air right at the point where Choundry's head would have been had he not dropped lower. A look of astonishment showed on his opponent's face even as Choundry's right foot made contact with the back of the man's foot, the one he was balancing on while he made his attack. Choundry's foot hit behind and to the side of the man's ankle and flipped his leg out from under him. The man slammed to the ground on his back and for a moment was stunned by the loss of breath and sudden impact. Choundry did not want to cause the man any serious damage, but he needed him out of the fight. While the man was on his back Choundry balled his right hand into a fist and brought it down solidly on the center of the man's chest in a blow that knocked out what air was left in the man's lungs and might possibly have fractured a few ribs. After the blow the man rolled to his side and curled into a ball to prevent any further damage. Choundry stood as the announcer called the fight. As he was leaving the ring, he walked past the young man and his friends and said as an aside " I hope you and your friends weren't too hungry."

Choundry had two more fights that day and he was able to win both. His opponents were both tough men but their fighting styles were such that Choundry was able to use what Dan had taught him to finish the fights both within the first five minutes of the bouts. Choundry did end the day with a cut over his left eye and he had several long scratches along his ribs. When he met Captain Johnston later that day, the Captain was in a jovial mood. "Ye did splendidly! Worth every penny that I paid for yer trainin."

"Now we're back to the ship and on to the next port. We's not going to make the same mistake that we did before and let your fame get ahead of us, we're going to move faster than word can spread."

When they'd returned to the ship, Choundry asked the Captain if he could speak with him in private. The Captain's face betrayed a quick look of suspicion but he agreed to talk with Choundry in the privacy of his cabin. On entering the cabin, the Captain put the bag that he was carrying into a sea chest located at the foot of his bed. He turned and sat down, leaving Choundry to stand in front of the door. "What is it ye want, lad?."

Choundry had thought through what he was going to say but, even so, he proceeded with a degree of nervousness as the Captain's pride was easily tweaked and, champion or not, Choundry could just as easily face punishment as any crewman if the Captain so wished.

"I know that you've made a great deal of money off of my fighting, and I appreciate that you've been placing bets for me as well. I am asking for the money that is due to me for my winnings in the ring. I think it only fair that I make my own bets going forward. If you'll tell me what you're betting, I'll still stand true to replace any losses that you might suffer should I lose a fight."

The Captain thought for a moment and, to Choundry's surprise, finally agreed. He said " I'll let ye have the money but only on one condition; other than to take back and forth to the fights and bettin, the money stays on board the *Merlin*, it's not to leave the ship." Choundry knew that Johnston was willing to give him the money because, with his powers as the Captain, he could take it back any time he wished.

The Captain went to his sea chest and retrieved the sack that he had placed there earlier. He withdrew a handful of coins and sat down at his table. "By my reckoning this be what I owes ye" and he proceeded to count out coins as he recalled verbally each fight and the bets placed and won. To his credit, the reckoning seemed to be fair and true and Choundry ended up walking from the Captain's cabin holding a fist full of silver and gold coins. When Choundry got back to his sleeping area, he managed to place the coins into the hidden compartment in his sea chest. He called to Andy and Darcy and pulled them aside to tell them that he had a wish to enlist their help to keep a close eye on his belongings. Both men said that they would be happy to make sure that no one bothered Choundry's sea chest, and they promised to talk with others who could be trusted to keep an eye open and watchful.

Chapter 9
Tensions Rise

The *Merlin* continued along its cruise and stopped at several new ports. These towns were all smaller than the one where Choundry had fought in the huge building, and the rings that he fought in were smaller as well. He was able to win each fight, and, in the process, he was able to double and double again his winnings. Choundry was also learning as he went, each opponent provided an opportunity to learn from the tricks and maneuvers attempted. Choundry did his best to not get over-confident and he entered each fight remembering his early victories where he'd been lucky enough to win bouts against truly more-talented fighters.

When not fighting or practicing, Choundry continued to seek out tasks aboard ship where he could learn new skills. He now regularly stood watch at the ship's helm and the Captain had taken to leaving him alone on deck as he went to his cabin for a meal. Choundry had begun to notify the Captain of things as they happened and one time he asked the Captain if he would like a sail tightened, when the Captain agreed, both didn't even notice when Choundry was the one to call forward to send men to tighten the sail. Even though the Captain was beginning to rely more on Choundry, he still did not include him in his meetings with his senior crew. He also never ordered Choundry to accompany him and others when they visited smaller vessels.

There was one incident that did seem to be a major turning point in Choundry's status with the Captain and his senior crew.

One day, when the *Merlin* had hauled up alongside a smaller ship and the Captain and some of his men went across, a woman's screams could be heard coming from the smaller vessel. After a period of time, the ship's boat began its return to the *Merlin*, and lying in the bottom of the boat was the huddled figure of a small woman, sobbing and obviously terrified. A man appeared at the railing of the smaller ship and began to call across, begging that his wife be returned. The man had obviously been beaten severely as blood could be seen on the side of his face and speckled across his shirt. As the boat came alongside the *Merlin*, Choundry and a few others of the crew stood and watched the scene below. Choundry stood in the entryway and, looking down at the ship's boat as two of the crew roughly cuffed the woman to stop her resistance. As they went to move towards the ship's ladder, Choundry stood with his feet planted wide. The Captain's attention had been centered on the struggling woman but he looked up at Choundry when one of his men leaned forward and said a few words close to his ear.

The Captain called up in a slightly slurred tone: "Jump lively, Choundry, and give a hand." Choundry looked down and at first did not reply but then said, "I know that with you being Captain that I'm to obey your orders no matter what. I've stood by while you and these men have plundered innocent fishermen and merchantmen, but I'll not stand by for the harming of a woman. Take her back now." A shocked silence descended over the ship and the men huddled in the ship's boat. The Captain's face had turned a bright red and his rage was building.

"I'll not take orders from any of me crew, ever, now do what I says or I'll have yer back striped with the cat."

Choundry stood still and only ventured to answer after a few moments had passed.

"You are the Captain of this ship and I agreed long ago to follow your orders, I've done all you've asked and I've turned a blind eye to things that I shouldn't. I've made you a great deal of money and in return I've learned a great deal. I will say this only once: you'll take the woman back to her husband and that will be that, and if you try and take the cat to me, ever, you'd better finish me because I will kill every last one of you miserable wretches."

Other members of the crew had moved forward at first timidly and then as a group had lined themselves up behind Choundry. Whether they would actually fight for Choundry was unclear but the mere threat of things exploding out of control was enough to tip the Captain into relenting.

"I never intended any harm to the woman" the Captain said defensively. "All I wished to do was bring her to dinner and then take her back to her husband, she didn't understand that I'm just a lonely sailor looking for a little gentle company. I sees that ye and she took my kind gesture wrong so, just this once, I will allow that maybe we should fix this misunderstanding and make everybody happy."

With that the Captain looked to the crewmembers in the boat and twitched his head in the direction of the smaller vessel. "We'll just take the lady back to her husband and we'll all be happy agin."

Once the woman had been returned, and the Captain had climbed back aboard, he started walking back to his cabin and, in passing, his eyes met Choundry's. The stare that he gave Choundry was hard, and it promised that he had not heard the last of this discussion.

For days several days thereafter, the crew seemed to tense as they passed one another. The men went about their regular routine, but the starter was used only sparingly and the ship did not track down any smaller vessels, even though several opportunities presented themselves. The Captain stayed mostly in his cabin and gradually things began to return to their normal routine.

Over the next several weeks, the *Merlin* called into several ports and Choundry was to fight only three times, winning all of them without sustaining any significant injuries. Choundry had been keeping rough track of his time aboard the *Merlin*. He was approaching the end of his second full year aboard the ship. Only one more year to go and his obligation would be fulfilled. An uneasiness was building within him, though, that he might not be able to finish his promised term.

There was a tension building on the ship and between him and the Captain. Ever since the confrontation over the woman, the Captain had been reserved and even more secretive. When the Captain did talk with Choundry in the course of the ship's duties, he kept the discussion to a minimum. It was during this time that from the core group of the senior crew, one man emerged as the Captain's favorite: a man named Cabot.

Cabot was a strongly built man whose one distinguishing characteristic was that he had not a tooth in his mouth and was forced to cut or mash most of his food. Now that the Captain was spending more time in his cabin, it fell to Cabot to relay the Captain's orders and to stand watch during his absence. Cabot was not well liked among the crew as he tended to be cruel over petty things. He seemed to take a genuine pleasure in tormenting the weak or more timid members of the crew. He seemed a cowardly man but, to be fair, he did know how to sail a ship and he had a real knack at finding just the right wind and angle to make the *Merlin* seem to fly over the waves. Cabot had little to say to Choundry and he seemed to avoid him whenever possible. Any interactions with Cabot were usually started with "The Captain says..." followed by instructions on what was to be done.

During this time, several of the crew began to seek out Choundry; to sit near him whenever they were off watch. Without any obvious attempt or forethought, the crew began to separate into two factions; the Captain's men and the rest of the crew that seemed to be collecting around Choundry. This situation continued for several weeks in which the Merlin moved along its usual southern cruise. This trip turned out to be somewhat unusual in that the *Merlin* did not stop in to Banti-town but continued on down the coast into territory that was new for the majority of the crew. The Captain warned both watches as they each came on deck to keep an eye on the coast and watch for any small boats putting out from shore. He told all that they were entering an area where "Savages and criminals were thick as fleas."

During one evening when the weather turned a bit rough, the Captain ordered the *Merlin's* sails shortened. As they were in unfamiliar territory the Captain opted to remain under shortened sails throughout the night to minimize chances of entering dangerous waters without the benefit of daylight to forewarn them. Although the *Merlin* rode a bit rough, it was a relief to not have to work the sails this night. The crew on watch sat about the ship and enjoyed the setting of the sun in a fiery blaze. Choundry was on the evening watch and he felt a pleasant excitement at being in strange waters and seeing new sights. He had discovered that he truly enjoyed traveling to places that were new to him. He enjoyed the experience of seeing new places and, whenever he had a chance to go ashore, to see new cultures and people in their natural surroundings. Choundry's watch finished in the middle of the night. Once the next watch had come up to relieve the men, there was a shifting of men in the darkness as those coming on duty went to their stations while others threaded through the familiar obstacles on the deck and made their way below deck and to their hammocks.

Choundry quickly went to sleep. He had learned to do as most sailors; sleep when one could because a full night of uninterrupted sleep was a rare thing indeed. At some point in the night Choundry was awakened from a deep sleep. He lie there trying to remember what it was that had caused him to awaken. He seemed to remember a noise that sounded like a low "thunk" of a solid piece of wood striking another piece of wood. He started to go back to sleep but ended up lying in the dark wondering what could have made such a noise. Above his head he could hear the measured tread of one of the watch as they slowly walked from one side of the ship to the other. All of the noises that he heard were familiar parts of a routine that he'd learned over many months. Nothing seemed amiss but he couldn't shake the thought that the noise that he'd heard did not fit the usual pattern of noises that he'd come to expect on board the *Merlin*. Feeling almost as if he had an itch that he couldn't scratch, Choundry rose from his hammock and padded on bare feet to the ladder that led on deck. He climbed quickly and poked his head up high enough to see around the deck within the limited light that came from the window in the Captain's cabin.

Choundry couldn't see anything suspicious but held back for a moment when he felt a slight tingling sensation go up his spine as he again heard a very faint noise that sounded similar to the one that had awakened him. This noise seemed to come from the rear of the ship, and included a section of the ship that was shrouded in darkness. Choundry stepped quickly to where the man standing watch was lolling listlessly while holding the helm with one hand and staring into the dark. The man was clearly startled when he saw Choundry approach but quickly relaxed as he saw his familiar face in the near dark. Choundry leaned close and said "Listen close, I fear something is amiss, alert the watch and send them to me and then go below to waken the rest of the men. Send someone to awaken the Captain but be sure to warn them to be as quiet as they can.."

With that, the man turned to look anxiously about and then make his way towards where several men could be seen on the starboard side of the ship. A few seconds after his shadow had merged with these men's outline, they all broke apart in separate directions to alert the others. Choundry stood holding the ship's wheel and hoped that he hadn't just disturbed everyone's sleep needlessly but felt certain all the same that something was wrong. Better to lose some sleep than fall prey to something sinister.

As he stared back into the darkness, his vision became a bit more sensitive, and he began to discern some slight movements in the shadows. He stood totally still but knew, with the light from the Captain's window, that he must be very obvious to anyone that might be looking forward from the stern. Suddenly he was certain that there was more than one person hiding in the darkness, just as several crew members made their way to Choundry's side, there came a rush of bodies from out of the dark. Whoever had been lying in wait must have realized that the alarm had been sounded and decided to move quickly before a defense could be raised. Choundry sensed more than saw at least a dozen figures rushing from out of the shadows. He could see the glint from what appeared to be raised cutlasses and he heard the sound of bare feet slapping hard against the deck. Choundry shouted a warning that the ship was under attack as he flung himself forward and down, rolling his body low and into the legs of the onrushing enemy.

Several of the attackers went down in a mass and this served to break the first wave of the attack and give the men of the *Merlin* a fighting chance while the rest of the crew made their way on deck. Choundry hit and kicked out at the bodies lying on top of him. He had only one advantage and that was that he knew that everyone he came into contact with would be an enemy while those who struggled to pull themselves from the jam of bodies had no idea whether they were coming into contact with a friend or a foe. Choundry flailed out and felt his fist come in contact with the bridge of someone's nose, sensing the snapping of the bone and cartilage. He grabbed out with his other hand and gripped onto the face of someone trying to rise from the deck. Choundry exerted a mass of pressure and forced the man first up, back, and then downwards with a crunching force to the back of the man's head as he came in contact with the deck. Choundry felt the slashes from several blades, and he suffered numerous bruises from contact with fists and hardened feet. Breaking free from the mass of bodies, he rushed forward only to realize that he had broken through the attackers and was now to their rear.

Searching around quickly in the dim light, Choundry was finally able to locate a belaying pin that could be used as a short bludgeon. With his weapon in hand, he began to move forward. He had the element of surprise as it was Choundry now attacking from the darkness and this time it was into the unprotected and unaware backs of the attackers. Choundry was able to bring three separate attackers down with short vicious swings of the club before the attackers realized their new threat. Several of *Merlin's* crew were down and Choundry could see that at least one of those would never rise again. Choundry kept pressure on several of the enemy while the remaining *Merlins* attempted to hold back the rest of the attackers.

At that point Choundry once again heard the sound of what must be another smaller vessel or ship's boat making contact with the hull of the *Merlin*. He knew that the attackers would be gaining reinforcements soon and that, once that happened, the end for the crew would only be minutes away. Not sure what he could do at this point to change this course of events, he redoubled his efforts to bring down the three remaining attackers that he was facing. A quick jab at one to force him to step backwards and then a follow through flat-footed kick to his exposed ankle brought a satisfying snapping sound followed by a scream from the now crippled fighter. Although he was now only facing two enemies, the time that it took for him to eliminate his third opponent had left him open to attack from the other attackers aboard the ship. Choundry felt a tremendous blow on his right shoulder and his right arm went temporarily numb. As a result, he dropped the bludgeon that he still retained from earlier in the fight. He also had a fist catch him a glancing blow to his chin. Shaking his head, he stepped back two steps to give himself a moment to clear his head and regain some of the feeling in his right arm. After a brief pause in which the remaining two opponents stood for a moment to catch their breath, they surged forward to resume their attack. Choundry formed his left fist into a wedge and, aiming at a throat, thrust it forward at the attacker on his right. He made a solid impact and felt cartilage crushing under his knuckles. The man stepped back and grabbed his own throat with both hands. He was making a strange gurgling sound as he continued to step backwards into the gloom until Choundry was forced to refocus his attention back to his remaining enemy.

This man appeared to be wavering after having just seen his two companions dealt with so severely. Just as Choundry was preparing for a last effort to drive his foe backwards, there came a rush of bodies from the forward part of the ship along with several crew members yelling as they rose from below decks. The man that Choundry was facing turned quickly and on seeing these new members of the *Merlin's* crew joining the fight he spun on his heel and ran back towards the rear of the ship. Choundry yelled, "Push em boys, there are more of them tying on to the back of the ship, the fight's not over yet."

With that, the crew surged as one towards the stern of the ship, voicing a savage yell. When they reached the railing at the end of the deck, they looked over and could see bodies jumping back into two boats or diving into the water. Within a few minutes there was not a trace of the attackers in the water except for the sound of oars being hurriedly applied as they faded in the distance. Choundry looked to his shipmates, and they all gave a yell; celebrating having survived such a close call.

As they walked back the length of the ship, they began to see that they hadn't been as lucky as they thought. Although a score of the pirates were lying about on the deck, one or two attempting to drag themselves to the railings in an attempt to escape their fate, there were at least half that number of the *Merlin's* crew who were grievously wounded or lying still. As the crew members moved among the wounded, some of them set about finishing off the remaining pirates while others searched the bodies for familiar faces or best mates. After serving together for many months, there wasn't a man among those slain who was not well known or considered a friend by many of the survivors. As Choundry was searching among those on deck, he stopped as he recognized a crumpled familiar form lying in the half light. Gently placing his hand on the shoulder of the quiet form, he slowly turned the body until he could see the bruised face of Darcy, eyes closed and strangely peaceful. The knife protruding from Darcy's chest was evidence enough that there was no point in checking further.

After a prolonged silence, the remaining crewmen of the *Merlin* stood and moved back away from the bodies. They looked around at each other and, after a few minutes, one man said, "Where are the others? I don't see the Captain either." With that, the crew moved together toward the Captain's cabin door. As they reached it, they didn't even bother to knock as was customary, and as the door parted it revealed the sight of the Captain and several of his senior crew, including Cabot, lying about the cabin; a keg of rum tapped on the table. These men who were supposed to be the leaders of the ship had slept through the attack in a drunken stupor. There was much heated talk among the crewmen who had just survived the attack that they should just take these men, one by one, tie them up with heavy lead shot in their pockets and pitch them into the sea. In the end the crew just walked away, not wanting to view any more of the death that had been visited on them in the night.

Chapter 10
A New Port of Call

As a result of the battle, for the next several days the *Merlin* had to be run shorthanded. The Captain never mentioned a word regarding the battle and the state that he and his men had been in. After waking, and seeing the carnage left on deck, they meekly went about tossing the bodies over the ship's side and cleaning the bloodstains as best they could.

The *Merlin* turned back from its trip into unknown territory. They'd be needing new hands to replace those lost and they were in no condition to fend off another attack. After a few days, they began to recognize some of the more prominent points of land and then finally they could see the telltale outward ebb of muddy water that indicated the entrance to the bay at Banti-Town.

Entering the harbor, the *Merlin* tied up. Choundry was still suffering the ill effects of the battle and the various wounds that he'd received, including a long slash down his ribs and a jagged cut across the back of his right hand. It seemed ill-advised for him to fight and even the Captain did not raise the subject as he prepared to go ashore. The *Merlin* stayed in harbor for four days during which time the Captain was able to recruit (or capture) seven new members of the crew. Two of the new men were real hard cases who thought themselves to be formidable. When the newcomers tried to bully some of the smaller members of the crew, Choundry was able to put them in line with only a few bruises and one black eye. The *Merlin* continued on back up the coast and along their familiar route of trade.

Their usual routine reestablished itself: sailing close along the coast, picking off the occasional smaller craft, and then moving on to the next port where Choundry continued to fight and win. His hoard of coins now filled the hidden compartment in his sea chest and he began to stash coins in a cloth sack that he placed in a small false support beam that he had fashioned in a little visited part of the ship. Choundry hadn't counted his treasure because he never had a moment's peace in which he could lay it all out. Even so, he knew that he was already wealthier than he'd ever dreamed he'd be. He no longer made any large bets when the Captain or any of his cronies were about. He hoped that he gave the impression that he was betting only smallish amounts so that the Captain's greed would not be excited. He even made a point to be seen by the Captain's men in the act of betting a copper or two on one of his pending fights. They would laugh and jest that he should have more confidence in himself, or the Captain might think he wouldn't give his full measure of effort. At these times he would have already bet what most men would have deemed to be staggering sums on his winning the fight. There were times that Choundry was hard-pressed to make it back to the ship without showing that he was carrying very large sums of money. He had taken to changing all coins into gold coins and bars to reduce the size of the space that he needed to hide his wealth. The bottom section of his sea chest was nothing but gold coins carefully stacked and rolled into the hidden drawer. Choundry was careful to be the only one who would move his sea chest as it would have been exceedingly clear to anyone lifting the box that it weighed much more than a mere chest of sailor's belongings.

Choundry had one scare that occurred as they were leaving a port and getting ready to set sail. The lookout called down to the Captain that he had sighted an English warship making its way down through the small boats and ships sailing in and about the port. The Captain called to Cabot, "That be an English fisherman casting his net for likely men to add to his crew, maybe we should lie about a bit and invite him over to take his pick of some of our little Mateys?."

With that the Captain turned to look at Choundry with a wicked gleam in his eye. He seemed to waver for a few moments, during which time Choundry realized that, if the Captain's greed for Choundry's winnings ever overpowered his lust for additional winnings at the fighting ring, that this was an easy way for the Captain to be rid of Choundry in such a manner where there would be little chance for him to refuse or even take his winnings with him. After some tense minutes where it was obvious that the Captain was taunting Choundry, he finally relented and ordered the ship to turn about and re-enter the port to wait until the English ship had left or had its fill of unwilling recruits.

Choundry reached a decision after seeing the English ship. He knew now that he was vulnerable and that the closer that he got to fulfilling his obligation to the Captain, the more likely that the Captain would use some form of trickery to separate Choundry from his winnings. As they sailed further up the coast, Choundry decided he'd have to act as soon as possible.

The next port they entered was Lisbon, and the Captain told Choundry to get himself ready for a fight. Choundry asked that he first be allowed shore leave along with the rest of the crew and in fact it had been a long period of time since Choundry had taken the opportunity to do something enjoyable. The Captain told him that he could go ashore with the first watch but to be careful not to eat or drink too much as he wanted him in top form for the fight. Choundry waited until the Captain and his men had left the ship and then he went below and gathered the majority of his savings into a double thick grain sack. He quickly left the ship and made his way along the wharf into the business section of the city. He walked along until he found the offices of a well-known shipping company. Entering the establishment, he walked to the counter and asked to see the owner. The clerk behind the counter looked at Choundry with a degree of disdain and, sniffing and coughing, seemed to imply that Choundry was exuding a strong odor, "My good man, Mr. Thompson is a very busy man, and he can't be interrupted without good cause. Pardon me for saying but I think that I can address any issue that you might have."

Choundry paused for a moment and then told the clerk, "Just tell Mr. Thompson that a man with a sack of money wishes to do some business with him."

With a look of surprise, the clerk decided that this situation was one for which he might regret not alerting the owner of the business. A few minutes later, Choundry was shown into the inner office. He saw a man standing in the corner who quickly turned and came to Choundry with his hand extended.

"You must be a caution, I haven't seen Edward so agitated in quite some time" the man said. "What can I do for you, young man?."

Choundry sat and took a minute to measure the gentleman in front of him. He seemed to be a good-natured man and Choundry sensed something solid about him. He decided to take a chance and said, "I've a bit of cash put by and I would like to invest some of it in shipping. Is that something that you could help me with?" The man looked at Choundry and, with a slight smile, said, "I can see that you are new to the business world as you get right down to it, no simpering and no playing around. Whether you know it or not, you've come to just the right place. I am in fact a bit short of cash as most of my money is in trade stretched across the two oceans. What is it you have in mind and how much can you invest?"

With that Choundry upended most of his feedbag onto the man's desk and the cascade of golden coins was truly impressive to see and even more than Choundry had expected. "Young man, you are either very wealthy or very foolish to carry such an amount around with you, why, that is a fortune!" Choundry looked to him and said, "I'm neither wealthy nor foolish as I have earned every penny of this money as a fighter in ports from here to London and back many times. I've yet to be beaten so I've done well with the bets. I have decided that it is no longer safe for me to have this money on board the ship with me so I decided to invest it so it will work for me. I hope that I can trust you to invest this money and that someday I will be free to return and work the investments with you. Is my trust well placed?"

The man looked at Choundry again and there was an odd look to his eyes. "Aye, you've placed your trust well as I'd not cheat a man who earned his money by his own blood nor a man who will accept my mere word in exchange for his life's savings. Let's count these coins and I will get Edward in here to write up a chit that shows the amount that you have invested. I will place this money into trade and shipping and hopefully, barring storms and pirates, you'll be an even wealthier man in a few years when the ships that we invest in finish their cruises."

After sealing the deal and tucking the written promissory note into his pocket, Choundry then left the shipping company and went to an investment bank nearby where he repeated the process except the end result was a round sum invested in the bank at a guaranteed annual rate of return. Leaving the bank, he then made his way back down to the wharf and walked up to where the *Merlin* was tied up. Returning the grain sack to the hold he kept sufficient funds in hand to place his usual hefty side bets at the upcoming fight. He felt strangely naked without having his savings at hand and he dearly hoped that he'd made the right decision. Now, in order to be safe from impressment on an English ship he had to execute the next step in his plan.

Choundry left the ship just prior to his appointed time and wound his way through the narrow streets, finally finding a street vendor selling olives from brine tubs and cheeses that hung down from strings. Paying the man for his purchases he then entered a store and purchased a half side of chicken and a small bottle of red wine. He walked down to the white sand that ringed the inner port and sat to enjoy his meal. He felt that he had done well over the past two and a half years, but he had to be very careful as it could all go to naught if he didn't watch the Captain and be prepared for what the man was obviously planning. Choundry knew that, if not for his potential to earn money for the Captain, the man would have long ago found some way to do him in, if for no other reason than that the crew held him in high regard while they detested the Captain. Choundry had challenged the Captain on his own deck and lived to tell about it. The Captain had not forgotten that day and he was just biding his time until events allowed him to seek his revenge without it costing him any coin.

That evening Choundry fought in a hall as huge as the one that had first awed him so many months ago. His fame had spread enough that it was hard for the captain to get good odds. Choundry was able to find someone willing to give him odds that would still provide him with a tidy sum should he win again. Some of the fights in this ring were slightly different from what Choundry was used to in that the champions would fight using blades. Although he had been practicing every chance that he'd had he still felt uncertain of his skills when using a sword; he had never been trained by a master as he had with his other fighting skills. Choundry declined a blade fight even though he could have earned a much higher set of odds had he agreed to the bout. Instead, he chose to fight in his usual manner and eventually won his fight. Choundry had decided that he must find someone who could teach him how to use a blade and build his skills. Looking ahead, he wanted to be able to face an opponent with any type of weapon if he were to ever be challenged by someone who considered themselves a "gentleman"; someone such as a squire or a squire's son.

Later that evening Choundry was just finishing his watch on deck and waiting for his relief to come from below decks when the Captain called for him. He proceeded forward and opened the cabin door, entering into the gloom of the candlelit room. Captain Johnston looked up from writing in a ledger. He seemed to be in a surly mood and quickly got to the point.

"Choundry, I can't get anyone to bet against ye anymore, I can't make money on ye and if I can't make money on ye yer worse than worthless to me. We has to sail to ports where your name isn't known. I'm takin a risk in doin that so I should get's more of a reward, I want some of yer winnings to offset the cost of the longer cruise."

Choundry had felt that something like this was coming so he was glad that he had taken action when he did. He shuffled his feet, looked down and tried to look sheepish. He looked back up to the Captain, "I have some put by but you know that I'm not one to put big bets on myself, I don't want to jinx the fight. What I did have put aside I've spent a good deal of on the ladies."

Captain Johnston looked at him and shook his head muttering something about "worthless scum," Choundry knew that the Captain was likely to believe his story about spending money on doxies in the ports that they visited because that is what the Captain and most of the men on the ship would have done had they the same opportunity.

Captain Johnston demanded some form of payment. When Choundry went to see what remained of his stash, the Captain went along with him. Choundry allowed the Captain to see where he hid his coins. Taking half of the coins from the few that he had managed to win from his last fight he turned and gave them to the Captain. "I'll gladly give you half if it allows us the chance to sail to ports where I'll have another chance at building some wealth, I've squandered what I've won so far, and I would dearly like another chance to make good." The Captain seemed satisfied with the coins that Choundry had given to him, especially since he now knew where Choundry kept his remaining few coins. On the other hand, Choundry felt that the loss of the coins was more than repaid by the elimination of the threat of being impressed onto an English man-o-war; the Captain no longer thought that Choundry might have a large sum of money worth stealing and therefore Choundry was of more value to the Captain if he remained on board ship and continued as his champion.

The *Merlin* continued on past its usual limit to its southern cruise and sailed once again down the savage coast where months before they had been attacked by the pirates. On this journey, the *Merlin* stayed well away from the coastline, keeping to deeper waters with sufficient maneuvering distance should they spy any suspicious vessels pulling out from land. The *Merlin* continued on for the next several days without spotting any other vessels. They rounded a series of high rocky cliffs and made in towards what appeared to be a large, sheltered bay. Making their way in towards the port, they eventually had to thread their way through a series of anchored ships. After they secured the ship, Choundry accompanied the Captain and several other crew members as they made their way ashore. Choundry brought along several of his remaining gold coins. He had decided to purchase a new set of clothes a step above in quality to anything that he had since he'd come aboard the *Merlin*. After separating from the others, Choundry went swiftly about making his purchases. He finally settled on a suit of clothes, two shirts and a new pair of shoes and stockings. Choundry had the packages wrapped tightly and tied with a strong cord, he had no intention of using the clothes any time soon and they needed to fit into the remaining space within his sea chest. After returning to the ship and placing his purchases in the chest, he went back ashore and made his way to a nearby tavern where he had agreed earlier that he would meet Andy and several of the others. On entering the tap room, it was obvious that Andy and the others had started without him and were well into their cups. Choundry ordered an ale and the house meal which turned out to be a passing decent lamb stew. The bread that came with the meal was piping hot and fresh from the oven with mounds of creamy butter. Within moments Choundry seemed to be in heaven.

He enjoyed watching the antics of his messmates as they caroused at the bar, Andy had turned out to be loyal friend and some of the others he had come to know as decent fellows. Over the past two and more years, Choundry had ample opportunity to get to know most of the members of the crew and he had been pleasantly surprised to find that some of them were truly stout lads who had come to misfortune as he had, although none of them had to swear years of service to the Captain. It was surprising to Choundry that these men hadn't chosen to leave the Captain's service at some point and join another ship. Although his time aboard the *Merlin* was certainly his longest service aboard a ship, Choundry knew that the *Merlin* was genuinely not a happy ship. The men were frequently tormented by several of the senior crew, although truth be told, this happened much less frequently as Choundry had become a force to be reckoned with. In fact, without realizing it, these men had started to spend more and more of their time aboard ship in close proximity to Choundry, sensing the strength and protection that he imparted.

Choundry had started to dare think of a future after the *Merlin*. His investments would hopefully allow him a good foundation to start his new life. He'd purchased the new clothes so that he could step ashore and assume a new life; no one would know where he'd been and what he'd accomplished, he would have a chance at a fresh beginning. Choundry was unsure as to what he would eventually do with his life but he knew that he dearly wanted to continue adventuring; seeing new places and learning, reading, and experiencing new places and peoples. He knew that he needed to be able to protect himself in the future so that he never had to allow any man's foot on his neck, as the Captain's had been for nearly the past three years. He wanted a life with a wife and family but that could wait until he had experienced the freedom that he'd been missing since he'd entered service at sea. He wanted to be able to come and go as he pleased and answer to no man. Mostly, he craved to accomplish great deeds, to become something that he couldn't even dream of today; he sensed a driving need to not waste the opportunities that his pending freedom would bring.

Choundry wiled the rest of the day away with Andy and his friends but was careful not to overindulge with food or drink. He still had a fight this evening and he wanted to be at his best. This was a new port and the fighters would hail from lands that Choundry might not even know of and they could have fighting techniques that he was not prepared for.

As evening fell, he walked Andy and the others back to the ship to make sure that they returned safely and were not robbed on the way. Moving along, Choundry asked a passerby where the arena was located and, after receiving directions, made his way through various streets until he came to a squat, single-story building with a high arched roof. The arena was just like most of the fight rings that Choundry had been in over numerous ports of call. It had the same dirt floor and the usual wooden walls. The crowd was somewhat larger than was usually seen at these fights and the dress of those attending seemed to be somewhat more refined and colorful. Several of the men sported large feathers sprouting from their hats and there were a few ladies sprinkled throughout the crowd. The ladies were dressed in such finery that they looked like tiny colorful birds perched on their seats; fans fluttering, and small scented handkerchiefs held to their noses to counter the smell of unwashed bodies. There was a hub of activity across the ring that broke apart into three men, two of whom were dragging an inert form from the ring. The third individual crossed the ring to Choundry's left where he could see that he stopped and talked with Captain Johnston. Choundry took this opportunity to find the nearest odds maker and, upon inquiring, found that he could get even odds on his own fight so he bet the rest of the coins that he had with him.

A few minutes later, the Captain approached Choundry and told him that he would be facing a local champion, that it was the only fight that he could find that would give decent odds. He told Choundry, "We've come a long ways and I has spent a good bit of money getting here, we'll have to take what fights we can so don't go complainin."

Although Choundry found this to be a bit odd, even for the Captain, he moved along as they approached the gate to the ring. Choundry stepped into the ring and heard the latch of the gate clicking into place as it closed. He strode forward several steps just as he'd done in numerous past events and waited for the announcer to start his wind up. After a moment's pause, his opponent entered the other side of the ring. At first Choundry could not discern what was different about the man until he realized that he was dressed in a very stylish set of clothes and sported a hat that was tilted rakishly to the side, hardly the dress of a man about to engage in what could be mortal combat. As realization started to dawn on Choundry, he turned to find the Captain had thrown a sword down into the ring, smiling at Choundry, "It's been a while since I saw fear in yer eyes going into a fight, tis a good thing for me to see, especially with all the trouble ye've been causing me, I still expects ya to win, lad. I'll admit that I'll not be wagering as much as I usually does on ye but this fight is special as I'll end up a happy man no matter how it ends."

Choundry knew the rules of the ring. He had entered and now he must fight or face punishment from an angry crowd that would most likely end up worse than what would have happened had he fought. Stepping back, he picked up the sword. He was thankful at least that the Captain had provided him with a good quality blade; mostly likely taken from one of the vessels that he'd plundered in the past. Choundry tried not to give the Captain the satisfaction of showing his dismay at this turn of events. He swung the sword back and forth, testing its balance and getting a feel for the weight. He'd practiced with Dan and his friends and had achieved a certain degree of skill but had little chance to maintain his skills while on the *Merlin,* as the Captain would have frowned on his having a weapon on board.

The announcer started the usual wind up to the match and finally called for the fight to begin. Choundry's opponent kept his body side-on, with the sword held forward in his right hand and his other hand placed on his hip. He moved in a practiced step that moved forward and slightly to Choundry's left. It was obvious that Choundry was facing an experienced swordsman, probably one well above what his training would allow him to match. Choundry realized that he needed to stay away from the man long enough to study his movements and try to find some way to counter his opponent's decided advantage. As they edged closer the man started a slow circling of the tip of his blade as if trying to decide where he would pick as his point of attack. Choundry attempted to show a calm and detached manner in hopes that it would cast some doubt in his opponent's mind. He forced a slight smile, and he moved first back then forward followed by a slight feint to this right. He tried to give the impression of self assurance; and that his taunting manner was designed to entice his opponent into a rash move. He tried to be as obvious as he could without giving away the fact that it was all an act.

The swordsman feinted forward and Choundry stepped back and to his right, allowing the blade to pass harmlessly by his side. His opponent had a slightly puzzled look on his face while he tried to follow Choundry's erratic movements in an attempt to discern a pattern or purpose. The man appeared to be in his early twenties and physically fit in the manner of someone who trains rather than works for his strength. This man obviously came from a different world than the one that Choundry had been raised in and certainly the one that Choundry had lived in for almost three years. He probably came from an upbringing with rules and behaviors that were "honorable and fair." Choundry had been forced to learn how to win; no matter what. Honor was all well and fine, but it could get you killed if you acted in the belief that all others would be honorable as well. Choundrey suddenly knew what he had to do to win; he had to do something that would be so alien to this man's world that he wouldn't expect it or know how to protect against it.

As his foe started forward again, Choundry stepped back but not quite fast enough as the tip of the man's blade cut a shallow slice up Choundry's forearm. Blood started to drip down his hand and onto the dirt floor of the ring. The swordsman smiled briefly as if he'd solved the puzzle. He started again to move in his previous pattern of forward and to the right, forward and to the right, inching closer with each step so that his blade would be that much closer for a telling thrust. Choundry waited. He needed the man to feel as if he were in control of the fight and that things had fallen into a familiar pattern. His blade flicked out again and Choundry's shoulder started to blossom a red stain from a puncture. Choundry gave an involuntary grunt but held his ground and started to swing a little erratically, in an exaggerated action that appeared as if he were trying to shield himself with the type of wild swinging that an unskilled man might use. His opponent stepped again and then raised on his toes' preparing to go on the attack. Choundry knew that he had to counter this, or he was likely to be mortally wounded or crippled in the next few moments.

As the man began his step forward, he went into a lunge, Choundry used his blade in a quick and deft motion to push his opponent's blade to the side and then out to his right in a sweeping motion. For a second Choundry and his opponent's blades were locked together out to the side, the sound of metal scraping on metal as they fought for leverage to win the stalemate. At that point Choundry implemented the move that he had hoped he would have an opportunity to employ; he stepped in and smashed his left fist directly into the young man's face. He followed up by stepping in under the man's blade so that the weapon was effectively useless, and the fight shifted to the type of pummeling that Choundery was familiar with. Within moments he had crushed the young man under an onslaught of blows that left him with an obviously broken nose and mashed lips. The man dropped his blade and stepped back trying to hold his hands to his face to ward off any more of the wicked punishment. Choundry stopped and stood, blade still held in his right hand, poised in front of his now defenseless opponent. With a quick flick of his blade, he touched the now blood-specked front of the man's shirt. He held the blade steady, "Do you yield?." With a quick shake of his head the man admitted defeat and tried to turn away. Choundry stopped him and told him "Let this be a lesson to you in trying to fight men who are not as skilled as you and who have but little chance. I have the right to kill you right now and end your life, remember this moment and how you feel the next time you think to face an unskilled man just for the amusement of your friends." With that, he walked back to the side of the arena and exited the ring. After returning the blade to the Captain he went off into the crowd, circled wide and stopped to collect his winnings.

He had been lucky again against a man with a much greater skill than his own. Choundry promised himself that he would not again be lured into the ring to fight with a blade until he had a chance to learn how to win without tricks.

The *Merlin* continued on its cruise going further into unfamiliar waters. Once, they had a close call as the ship brushed against a coral head that, had it not broken off, would have crushed the hull of the ship and most likely sent it to the bottom. The *Merlin* had no cannons and the swivel guns that were in the hold had long been neglected and were lying rusted among the ballast stones. There were several muskets and handguns along with a chest full of cutlasses and axes. Belaying pins were located in several spots around the ship. The crew of the *Merlin* could put up a fight against raiders using smaller boats, but the ship would be almost defenseless against any ship of size that sported larger armament. Captain Johnston relied on evading larger ships and staying in waters that he knew where and how to hide; places where a ship of the *Merlin's* size could go that might tear the bottom out of a larger ship.

It became apparent as time went by and the ship went further into strange waters that they were taking great risks. The crew started to become anxious and eventually word made it to the Captain who, walking the deck one evening said, "We'll go to the next port and then we'll make our way back to home waters. Bear with me lads. The next port is greater than any we've ever seen, and the women are the most beautiful ye've ever dreamed of, and willin lasses to boot!"

At that moment, the lookout yelled down that two sails had been sighted just emerging over the horizon slightly to the west of their present course. Although they could be mere merchantmen making their way down the coast, it was also very possible that these were war ships spaced in such a manner to be sure that they could come down quickly on any prey making their way along the coast. The Captain called for his eyeglass and after climbing partway up the ropes, he wound his arm and leg around the rope and held himself dangling above the deck as he scoped the distant ships.

After a few minutes, he allowed himself to slide down the rope slowly, heedless of the tar being ground into his clothing.

With a sigh, he said "Alas, lads, we'll have to save those women fer our next trip, there be scoundrels who have likely heard of the *Merlin* coming this way and they be waiting to do a villains work. As much as I'd dearly love to stay and teach them a lesson, I think that it be a better idea to reverse our course here and make our way to our usual home waters."

With that, the *Merlin* was put about and started the long journey back. They did stop again in the same port where Choundry had his battle with the blades, but he told the captain that he was dealing with a stomach malady. The Captain was fairly apoplectic when he heard that Choundry was not to fight again. He still had the cargo on board that he shipped when they first stopped in this port so that meant he had no means of making a profit at all and that the last leg of his southern cruise had been pointless.

The Captain ordered the ship made ready and then they sailed out to head north again. The *Merlin* did stop in two ports on the way back up to their home waters. In both ports Choundry was scheduled for fights. Choundry made a point of assuring himself that no weapons would be allowed in either ring before he agreed to fight. He won both fights handily and was able to collect his winnings without the Captain realizing that he had made substantial side wagers. Finally, the *Merlin* was back into waters that had long been their usual routes for trade. The Captain had shipped a large cargo of fruits at the southernmost port of call that they has visited and he was eager to sell his cargo as quickly as he could to avoid spoilage. He pushed the crew to move on to the next two ports where the *Merlin* entered, quickly unloaded what cargo the Captain was able sell, and then left without any of the crew being allowed ashore. The Captain seemed frantic to get to the next port and sell his cargo before it all wasted in the hold. Choundry had recognized the last port that the *Merlin* had entered as being one just down the coast from his hometown. Choundry stayed away from the Captain, trying not to remind him of his presence and therefore the reason they'd avoided this particular port of call these past years. The Captain's greed kept him focused on driving the crew on to the next place to sell his goods; it appeared that he was not paying attention as to what ports were next but he was instead only interested in how much farther he would have to go to make his next sale. As a result, it was for this reason that when Choundry had raised his eyes to the horizon the following morning he finally saw his home port coming into view.

Chapter 11
Return to the Present and a Homecoming

After having words with Captain Johnston, Choundry went below to gather his belongings. He quickly unbundled his new suit of clothing and, after donning the clothing and his new shoes, he placed his pistol in his belt on one side and his sword in the other. He half expected the Captain to attempt to rob him or go back on their deal. Choundry was ready to fight his way off of the ship if need be. After he had repacked his belongings, Choundry shouldered his sea chest and made his way on deck. Looking about, he could see that there were several of his mates who looked genuinely distressed to see him leaving. Andy came up and said, "I can't say that I blames ye for going Choundry, ye'll be missed and the ship will not be the same. I can't say that I look forward to what the Captain and his mates will do when you're gone."

Several of the crew gathered around Choundry to wish him farewell. Choundry told them, "I'm not sure what I'll do or where I'll settle but you men could sail with me any day that you wish, I'd welcome any one of you." With that he lifted his sea chest and strode to the front of the ship. Captain Johnston was watching him from his usual post on deck; "Begone with ye, a useless lubber ye came on this ship and in my mercy I took ye in as if ye was one of me own kin, now yer deserting me. Well, good riddance! It's time I got this ship and crew back to the way they used to be, enough of the Christian charity that's been goin on. Get off me boat or I'll have ye thrown off."

The Captain had obviously remembered why he had chosen to avoid this particular port in the past three years as he told his crew that they would tie up and conduct their business and to be ready to sail within an hour.

As the *Merlin* touched the wood of the dock, Choundry stepped off and strode several steps. He turned to look back at the ship that had been his home for the past three years. Much had happened since he'd left this same town. He had learned much. He couldn't imagine ever missing this ship, but he would miss some of his comrades and he would take much from the experience into his new life. With a last glance, he turned and started up the familiar street into town.

Choundry had changed much in the past three years; he'd grown another three inches in height, he had grown the breadth of his chest and arms, his hair was now much longer and worn in a queue down the middle of his back, and he carried numerous scars from all of the battles that he had fought. It was no wonder that the people he passed as he walked through the town did not seem to recognize him; especially, Choundry realized, as these people would have marked him as dead many months ago. Choundry made his way up through the street where he used to run and play as a lad. The memories came rushing back to him and he felt a lump rising in his throat. He had schooled himself to not think of home for the pain that it would bring or the fear that it would somehow "jinx" his chances of returning. Now that he was actually here, the walls started to crack, and the emotions started to well up. He had to stop for a moment to collect himself before he could move on. He coughed roughly and blinked his eyes clear. As his steps drew him nearer to his family home, he suddenly came to a halt. He found himself consumed by the thought that he had always dreamed of returning home to his family but had never considered that something could have happened to them in his absence. When he had left home three years earlier, his mother was already showing her age and she had experienced several bouts of sickness that seemed to take longer each time to pass. What if he had returned to an empty house? To find that no one here even remembered him? What then?

Choundry hunched the sea chest higher on his shoulder and his look hardened, whatever would be would be and he must find out. If it were so, then he would just have to accept what was. With a silent whisper he asked God for just this one time to show him His grace and allow him to find his family again. He dearly wanted to have back what was stolen from him.

Choundry eventually found himself standing outside his family home. He felt confused because he didn't know whether to knock or to just enter as he used to. Placing his sea chest on the ground nearby, he finally reached out and rapped roughly on the door. For a moment he couldn't hear anything from inside and then he heard a slow and soft tread approaching the door. His heart soared because he remembered that sound from so many nights of lying in bed and hearing his mother walk softly about the house tending to her never-ending chores. He heard the click of the latch as it was opened and then the door swung back to reveal the face of his mother.

At first, she gazed up at him with a puzzled look and then she started to search his face, at first slowly and then frantically. Her hand shot to her mouth and she took a step backwards. Visibly shocked at what she saw, she could only mouth weakly, "Choundry…Choundry…is that you? It can't be …dear God make it so."

He smiled and tears came to his eyes, "Aye Momma, it's me, back home." He took a step and then tentatively held his arms forward as if he were afraid of her response.

"It is!" cried his mother as she flung herself forward and gripped him as if she were drowning. Emotions seared through Choundry; the joy of homecoming and the distress of the pain that he had made this good woman endure. How foolish he had been in his youth; how prideful. He vowed at that moment that he would never again hurt this woman by his foolish deeds. He was being given another chance to do right by her and by heaven he wouldn't waste it.

After several moments of crying and holding Choundry with all her might, his mother backed up a bit and looked up at his face. Her manner changed slightly as she reached up and gently traced several of the scars on his face. Her fingers trembled and she bit her lower lip as if to stay its quivering. "My son, where have you been? What has happened to you? Oh my son."

Choundry reached up and gently took her hand in his. "It is over, and I am back now, a little older and much the wiser. I have dreamed of this moment for so long, mother, I hope that you will forgive me for all that happened, I promise to make it up to you." His mother tilted her head and smiled at him, "My prodigal son, I welcome you back with all my heart, there is nothing to forgive; just many thanks to be given to God for your return."

Picking up his chest, he stepped into his old home. His first impression was that the main room was much smaller than he had remembered. There was almost a dreamlike feeling to be looking about at all of the familiar objects and memories from his youth. He sat at the table and his mother sat close by, still holding to his hand as if she couldn't bear to let him go.

After a few minutes of enjoying the sensation of being home, Choundry began to tell his mother what had happened during his abscence. He glossed over much of what he had endured during his time aboard the *Merlin*; he didn't want to cause her any more distress on his behalf. His mother stayed quiet all during the telling of his tale; she seemed to just enjoy the sound of his voice. When he was finished, Choundry looked to his mother "How have you been, he asked? Where is Catherine and Kyle?."

Choundry's mother averted her eyes slightly before she answered him. "Your sister has been married these past two years and she has a young son already. She found a good man, a local farmer. He is not a wealthy man, but he does care for Catherine and he is a solid man. I think that your father would have rather she married a bit higher, but he would have approved of the match."

Choundry sat back and thought, "So much to have happened, his sister gone from home and he an uncle! He would have to visit her as soon as he could manage."

"And what of Kyle? Is he at his shop?." His mother answered, "Yes, he has done well and many of the gentry are coming from a distance to order his wares. He even has an apprentice now and he lives in a fine house just down the street from his shop." Kyle lives in another house? He must have become very successful indeed. Realizing that his mother now must live alone in this house, he looked about and could see the telltale signs that things had fallen into disrepair. The house was as spotless as ever but there was a cracked windowpane and the sills all could use a good scraping and painting. There must also be a leak in the roof at the southwest corner as the ceiling showed staining. His mother stood to place a kettle on for a pot of tea. Choundry lifted his sea chest and took it into his old room. He was surprised to see everything was exactly as he had left it. His mother came to stand beside him and looking into the room said, "They all wanted me to sell off your things, especially when we tried to put together a respectable dowry for your sister. I wouldn't have any of it. I prayed for you every night. When you first went missing, I dreaded each tide as there was talk that your body might wash ashore someday. When it didn't, everyone just accepted that you were gone but in my heart I knew that you were out there somewhere. My prayers have been answered today!"

Later that day, Choundry decided to walk downtown and visit his brother at his shop. Again, as he walked the streets it was obvious that folks didn't recognize him as the youth who had come to a bad end. He stepped into his brother's shop with the accompanying sound of a small bell announcing his entry. A young man was seated at the counter looking over a small leather-bound ledger. He seemed a decent lad and when he looked up, he quickly smiled and asked if he could be of any assistance. Choundry asked if Kyle was available. The young man, apparently the apprentice that his mother had mentioned, said that his master was in the back working on an order. Choundry asked the young man to tell his brother that an old friend was here to see him. After disappearing into the back of the building the young man returned a few moments later accompanied by Choundry's brother, Kyle. He didn't look much different, other than he was wearing glasses. As his brother entered the room he stopped dumbfounded and stared at Choundry. His eyes went wide.

"Oh, my Lord…it can't be" he said, taking a couple of steps forward and stopping again. "Is that truly you? Is it Choundry?." At that moment he quickly stepped forward and grabbed Choundry in a strong embrace. "I can't believe it is really you! Where have you been all these years?"

Choundry stepped back, somewhat surprised at the warmth of his brother's welcome. Before he could answer, his brother stepped back and looked at Choundry, obviously seeing the changes that had been wrought in his brother these past years. The impressive breadth to his shoulders, the scarring of his face and the tanned complexion. "It must be quite a story indeed, please come and sit, you must tell me all that has happened to you, but first you must tell me how you came to leave us."

Choundry and his brother sat for several hours as he told him of what happened that night long ago, his suspicions as to who had paid to have him beaten and taken away, and he talked of much that had occurred. He felt curiously reluctant to talk of his wealth and investments, so he left that out of his story. Soon enough he would share that part of his story when the time was right. Choundry's brother looked to him and said, "Brother, I must confess that your returning has lifted a terrible weight from my shoulders. I always blamed myself for the words that we had when last we spoke and for allowing you to walk into danger alone. I cannot tell you how your returning has made me a happy man. I felt that I had let you down and our father as well. It has been a sad three years since you left. I have accomplished a great deal in my business, but it has all been as sand in my mouth since I feared that you'd been killed. It didn't help that the squire's son has hinted on occasion that he had his revenge on the man who'd made him a cripple."

At that, Choundry's brother sat back and said, "That is something that we must consider. The Squire and his son will not be pleased to have you back. He will not be eager for the talk that might come about regarding the role that they had played in planning your murder."

Choundry thought for a moment. "Now that I am home, I no longer have any wish to stir up that old account. I'd just as soon call that account settled as the Squire's son and I will both bear the marks of what happened for the rest of our lives. I'll not bring sorrow to you and our family again. I've changed since I left home, I have plans for the future and I'd rather not look back."

His brother looked relieved and said, "That is certainly welcome, brother, I am happy that we can enjoy your return for now, although we'll have to deal with the Squire at some point if you wish to make your home here again."

Choundry waited a moment and then replied, "That's just it. I have dreamed of coming back here but I have found something inside me that craves to see new lands and seek out the excitement of travel. I will stay if that will help you and mother but I have to admit that I am hoping to use some savings that I've put by to finance some trading ventures."

His brother sat back with a thoughtful expression. "Hmm, that might suit more than you think. I have some funds set aside as well and I have much more inventory than I can sell around these parts. I would have tried selling in distant ports, but I've no one that I trust enough to hand over silver objects with any degree of assurance that I'd ever see the money from the venture. If you are of a mind to go trading, I would be very happy to invest as well. I have big plans, Choundry. I want to grow my business and become secure enough that men like the Squire cannot harm our family so easily. The lords of the manor have lands and they have revenues but they are not as wealthy as they used to be, they have bred poorly and their sons and daughters cannot be bothered to manage their estates. They are bleeding their tenants dry and as a result much of their land is now lying fallow. Merchants and their wealth will someday be the new gentry! I plan to be right in there amongst them. I want those like the Squire to come to our family when they need funds, I want to make them beholding to us and be damned to them and their ways. We will someday be the ones living in the fine manor and they can go and whistle for their supper if they've a mind."

Kyle had spoken this last part very passionately as if it were a dream that had long been dear to his heart.

Choundry looked to his brother and said, "Aye, Kyle, let us agree that you and I will work together as one with an eye to building our family fortunes. I did not mention it before, but I have actually managed to win a great deal of money from the fights that produced the many scars that you see on my face and many that you can't see. I bet wisely and I managed to invest most of it in a far port. I believe that I chose a partner wisely and, with any luck, my investments will be building. We can put together some trade packets and with your silver wares we will have a grand start. We can talk of this later. First, I would see our sister, I'd like to add to the dowry that she received, and I want to fix a few things around our mother's house. I think it best that I keep my presence here as low key as possible and move on as quickly as I can as I don't want to goad the Squire into action."

By that time, it was early evening and Choundry decided to start for home. Although he wanted to keep a low profile in town, he felt that the least he could allow himself was a quick drink in his favorite ale house. It was still early, so there were bound to be only a few patrons. The one man that he wanted to avoid was the Squire's son, so he glanced around to make sure that none of the occupants were gentry and then went to the far corner of the bar, sitting next to a small partially hidden back entrance that Choundry had used more than once in his youth. He called for an ale and sat back to look around the room. There were three other men seated at a nearby table and another man sitting alone with his head slumped and almost touching the tabletop. There was something familiar about the man that sat alone so Choundry sat and studied him for a few moments thinking that it might be an old drinking buddy from his early days. When the man glanced over towards the bar at one point, Choundry could clearly see his profile. He was shocked to see that it was his friend Andy from the *Merlin*! Moving quietly to stand beside his old crewmate, Choundry said quietly, "I thought I'd never say that I'd be so glad to see such a sorry face again, but, welcome my friend!"

Andy looked up quickly and a broad smile sprang to his face. He started to stand and greet Choundry but held his place when Choundry leaned down and whispered, "I am trying to keep some from knowing that I'm home as yet. Let's drink a glass and then go someplace where we can talk." The two quickly finished their drinks and Choundry paid up both of their tabs.

After leaving the tavern, they made their way along the lane leading to Choundry's mother's house. As they walked, Andy told him of his decision to leave the *Merlin* since he knew that Choundry's leaving would bring back the evil times prior to his friend's arrival. What Andy didn't know was that he wasn't the only one of the *Merlin's* crew who felt the same way, and, as a result, at least seven of the *Merlin's* crew had stepped ashore with their belongings right after Choundry had left the ship. Most of them were able to sign on quickly with other ships in the harbor; unfortunately, for Andy, his build and age had limited his usefulness, and since he was not much of a man for handling sails in rough seas, he wasn't able to find a berth as the others had. He'd all but given up trying for the day and went to spend the last of his savings on a good pint of ale. He had a thought to look Choundry up for advice in finding a ship but hadn't any idea where to start looking for his old friend.

Choundry was surprised to hear of the other crew members leaving as they had. Captain Johnston must have been enraged at the loss of his crew, particularly because the ones who left were his prime hands, the ones willing to bend a back to do a decent day's work. Choundry looked to his old friend and said, "Andy, you've spent a good bit of the past three years watching my back and being a good friend. I can't promise wealth but if you will throw in with me, I can promise that you'll never be bored again!"

Andy seemed genuinely pleased at the offer and quickly accepted.

"We will be staying in town for a few days," Choundry explained. "I am sure my Mother wouldn't mind a house guest and you can help me do some repairs around her house. I will also need your help to purchase what's needed without showing my face about town. I will make a quick visit to my sister's and then back again to the sea, although this time we'll be buying our passage instead of working the ship!"

Choundry's visit to his sister, Catherine, took longer than he had anticipated. He decided to stay for several days to help with the harvest. He quickly took a shine to his new brother-in-law; Mathew and could see why his sister had chosen the man over several others who'd been courting her before Choundry's departure. The farm where they lived was modest in size and they were forced to rent extra land. Being a tenant of the gentry was not pleasant at any time, but the rents had risen in recent years and they were hard-pressed to make ends meet. Although they worked from sunup to sundown most every day, his sister and her husband were fighting a losing battle as the price of the rents would not allow enough profit to ever hope to better themselves. Choundry went to talk one day with a local landowner and ended up purchasing several acres that adjoined the land that his brother-in-law owned. When he returned, he gave the deed of the property to his sister. This would allow them to farm their own land in sufficient amounts so that they could afford to drop the rented acreage and focus on bettering the land that Choundry had bought for them. Although this took half of the funds Choundry had with him, he felt that it was money well spent. The plans that he and his brother had for the future were what he wanted to focus his energies on but wherever he could, he wanted to make sure that his family was secure before he set out on any new endeavor.

When he returned to his mother's house, he found that Andy had made himself useful and seemed to be thoroughly relishing the feeling of having a home and being part of a family. The house was neat and shiny only in a manner that a sailor fresh from the sea could make it. The windows fairly sparkled and the metal fittings throughout the house not only worked but they had a shine to them greater even than the day that they were purchased. The roof had been fixed and all of the rooms had a fresh coat of paint. When Choundry came up to the house he found Andy reclining in the sun under the porch, his feet up and a sweet muffin in his hands nearly as big as his head. Andy was dozing but obviously enjoying himself immensely. Choundry stepped up to the porch and said, "If I didn't see the proof of your work, I'd think that you had lazed since I'd left and eaten my mother out of house and home."

Andy sat forward quickly with a sheepish grin and said, "Aye, it has been a real pleasure doing work for your mother. She don't use a starter but I'd work harder for one of these sweets than I'd ever have done for the Captain. I think that I've fattened up a bit since ye left, if'n we don't get going soon I may not be able to fit on a ship."

When Choundry went to his brother's shop, he found that all was ready for him. Kyle had purchased trade goods as well as packed up a large shipment of his silver goods. Choundry went down to the docks to seek out any ships that might be headed toward the ports where Choundry wished to travel. He needed to start making trades, but he also wanted to visit Lisbon to meet with his partner to see how his investments had fared.

Chapter 12
Life Abord the *Lucky Miss*

One of the ships that he visited was a brigantine similar to the *Merlin* but much newer and it looked as if the bottom had been newly coppered. It seemed that the ship would be a fast one and, although he didn't know it when he boarded, the Captain and first mate were familiar to him from the arenas. They remembered Choundry and were eager to discuss booking passageway for Choundry and Andy as well as their cargo. Knowing that this ship must have a regular route, Choundry asked of the ports that they would be visiting and the types of goods that the ship was carrying, it wouldn't do for Choundry to be competing directly with the Captain for sales in the ports that they visited. It seemed all was well, and they sealed the bargain with a handshake.

The Captain said, "I have given you a good price for passage as I can always use a good fighter among the crew and you certainly be among the best I've seen, if not the true best of the bunch. I know you to be of good character to boot. We may have need of your skills this trip as the thieving pirates have been getting closer to the main shipways and they be getting bolder, going after bigger and better armed ships all the time. I have shipped six eight-pounder cannon for this trip, it will cut down on our cargo but the merchants are becoming anxious about their merchandise being stolen so I can charge a bit more if I show them that we have some teeth to the ship. Since the cannons are new to the ship, I'll need to practice the crews a bit so I hope you don't mind the flash and bang of the cannon. None of my lads know how to use them and they'll need to burn some powder before they would be of any use in a fight."

Choundry assured him that he and Andy would welcome seeing the cannons in use, and he added that he would consider it a favor if they would allow him the chance to practice with the crew. It was agreed and the loading of Choundry's cargo was arranged for later that evening. Choundry asked that some of the ship's crew go to his brother's shop to pick up the crates, saying that he had other duties to attend to before they shipped out. The Captain of the ship, which turned out to be called the "*Lucky Miss*," told Choundry that they would be sailing with the morning tide and to try and be onboard in time as they would play havoc trying to get out of the harbor without a favorable wind. The Captain felt that there was rough weather approaching that might hold them in harbor if they did not get to sea in time.

Choundry spent much of the rest of that day purchasing trade goods with his remaining funds. He asked Andy to make sure that these crates were added to those that were already on board the *Lucky Miss* and then he left to go home for the remainder of the evening.

When he sat to dinner later that evening, he told his mother about his plans. At first, she expressed disappointment at Choundry's pending absence but was elated to hear that he and his brother had grown close so quickly and that they were working together to better the family. Kyle came to the house and the four of them stayed up into the early hours reminiscing about the early days when the family was whole, and their father was still alive. His father had been a lively man with a great sense of humor, always singing and he would occasionally, in the privacy of his own home be caught giving his wife a little pinch on the bottom when he thought no one was watching.

Choundry and Kyle parted with many handshakes and embraces, promising good fortune to them both, Choundry embraced his mother and Andy did as well, in turn. He told them that he would send word whenever he could but that his ventures may take him several years before he could set foot in this house again. He asked them not to worry as he would be living as a merchant now without the need to risk his life in every port he visited. When they finally parted, Choundry shouldered his sea chest again and started down to the ships.

As Choundry and Andy walked onto the ship, the Captain, whose name was Thomas Evers, greeted them as they came on board. Choundry started to lift his hand to salute the Captain but caught himself before he had gone too far; although it was obvious that the Captain had noticed his movements and recognized them for what they were.

"Aye, now that you are joining the ship as a man of substance, I'll be needing to introduce you by your full name, I've never heard you called naught but your given name; what be your last name?."

Choundry smiled at the pleasant sense of camaraderie with the Captain and replied, "Anders, my last name is Anders, and well met to you Captain, I hope that we all shall fare equally well on the *Lucky Miss*; and I must say that she is as well found and pleasant a ship as I've seen."

The start of their journey went well with stops at several of the ports that the *Merlin* used to frequent. Although he had never participated in the bargaining, Choundry was familiar with the shops and residences of the local merchants with whom the Captain had done his deals. Many of them remembered seeing Choundry among the crew and, even if the scars on his face were not proof enough, they were familiar with his reputation as a fighter. It was obvious that they didn't wish to anger this man and that they welcomed new trade. As they sailed from one port to another, it became apparent that the silverwares from his brother's shop were becoming more popular the further they sailed. At one point, Choundry wrote to his brother and asked him to ship additional goods to Lisbon, where he hoped to eventually link up with his partner.

At various ports, Choundry was tempted to try his luck in the arena if for no other reason than to gather in more coin for trade and goods. He finally decided that he would not risk the arena and that, unless he were reduced to poverty, he had left that life behind along with the taking of foolish risks. He began to worry that he would suffer boredom aboard the ship if he did not have a duty post to man. When he mentioned this to Captain Evers one evening as they were sharing a meal, the Captain offered to start training Choundry in the rudiments of navigation and other skills necessary to the running of a ship. Choundry eagerly agreed to the arrangement, and they started that very evening. Choundry had always been quick with sums but the type of math problems that he was being introduced to were totally alien to him. He was pleased when the Captain loaned him some of his books and charts to take down to his cabin to study at his leisure. He also allowed Choundry access to one of the ship's precious sextants. At first, Choundry had trouble mastering the process of fixing the ship's location, especially when any variance from true in any of the tasks or calculations could place them hundreds of leagues from where they actually were. The Captain told him that, although he felt that the teaching of these tasks came easier to a younger mind, Choundry wasn't too ancient to find his way through. It was during this time that Choundry also worked with the crew to practice on the guns. He surprised many when he doffed his shirt to aid in the working of the gun, his muscles were impressive and he laid to the work with an enthusiasm that was contagious. Many of the crew were fascinated by the numerous scars that crisscrossed much of his torso, especially the one that was directly over his heart and looked as if whatever had caused the wound had sliced in several different directions. The crew were amazed when he showed them how the scar on his hand matched up with the one on his chest and were then told how he had almost perished in his first arena match.

Meanwhile, the skill of the gun crews gradually improved. Choundry showed some skill at aiming and ended up being named gun captain for one of the forward guns. Choundry offered and the Captain and crew quickly accepted, to provide lessons in fighting without weapons. He would spend at least two hours a day on the upper deck going through the various maneuvers and techniques that he'd learned. This made the crew feel more capable of handling whatever might come but it also allowed Choundry to practice and maintain his skills at a high degree. Occasionally, Captain Evers would offer to do some sword practice with Choundry and, although Choundry learned a great deal during these bouts, he knew that the Captain was good but not at the level of some of the swordsmen that Choundry had seen in the various arena matches that he had witnessed.

The *Lucky Miss* continued on about its usual course and stopped at several additional ports. Now that Choundry was privy to the Captain's maps and charts, he began to study the names of each port and to look ahead to their next ports of call. When he had worked as a member of the ship's crew on the *Merlin*, he had been forced to focus on the work at hand and eventually one port blended into another. The crew had come to know each port less by the name and more by a unique characteristic or an event that had happened there on an earlier visit. Now Choundry took the time to study the coastlines and learn the names of the various regions and countries that they were coming to. The *Lucky Miss* tended to cruise further than the *Merlin*, and the ports were more numerous as well. Some were actually in countries Choundry had never visited and he would be hard pressed to conduct business as the only languages that he knew were English, some of the old Welsh words and a smattering of Spanish and Portuguese from his visits to Portugal. Now he began to wonder why Captain Johnston had steered clear of any of the French ports?

After the *Lucky Miss* had been at sea for several weeks, they came to the city of Portsmouth. The size of the city was much larger than any English city that Choundry had ever visited. When they tied up at the wharf, Choundry made his way to the local merchants row and stopped in to determine who was buying. He was running low on some stock so he also inquired regarding what merchandise might be available for sale. This took him the better part of the day with the final outcome that he had traded approximately half of his remaining stock for merchandise that he thought would be welcome in the ports where they were headed next. Choundry asked Andy to accompany the store owner's men to the *Lucky Miss* and make the exchanges in goods. In the meantime, he decided to walk the streets of Portsmouth and eventually ended up on a rise overlooking the harbor. Close on to where he was standing and far off to his left lay parts of the English fleet. He could see numerous small ships and boats plying the waters, carrying red-coated soldiers and others wearing powdered wigs and hats. The ships scattered about were almost too massive to believe, some had two and three rows of gun ports and their hulls were so large that it seemed impossible that they could float at all. Thinking of the many thousands of men like him that were tasked to man those ships with little recourse or freedom, Choundry was suddenly thankful that it had been the *Merlin* and not a visiting warship that had scooped him up and taken him to the sea; as bad as the *Merlin* had been, at least he had been able to win his fortune and eventually his freedom.

Making his way back to the *Lucky Miss*, Choundry boarded the vessel and assured himself that all of his new supplies were stowed to his liking. He had an early dinner with the Captain after which the *Lucky Miss* left the port and set a full set of sails as it moved further up the coast. They would be touching in to two other ports before crossing the channel to make trade on the French coast. Trade with the French was frowned upon by the English but not forbidden.

Tensions had been running high between the two countries again and some ships had been lost under suspicious circumstances.

Sailing that evening was very pleasant indeed as there was a slight favorable wind that brought a freshness to it and the smell of the ocean. After the gutters, mud flats and sewers of the town, the change seemed heavenly. The Captain maintained running lights fore and aft as was the custom for ships at sea. The night was dark and only a sliver of the moon could be seen. A low cloud bank was moving its way in from the north. After all his time at sea, Choundry could tell that the low clouds most likely did not bode evil or indicate any savage storms. It seemed that they might be in for a few rain showers so he remained on deck to enjoy the air as long as he could. He was mildly surprised when he saw the flashing of what appeared to be lightning in the direction that they were traveling. He walked to the middle of the ship to stand beside

Captain Evers as the Captain called up to tighten one of the sails.

Chapter 13
A Life Saved

As they sailed on, the lightning on the horizon caught the Captain's attention and he moved briskly to the fore of the ship. Choundry walked along with him as he sensed something was amiss. Captain Evers stared ahead and said, without turning his head, "Unless I'm wrong, that be small cannon fire. I'm afraid that someone is catching it and by the looks of it, it's a one-sided fight."

Choundry expected the Captain to haul off and change direction away from the battle. Turning to Choundry and the crew, Captain Evers called out, "There are folks yonder being mauled by someone over there. We aren't a fighting ship by far, but we do have the six pounders now, I'll not take us into a battle as we aren't ready for that but if you all are agreeing, we'll see if we can offer some assistance to the poor souls under those cannons. We will most likely be too late to do any real good and if we see that there is still danger when we arrive, why, the *Lucky Miss* is faster than any other ship that I know of and we can outrun any ship of a size that would dare to tackle us. What do ye say, lads, do we go in?"

The crew were all willing to go forward to help if they could. Choundry assured Captain Evers that he was more than willing to do as he suggested. With that, the *Lucky Miss* continued on under full sail. As Captain Evers had predicted, the firing stopped before they were anywhere close to where the battle must have been occurring.

An hour later, they cruised forward with the lanterns turned off and the crew warned to silence. There was no sign of any battle or of any ship having been in the area. Choundry was beginning to doubt that anything had actually happened here when one of the crew came padding on bare feet to whisper to the captain that there was some wreckage to the port side. The Captain ordered sails reduced and the *Lucky Miss* drifted forward silently. Choundry was standing at the front of the ship along with Andy and the Captain when he thought he heard a creaking sound off to his left. He touched the Captain's arm and pointed in the direction of the noise. The Captain listened for a moment and then ordered a slight change of course. In a few moments, the vague shape of a ship's front could be seen emerging from the gloom.

The creaking noise was coming from what was left of the rigging and tackle as it swayed in shreds from what remained of the mast. The ship was obviously in a bad way and it could be seen settling quickly. The Captain ordered the helm over and said that he would risk the noise of touching the *Lucky Miss* to the sinking hulk so that they could climb to the other ship to see if there were anyone to be saved. As they touched, Choundry, the Captain and two of the *Lucky Miss'* crew jumped aboard and started to search. What had first appeared to be bundles of the shredded sails littering the deck turned out to be the prone bodies of men lying about. All was quiet and after checking several of the huddled shapes they determined that they were all dead. Each man had his throat cut as if to make sure no one survived to bear witness. Choundry thought that the ship might be Spanish or Portuguese in origin. He moved forward and was ready to go below when he thought he heard an odd noise coming from the upper deck cabin. Placing his ear to the door, he could hear a faint sound that, as he listened carefully, he was finally able to make out as the sound of someone crying softly. Motioning to the Captain, Choundry slowly opened the door and then entered softly.

He wished now he had brought his weapons with him but now was too late to go back and gather them. The Captain entered with him and they both stood, listening to the sound of weeping coming from a dark corner of the cabin. Captain Evers slowly closed the cabin door and said, "We'll risk a light to see what we must, this is obviously someone needing our assistance, and we came here to help."

He quickly worked in the dark and brought a small flame that he transferred to a candle. Once they were ready to move, they crept slowly forward. The crying kept up in a monotonous way that started to bring a shiver to Choundry's spine. As they drew near, the candle flame showed the remains of various pieces of shattered furniture, glassware lay shattered over the floor and splotches of what appeared to be blood could be seen pooled in several places. It was obvious that a terrible fight had taken place in these close quarters. As they looked past the wreckage, they could see a pair of twisted legs showing from under a shattered cabinet. Moving closer they found a man's head and shoulders emerging from under the other side of the cabinet; he too had been dispatched in the same manner as the rest of the crew.

The sobbing noise continued. Leaving the dead man where he lay, they moved forward until they reached the far end of the cabin. There they found, lying on the remains of a shattered bed, the reclining form of a young woman. It was she who was sobbing quietly. At first Choundry felt that he should avert his eyes as the woman was wearing only small shreds of what must have been a nightgown. She had obviously been abused badly and had suffered terribly. Besides numerous bruises and cuts, she lay amidst covers that appeared to be soaked in blood. Her eyes were closed and she was whispering to herself, the sobbing having stopped when the candle came close. The poor woman was clearly close to passing but she held a bundle clutched tightly to her chest. Captain Evers stepped forward and, holding the candle close, asked the woman if there were anything that he could do for her. The question did not bring any response. Choundry, following up on his suspicions regarding the origin of the ship, stepped forward and asked her the same question in his halting Spanish. The woman gasped briefly and turned her head towards Choundry and the Captain. Her eyes weakly opened, and she started whispering in an urgent manner.

Choundry could barely keep up with translating the woman's words, but she first thanked God for sending his angels. Choundry told her gently that they were sailors who had come to help and to not worry as the ones who had done this were now far away. The woman looked to them both and, as the ship gave a heave and started to list further to the side, she told Choundry that "She and her husband…..," with this, she glanced over to the cabinet laying on its side, "had been looking for a new home and that she wished that they had never left, she went on to say that she knew that she was dying and that it would be a blessing as she didn't want to live without her husband," she hesitated and then added that "She had one great request to make of these two men standing before her; she told them that God had sent them to save her baby girl Isabella and, she asked them "to accept the charge that God had laid at their feet and see her child to safety."

Choundry translated this to Captain Evers who could only stand and watch the suffering of the poor young mother. Captain Evers asked Choundry to ask if the child had family to send her to and the woman shook her head, saying, "We traveled because we had no one left who was holding us to where we used to live. We were looking to find a place to grow our family, now it will not be so and only our little Isabella will go forward."

Choundry looked to the Captain and he stepped over to the young woman and knelt beside her. He reached out to touch her hand gently and, smiling, he nodded his head to show that he would accept the charge of caring for the little girl. With that, the woman smiled slightly and glanced briefly down into the bundle that she held close. The injured mother seemed to calm visibly, laying her head back on the torn and bloodied bed sheets. Though her arms still held tightly to the little bundle, she was obviously passing quickly.

Choundry and the Captain stayed by her side until they were sure that she had gone.

Captain Evers reached forward and gently pulled the tiny bundle from the dead woman's arms. As he held the bundle up, he could see two tiny eyes staring at him from deep in the folds of the blanket. Holding the infant as if she were made of the finest porcelain, the Captain stood and they slowly made their way to the cabin door. The ship gave another lurch and both men knew that the hulk had only moments left before it would slip below the waves. They hurried back over to the side of the ship and Choundry stepped over to the *Lucky Miss* and then turned to receive the infant as the Captain handed her across the widening gap between the two ships.

After the Captain had stepped across and down onto the deck, he moved to Choundry and took the child back into his arms. Neither man had spoken since the woman had died. Standing on the deck in the gloom they were suddenly unsure of what to do. Probably for the first time in many years, the Captain didn't know what to do on his own ship. Choundry looked to the Captain and said, "With your permission, I will get us underway so we can be free and moving in case whatever ship that did this were to return." The Captain nodded his head and went slowly forward to enter the doorway to his cabin, still holding the bundle close to his chest.

They quickly got the ship under way and Choundry and the first mate did their best not to disturb the Captain. About thirty minutes later, Captain Evers emerged from his cabin, gently closing the door behind him. He went to the middle of the ship and asked that his crew gather round. He looked out at his men and announced, "Mates, I know that I am your Captain but I have something that I would like to ask you all; a favor that I wouldn't hold it against you if you refused. The wee lass in there, nodding toward his cabin, needs a home and my Dorothy has always wanted a child, although the Good Lord has never seen fit to bless us with one. I would ask you all that we return to Portsmouth so that I can bring the little one to my wife. Most of you have shares in this voyage so the delay may cost you some earnings, what say you all?"

To a man they all agreed to the delay. It was obvious that Captain Evers was well liked and that these men were all very happy for the good fortune coming his way, even under such tragic circumstances. The Captain seemed truly touched at the support of his crew.

Turning to Choundry, he said, "I should ask you as well, since you have a stake in this trip too. Are you willing to accept the delay of returning?." Choundry could feel the emotions welling up in this strong man and was touched by the pleading in his eyes.

Choundry responded, "Aye, but only on one condition. I was there when we both agreed to accept the burden of making sure that this child was safe, I would ask to be named her Godfather if you and your wife would agree." Captain Evers smiled, and his eyes grew misty, he turned with a cough and said, "That would be an honor, lad, and well spoken."

As the Captain started walking back to his cabin he stopped and turned as if remembering something, "One more thing, lads, before you go back to work. We have three days to Portsmouth, does any man of you know anything about caring for a wee one?." They all looked at each other and no one spoke until Andy stepped hesitantly forward and raised his hand, "I had three baby sisters growing up and I had to help me mum with em. I knows how to do the fix ens and the food. We've no cow's milk aboard so I'm not sure what we'll do though."

One of the other men stepped forward, "We has the little nanny goat in the forward hold, that might work and I'll be milking her as soon as ye like." After some thought, Andy added "We'll need soft clothes for the diapers and a cradle for her to sleep in." The ship's carpenter spoke up and said that he would have a cradle and a bed to boot, made up in no time. Other men offered personal items of clothing that could be taken apart and made into clothes for the infant. The man in charge of mending the sails on the ships offered to take charge of the making of the baby clothes. Andy looked as if he were relishing his role of being the lone "expert" and man in charge. Finally, with a chuckle, he looked around the crew and said, "Well, there is one last thing that we'll need and luckily I has an idea how we'll fashion one as I'm pretty sure that none of ye has this in their sea bags, and that's a nipple!." With that he turned and strode towards the Captain's cabin with a strut that clearly conveyed his momentary sense of importance.

Although there were many anxious moments over the next two days when little Isabelle had initially refused to accept the new milk or the small pouch of fine silk that had been sewn onto the top of a small flask to serve as an infant's bottle. Her cries were pitiful to hear and many of the crew paced the deck, worried that their hopes would be dashed and that Captain Ever's dreams for the future would come to naught. It was on the second day that a quiet fell over the ship, and after an hour had passed Andy stepped out to give the good news, "The little babe finally got hungry enough to eat! She is a little tar, she is, she ate that down like it was peas and gravy!." He chuckled, "I don't know who fell asleep first, the Captain or the babe!"

The crew spent the rest of the day walking on bare feet and whispering whatever orders had to be passed. It was as if the ship did not even need someone in charge during this period, they were all focused on getting the ship back to Portsmouth and each man had sailed with the Captain for many years. Choundry's opinion of his fellow man, in general, changed during that voyage, after years of seeing rough men at their worst, he hadn't realized how jaded his opinion of the common man had become. Seeing these men give selflessly to their Captain was a true testament to not just these men but to the good nature of most sailors.

When they reached Portsmouth on the third day, the Captain went into his ship's boat with Choundry and several of his crew. Each man was tasked with carrying the items that had been made for the baby. They made a very curious procession as they wended their way up the street, one man gently carrying a wrapped bundle followed by a small parade of rough sailors, one with a baby's crib, one with a bed, and the others carrying armfuls of baby clothes, much more than any one child could hope to wear before it grew too large to fit in them all. Word must have spread to the Captain's wife regarding his unexpected return. She was standing in the doorway to their modest house as the small parade reached their front gate.

At first, Dorothy's face betrayed a worry that something bad had happened to the Captain but this quickly changed to one of puzzlement as the Captain bent forward to give her a kiss on the cheek and to whisper in her ear. Her expression changed to one of sheer joy. The Captain turned to Choundry and his crew and told his wife loud enough for all to hear, "These men helped to save this dear little soul, they gave of their own and they all helped to make sure that little Isabella has all that she needs." He went on, "All that she needs, that is, except the one thing that she needs dearly the most, and that is a Mother."

He turned to his wife and gently handed her the little bundle that by now had started to wiggle and make small mewing noises. Dorothy took little Isabella and looked deep into her eyes and then gently held her close. "Oh Captain Evers," she said, "it is only a man as wonderful as you and as clueless as any sailor can be would make me worry so and then hand me a blessed child such as this."

She then turned to all of the men who had accompanied baby Isabella, "I thank you all, you've made me a very happy woman and you've answered my prayers." With that, the men carried into the house the furniture as well as all the and belongings that had been fashioned during the trip. Captain Evers thanked his men and told them that he would meet them in the tavern that evening for a dinner for all.

As the crew turned to leave, the Captain asked Choundry and Andy to stay behind. They went inside and Captain Evers introduced Andy to his wife and explained that Andy had been the one who had cared for little Isabella during the journey. He asked Andy to help his wife to unpack each item from the supplies that were brought from the ship and he asked him if he would be willing to go to the store and fetch whatever his wife thought might be needed for the baby.

Dorothy fussed over Andy and they laughed and made little "ooh and ah" noises as each piece of tiny clothing was brought forth from the pile that had been left on the kitchen table. Choundry and the Captain sat quietly just enjoying the sense of home and pure happiness that pervaded the little house. Once Isabella had gone to sleep and Andy had set out on his errands, Dorothy came to sit with the two of them. It was then that the captain told his wife how they had come to find the baby. He did not go into details about the condition of the crew or the ship but he told of how he and Choundry had been sworn to keep little Isabella safe; that there were no family to find and return her to and therefore she was theirs to keep and raise should they choose. The Captain went on to explain how they had left the stricken ship and then returned home. He looked to Choundry and said, "And, as this lad was there and swore the same oath that I did, he has agreed to be little Isabella's Godfather, and a better man we'd never find."

With that, Dorothy came forward and kissed Choundry on the cheek and thanked him for what he'd done and told him that she was "very happy to have such a good man to watch over the baby." Captain Evers looked to his wife and told her "She's not just a baby, dear. She is our daughter. I've always wanted to say it and now I can; tis good to be home Mother Evers."

Chapter 14
A Return to Lisbon

They stayed in Portsmouth for three days and then the Captain called for the ship to resume its cruise. They put to sea and headed straight up the coast, passing the ports where they'd stopped previously. Eventually they came to their next port of call. Here Choundry again made some additional trades that, although not resulting in gaining any coins, did add to the size of his merchandise stored on the ship. Three days later, after one final stop on the English coast, they turned and started their journey across the channel. They saw several of His Majesty's fleet during their crossing and what looked to be a convoy of ships coming up from the Mediterranean. Captain Evers had very specific ports on the French coast that he visited routinely. His connections were solid ones that he trusted to sell him quality goods. He told Choundry of the various ports, the merchants they would be meeting, and the types of goods that would be most sought after. Although much of what Choundry had shipped was not going to be of high demand on this coast, there were a number of items that he had in his stores that would be welcome and Captain Evers felt strongly that the silver wares from Choundry's brother would fetch a very handsome price as the French valued fine craftsmanship and they were inordinately willing to pay for what they considered to be objects of beauty.

Their first port was LaHavre where they anchored well away from the docks and rowed ashore. Captain Evers mentioned that, although things were much better than they had been in the past, recently tensions had begun to build between France and it's ancient enemy England. He still felt that his contacts were trustworthy, but he didn't want to place temptation under the noses of the local government.

Captain Evers had mentioned earlier to Choundry that he would be wise to ship as many quality wines from this port as was possible. He warned Choundry that the wine market was a very dangerous place for an inexperienced merchant to venture and to not make any deals without first consulting him. "A wine made in one year may be worth a fortune to the right people, yet the same grapes a year later may produce something only fit to give to the hogs" he explained. It is also very important to know how the wine has been stored and you should know that there are many varieties of wines, each thought of differently by those who value such things."

Choundry took the warning to heart. When he went on shore to bargain, he usually accompanied Captain Evers and studied what he did as well as learned the various merchants who could be trusted. Choundry eventually traded for a large quantity of wines of various types and years. True to Captain Evers' prediction, Choundry's silver wares were in high demand and by the time that they had left the first port in France, he had sold or traded his last remaining silver stock. Before leaving Le Havre, Choundry found a ship that was headed back to England and then up past Choundry's home port to Liverpool. He posted a letter with the Captain who promised to drop it off in Swansea as he passed. Choundry wrote to his brother of his success and of the great demand for his wares. He again mentioned that he would be traveling to Lisbon in hopes of finding a shipment from his brother but asked him to ready even more goods which he would collect on his next visit home.

The *Lucky Miss* traveled down the coast of France stopping next at Brest and then later at Aracachon where Choundry purchased several dozen crates of Bordeaux wines. Choundry had done well with trading. His cargo of merchandise from England was mostly still intact and he had traded and purchased a very large cargo of various wines. He knew that he would have to hold the wine until the ship had nearly completed its trading route and returned to home waters where the wines would be in high demand.

As the *Lucky Miss* entered Spanish waters, Choundry began to recognize some of the ports the *Merlin* used to visit. He felt more comfortable negotiating for trades or sales in these ports now that he had a modest proficiency with the language and he knew some of the local customs. He continued to make deals, finally selling off some of the merchandise that he had been fearful as to its true trading value. It seemed that if you held onto something long enough and traveled far enough, you'd eventually find someone who would be excited to purchase whatever wares you might have.

One evening Choundry was having a late dinner with Captain Evers. He talked of their eventual visit to Lisbon and of the man whom Choundry had entrusted with the majority of his fortune. When Choundry mentioned that the merchant's name was "Thompson" and described where his shop was located, Captain Evers smiled and shook his head. "You must be a very shrewd man or a very lucky man," he said. "You probably found the only honest man that I've ever met in that port. I've known William for many a year and we deal whenever I come to his home port. He has quite a number of ships plying all of the surrounding seas and I've carried his cargos more times than I can count. If you left your money with him, you can count it safe, and that man dearly loves making his money work, so I wouldn't be surprised if your investment has done well. If I'd known that William was accepting investment money, I would have talked with him long ago."

So it was that when the *Lucky Miss* entered the port of Lisbon and tied up at the docks that Choundry and Andy were first in line to step ashore. Choundry was eager to see how his investments had fared, so they made their way quickly up the street and found their way back to the shop that he'd visited so long ago. When Choundry entered, he saw that the same familiar clerk, whose name he remembered was Edward, was tending the front counter.

Choundry walked to the front of the store and asked whether Mr. Thompson was available. Edward gave him a look that showed clearly that he didn't remember Choundry from his earlier visit. This time he didn't show the same level of disdain toward Choundry as he had during his first visit since Choundry was now dressed as a modestly wealthy tradesman. Edward smiled broadly and offered a swift assurance that he would fetch the owner. When Mr. Thompson came out from his office, he immediately recognized Choundry and greeted him with a smile. He held his hand out and they shook hands briefly.

"At last, the elusive Mr. Anders, I've been expecting you for several days now," said Thompson. "I can see by your puzzlement that you don't know yet that I've received correspondence and a rather large shipment from your brother. Please come in, I am sure that you are curious as to how your investments have fared."

He called for some hot tea, and they entered his back office, where Mr. Thompson sat and offered a chair to Choundry. Andy had stayed in the store to browse the wares.

"You will be pleased to hear of your successes."

As the tea was delivered, Mr. Thompson brought out a thick canvas-covered ledger and started to run his finger down a set of columns. "As of now you have a rather large shipment coming in from the Spice Islands," said Thompson. "If that ship and cargo go as I've planned, we will both surely see an immense profit as the rewards for those types of cargos are based equally on the risks of running the gauntlet of storms and pirates throughout that journey. I have high hopes for news of their arrival at any moment. Even without that cargo, you have been invested in at least six different endeavors across much of the surrounding coasts; one large shipment going to Italian ports, and you have a minority portion of a plantation that is being built in Hispaniola. All of that plus a tidy sum here waiting for consideration and investment."

With that, Thompson pointed to a figure on the ledger that was almost equal to the original sum Choundry had invested. "We've been lucky, it has been a rare season when we have yet to lose any major cargoes," he continued. "I can't promise the same results year over year but I would venture to say that you arc easily ten times wealthier than you were when you last left here and if the spice ship arrives as I hope, you can easily double that amount."

Choundry sat back, stunned by the amounts that Mr. Thompson had mentioned. At first, he wasn't quite sure what to say but finally asked, "You've done main well with all that I entrusted to you, if it not be too much to ask, would you mind our continuing this arrangement? I have a friend who knows you well and he tells me that I could never find a more trustworthy man than yourself so I would like to continue our partnership."

Mr. Thompson seemed genuinely pleased to continue their arrangement. He asked who their mutual friend was and when Choundry named Captain Evers, Thompson smiled and said, "I've known the man for many years, and it is a real pleasure to name him as a dear friend. His Dorothy is a cousin to my wife. We first met in Portsmouth when I was just a young man like yourself making the rounds trying to make my stake in the world. I met Anne one day on the wharf when she had gone a visiting to John's ship. I took one look at her and I was never a free man again." He finished the last statement with a wry smile and chuckle.

"Now that you have an initial reckoning of your worth, I would say that you must feel very good to be such a wealthy man at such a young age. What are your plans going forward?"

Choundry thought for a moment and then answered, "I want to send some funds to my brother to repay him for the silver wares that he has invested. He has entrusted much to me and I'll not beggar him waiting for his return investment. Is there a way to get funds to Swansea where my brother can reach them?"

"Aye," Thompson replied. "I have at least two ships headed that way, and I can either have them carry the moneys with them or have a draft on a local bank. Which would you prefer?

Choundry chose the latter since there was always a chance of piracy or losing a ship in a storm. "Now that I've done right by my brother, I'd like to check on some funds that I have here in the local bank and then I'm unsure whether to continue my journey with Captain Evers or if there is something that I can do to better my…our investments."

Mr. Thompson looked slightly pensive and told Choundry, "Why don't you enjoy Lisbon for the day and let me give that some thought. I have been thinking of a few new endeavors and I might have need of a young man who is unknown to those who normally do dealings with me and my staff."

Leaving the shop, Choundry and Andy made their way to the bank where Choundry had placed some funds on his visit to Lisbon. After checking on them, he decided that he would deposit some of the moneys that he had gained so far in this journey. While he was there, he pulled Andy up to the counter and called over a bank clerk. Choundry asked the clerk to write up an account for his friend and when the documents had been written up he placed a deposit of 50 pounds in the account under Andy's name. Andy stood dumbfounded at what had happened; 50 pounds was enough to buy a small home somewhere or purchase an interest in a tavern, which had always been his dream. Andy looked to Choundry as if he couldn't comprehend what was occurring.

Choundry told his friend "Andy, you have been a true friend and a boon companion. You have helped me in my success and I acknowledge that I owe you a debt, and not just the pay that you've been receiving, I am placing this money in an account that you can't easily reach as I don't want you tempted to gamble or spend it on women. I want you to someday have your dream and I'll place money here every year that we are successful, you'll share a percentage of what we make and some day, if we both live, you may retire a wealthy man." Andy started to speak but choked up. Choundry slapped him on the back and told him to sign the documents.

After they were done, they decided to go for a late lunch along the main boulevard through town. They sat and had dinner at an open air café and both men ordered hearty meals. Then they strolled through the town and the local market where Choundry was able to find a few small items for his mother and sister; one a lacey shawl that looked as if it were almost as fragile as a spider's web, and the other several carved seashells with pictures of seascapes and exotic animals.

Several times Choundry passed local women who tended to be short in stature and who invariably had long black hair. Some of them returned his glances rather boldly. Choundry had held his emotions in check for so many months and years that, now that he could finally begin to relax and enjoy the fruits of his labors, he was finding thoughts and urges flooding his mind. He dearly wanted the company of a woman, even if it only meant just talking. If he had stayed at home the past several years, he would most likely have done his share of courting the local girls and would probably be married by now. He had missed out on what would have been, and he had chosen a voluntary lonely life rather than spend time with the women who had routinely been available to him and all of the other sailors in the ports that he had visited. He had seen the effects of the pox that so many sailors suffered from and he had promised himself that he would not fall to that vile disease.

Walking the streets, he found himself frustrated; back home he had been able to flirt with the local girls and he had even spent time with several of the willing lasses. He had thought himself a man of the world in his youth and now, here he was several years later tongue-tied at the thought of trying to talk to one of these local women. The frustration was boiling in him, and he drove on through the crowd until he noticed the labored breathing of Andy trying vainly to keep up. Choundry stopped and told his friend that he was sorry for being so thoughtless; as he said that, his eyes roamed to a spritely looking young woman who sauntered her way by the two of them. To Choundry it seemed as if she were some untouchable Goddess who surely ignored lesser mortals, while the more experienced Andy could detect the twinkle in the young lady's eyes and the little extra sway that was added to her walk after she had passed them by.

Andy looked to Choundry and thought for a moment, "Lad, ye have a sharp mind for business and ye know how to fell a man with one blow in ways that most men couldn't even imagine, but ye don't know how to deal with women any more than the smallest ship's boy. We'll start ye on the right track, but I'll not let ye fall afoul of anyone who'll pick yer pocket or steal yer heart, leave it to old Andy to find the way."

Choundry looked to his friend and laughed at the absurdity of ever needing someone to teach him about women; he might be rusty, but the blade could still cut!

"Thank you, Andy, but I'm fine and all things will happen in their own due time."

Later that afternoon they returned to Mr. Thompson's store and Choundry again entered his offices. After they'd been seated, Mr.

Thompson said, "First things first, now that we are business partners in these ventures, I think it only right that we call each other by our given names, I know yours, but I would take it kindly if you would refer to me as William from now on. Choundry agreed and they continued on with their meeting. "I have been thinking of our earlier discussion and your offer to assist with some of our business ventures, I would like to propose a slightly different course of action, if I might. I have an acquaintance who has been asking me to invest funds and the use of one of my ships for a period of several years. He promises a huge return on the investment, and I am tempted to agree since he comes from a titled local family. He and his family have fallen on bad fortunes recently and he is trying to recoup his lost wealth. It shows the level of desperation that he must feel to engage in business as these old families usually refuse to soil their hands with real work, rather relying on others they hire to conduct their business, a practice I must say is rather risky and often ends poorly."

"My acquaintance is named Don Alfonso Martinez. He is the son of a past governor of this province. He is proposing that I invest my funds and send a ship to the trading post that he has set up along the Ivory Coast. He tells me that he is making a small fortune trading elephant ivory and exotic hides with the locals, and he would prefer to expand the endeavor and reap an even greater reward. In all good faith, I cannot just dismiss him out of hand. There may be an opportunity here worth pursuing, but I have my doubts regarding the Don and I am reluctant to invest or make any decision until I know a bit more. I need to have someone that I trust, who has good judgment, and who is not known to be one of my agents. I need someone who can take a look at this trading post and see if the opportunity is as I've been told. I would propose that you travel on as you have, in one of my ships, posing as a merchant with your wares, and stop at this port as if you were on a journey down to the Cape and back. You should have a chance to see what this business venture is based on and whether there is a sound reason to invest money; mine or, if you chose, some of yours as well."

Choundry thought for a moment and, seeing that this would be an opportunity to learn more about business, travel to ports that were farther along that coast than he'd ever traveled with the *Merlin*, and to be of real value to his business partner, he quickly agreed to make the journey.

"Excellent," said William. "If you'll shift your belongings and cargo from the *Lucky Miss,* we can place the majority of it in storage or send it out with some of our other shipments. I am afraid that you'll have several days on your hands before the ship is ready to start its journey down the coast so I'd advise that you choose one of the inns along the Mainstreet frontage as they are all excellent and I will know where you can be found if needed."

Choundry agreed to check in daily and to notify Edward where he was lodged. He then thanked William again and headed out of the store and down to the wharves. Captain Evers seemed truly sorry to hear that Choundry would be leaving the ship. He promised to check in the next time that he was in Lisbon to see how he was faring and Choundry promised to stop into Portsmouth periodically to see how his little Godchild Isabella was doing. The two men parted as friends and Choundry left instructions as to where his merchandise could be sent.

Before Choundry left the ship Captain Evers came to him with a book. "This is a manual that my Dorothy gave me years ago," he explained. "It is written on the ways of the sea and ships, it teaches some of the math needed to learn navigation and it has some of the older maps of the coasts. Beware not to trust those maps too fully as they are older versions and need much updating, I used to make corrections to them when I could, but I eventually was able to afford the newer nautical maps that were far more accurate. It will do you well enough in your search to learn more about mastering a sailing ship."

Choundry settled on the inn that was closest to the wharves and to William's office. He signed for two rooms and moved his belongings into the room that was toward the front of the Inn and allowed a full view of the harbor and the ships that were moored close to the shore. Choundry was in his room for no more than an hour when there was a knock on the door. Choundry opened the door and was passed a note from the owner of the Inn, "This was just delivered for you senor."

The note was from William, inviting him to a dinner and dance that was being put on by the town; it was a yearly event and one that William felt Choundry might enjoy. After reading the note, Choundry looked up and found Andy leaning against the doorframe smiling. He nodded to the note and said, "Well, I guess ye have a dance to go to, now alls we needs to do is find someone to teach ye to dance!"

Early the next morning Andy stepped out on his own and returned in less than an hour. "Edward has set us up with a young gentleman who tutors the local children in dance and ballet, he lives several blocks from here and we have set a ten o'clock appointment with him."

It was obvious by now that Andy and Edward had both schemed to bring Choundry out of his shell and into gentle society. Choundry agreed to go to the appointment but felt slightly foolish, half hoping that the appointment would need to be cancelled. Andy seemed to be in high spirits as the hour approached for Choundry's dancing appointment. He laughed and made snide remarks about Choundry learning to be light on his feet and "dance on his toes" as he led the way to the appointed place.

Upon entering they were greeted by a slender man in his late twenties. After turning over the required fees, Choundry told the man that he just wanted to know how to not make a fool of himself in public when he attended the dance.

"Anything else that you can accomplish would be grand, but unlikely," he said.

The tutor moved gracefully about the room and with dramatic gestures. He started with some demonstrations of the local dances and the steps that were required in each. Many of the dances were somewhat repetitive and followed a specific step sequence. When he finished the demonstration, he walked to Choundry and Andy and stated "Attention! We must begin." Looking to Andy he said, "And you, sir, will take the part of the senorita so you must be quick to move with your lead; the young Gentleman here." Andy stepped back as if attempting to flee but Choundry turned to him with a laugh and said, "Yes, senorita Andy, you must dance with me, but be sure to follow my lead and be light, oh so light, on your feet!."

Andy knew that he was trapped, so, looking around to assure himself there wasn't any audience, he agreed, but said, "I'll do this the once but if anyone ever says a word I'll bust his nose fer him." all the while glaring at Choundry. They practiced well into that evening and, taking a break for dinner and a night's rest, they resumed early the next day. At one point during a break, Choundry thought to ask the young tutor if he knew of any men proficient with swords who would be willing to provide tutoring.

After a thoughtful pause, he said, "I know of one who is simply amazing with a sword but he is out of the country and is not expected back for several months, I can think of no one better to teach dueling but he usually does not take students as he is a very wealthy man. His name is Don Alessandro and he lives in a small town up the coast." After a pause he went on, "I can say, though, that our lessons will make any training in fencing all the easier as the art of footwork is much needed in learning how to fight like a gentleman. What we learn here today will be a good start to anything that you might learn later with any teacher." With that they started again although Choundry now showed a more keen interest in the session.

On the day that the dance was supposed to occur, Choundry and Andy began their usual morning walk but Choundry led out along a direction that they didn't usually follow, it was their usual pattern to walk the wharves inspecting the various ships to see who had tied up during the night and to see if they recognized any of their old crewmates in the masses of sailors. This morning's route took them into the town's storefront area and Choundry eventually broke their morning walk by stepping into a local clothing store. He glanced thoughtfully at the clothing on the racks and walked back to the counter at the rear of the store. The tailor put down his scissors and came forward, "What can I do for you two gentlemen?." Choundry gestured to Andy and said, "My friend here has newly arrived, and his baggage was delayed. He will need a new suit of clothing and matching attire so that he may be dressed appropriately for the dance tonight. I will leave him here with you and return in two hours to see what has been decided upon, I would also like to order him a sturdy set of clothes for an extended voyage that we will be undertaking.

Andy stood quietly as Choundry turned to him and said, "Now that you know how to dance we must make sure that you are presentable as well for the ladies, the only thing that you must remember to be sure of is to lead when you dance as I must say that I've seen you dance and you dance like a little girl!."

With that he left Andy to the skills of the tailor.

That evening saw Choundry and Andy dressed in their finery, standing just inside the door to the building where the dance was to be held. It was a large community building that appeared as if it were designed for just such an event. After giving the man at the door their names, they were announced as they entered. There were quite a few people and there seemed a balance between what the locals might consider "gentry" and the other half of the crowd seemed to be wealthy members of the community; probably merchants or artisans and their families. Off to Choundry's right he saw William approaching, Edward slightly behind as if in tow. The two men greeted Choundry and Andy and after a few gentle jibes at Andy's expense regarding his new attire, they decided to retire for the dinner that preceded the dance. Choundry watched William closely to be sure that he did not forget any of the graces that his mother had taught him so many years ago. He was eventually seated in the middle of a very long banquet table. To his left sat William and to his right sat a fat merchant who was totally engrossed by, and leaning over, the young lady who sat to his other side. This left Choundry looking ahead to where two women were seated directly opposite him. One was a matronly woman who wore a black lace shawl over her hair and frequently fanned herself with a gilt-covered fan. She had numerous glittering rings and a necklace that looked as if its sale could purchase a small ship. Seated next to her and directly across from Choundry was a woman who looked to be in her late thirties and she wore little jewelry and no covering on her piled ebony-black hair. She was dressed in a golden-colored gown that was cut somewhat immodestly low in the front. Choundry introduced himself to both ladies. The elderly woman looked to her left with a sniff, fully ignoring Choundry's words, but the woman to his front smiled and introduced herself as Maria Alvareze. Maria introduced her male cousin who was seated to her right and was therefore present to serve as her escort, as was only proper. Maria's cousin appeared to be well into his cups as he'd downed two glasses of wine since the time that they had sat down.

Partway through the meal, and after a brief discussion with William regarding the still late to arrive ship from the Indies, he found himself sitting quietly awaiting the next course. Maria smiled at him and asked, "Tell me Mr. Anders, what is it that you do?"

Choundry told her that he was a merchant who had originally come from the coast of Wales but was newly arrived in Portugal and now in a partnership with Mr. Thompson. Her gaze narrowed slightly as she said, "I hope that you will not find me rude in asking this, but I can see that you carry the scars of an active and seemingly dangerous life. Are you a duelist of some sort. A man of adventure? What kind of man are you?"

Choundry did not want to admit to his past as an ordinary seaman and fighter in the ring and after a moment's consideration, he replied, "Let's just say that I have been many places and been many things and that I try to be the better man for it."

Maria seemed to accept this answer although a new look of consideration came into her eyes. They had little chance to talk further as there were several toasts being made at the head of the table and then the main courses were brought out.

Following the meal, they all enjoyed a small glass of a rather sweet liquor that was unfamiliar to Choundry. Following the dinner, the ladies went toward the rear of the building while the gentlemen either smoked on the veranda or talked in small groups. When the dancing eventually started, the room began to fill, and couples made their way to the dance floor. Choundry watched the dancers to make sure that the steps being used were familiar to him. He started wandering the crowd and soon came to a group of women sitting in the far corner of the room. As he started forward, William stepped to his side and told him, "Do not waste your time with yonder women, they are part of the aristocracy here and they would deem it below their status to talk with such as us let alone be seen dancing with one below their status." Choundry thanked William for the warning and proceeded on towards the other side of the dance floor.

He was able to find several women who seemed very willing to dance with the very tall mysterious foreigner. He tried his best to match his steps to their much smaller gait but found himself almost tripping at times in his efforts to not step on their toes. He colored slightly and thanked the young ladies. He had enjoyed the sensation of their soft hands in his during the dance moves but had found that he felt somewhat oafish and uncoordinated; the tutoring had not prepared him to dance with someone so small in stature.

He had all but given up on dancing that night when he saw his dinner companion seated at a table along with her now obviously inebriated cousin. He walked up to her and asked her if she would be willing to dance. She smiled what seemed a very relieved smile as she glanced at her cousin, who barely noticed their conversation. "Yes, I would love to dance," she said taking his proffered hand. As they entered the dance floor, Choundry noticed that Maria was taller than most of the other women on the dance floor. He said with a smile, "I am so relieved to see that you are taller than I thought, I am new to dancing, and I am afraid that I have not enough grace to manage my steps well."

She gave a slight smile and said, "I am glad that I am such a giantess that I am not like other women, that has been pointed out to me in my youth many times, but I had come to forget." Choundry apologized for his rude remark and felt rather foolish as they started their dance. Maria smiled and told him, "Please forgive me, I know you meant no harm in your remark, you are unpolished and rather honest in your manner. I am not used to men who say what they think."

They finished the dance and another and then took seats with Choundry sitting at Maria's table but with her cousin seated in between. Maria looked to Choundry "I am surprised that a young man such as yourself would spend his precious evening with an old widow such as myself," she said. "Surely there are many women here who would love to speak with such a handsome man as yourself."

Choundry smiled and replied "As I mentioned, I have lived quite an eventful life these past years and as a result I find the thought of idle chatter with a woman barely into her adulthood not that enticing. I had mostly wished to have a few moments enjoying the company of a woman who could remind me of the finer points of life that I've been missing. I hope that you do not mind if we talk further but I do not wish to create any scandal as I am not familiar with the local customs."

Maria smiled and said, "I am afraid that tongues are already wagging all across the room, especially in the far corner." She indicated the group of ladies within the circle of aristocrats. "Besides, there has been ample talk about me and my unwillingness to marry again. I have enough lands and money to live comfortably for the rest of my life and I've no wish to hand all of that to some jeweled fop who would waste it on wine and whatever else suits his pleasure. I have chosen to live as a marked woman but even I must maintain the customs to some degree so therefore I must be chaperoned by my trustworthy cousin here."

They talked further on into the evening until it became clear that the event was coming to a close. Choundry began to take his leave of Maria but sat back again when she said, "You must have a ways to walk to your Inn, please allow me to offer you a ride in my coach. We must be circumspect though as there would be much scandal should we be seen together without an escort. I will have my cousin along, but I am afraid that he no longer fits the definition of someone capable of defending my honor."

Although the distance to his lodging wasn't too great, Choundry found himself agreeing readily to the offer. He was instructed to meet the coach on the corner just down from the dance building. Choundry made his leave and, on the way out, told Andy that he was going for a walk and not to worry about his whereabouts, Andy hid a knowing smile and made his way back for a last glass of sherry.

Choundry waited impatiently on the corner, trying to be as inconspicuous as possible. After several minutes, a covered coach, drawn by a team of six pulled up to the corner and Choundry entered when the door swung open. Maria's cousin was slumped across one of the benches, obviously no longer conscious. This meant that Choundry had to seat himself beside Maria. As the coach was of a smaller build, the bench was a tight fit for one of Choundry's size and thus their shoulders were touching as they got underway.

Maria turned to him and appeared close to crying, "I am sure that you must think me worse than the commonest woman on the street. I assure you that I do not make it a practice to act in this manner. It is only that I have been widowed for the past seven years and I am going mad with the loneliness."

Choundry wrapped his arm around her gently and assured her that he thought her a wonderful woman and one to be admired for her independence and strength.

He realized that they were traveling through town and he had not mentioned where he was staying. He stayed his tongue as it came to him that he was being taken to Maria's home. He dared at last to bend down and kiss her gently on the lips. She responded with a surprising vigor that left them clinging tightly to one another. Their embrace and passionate kisses continued until Choundry heard the coach enter a courtyard. A large gate swung closed shortly after they'd come to a stop. Maria stepped out and motioned for Choundry to follow her through a side door. She left instructions to take her cousin back to his residence and give him several bottles of wine for the rest of his evening. Maria then entered the doorway that she had sent Choundry through and, grabbing his hand, pulled him along an empty corridor.

They finally entered a side room that turned out to be Maria's bed chamber. She turned to Choundry and resumed their passionate kissing. After a moment, she pulled away and said breathlessly, "I will be right back, please do not light any of the candles, I would prefer the dark for now." Maria then went into a side room. Choundry waited impatiently until a few minutes later Maria returned dressed in a silken nightgown. Choundry stepped to her and could almost not breath with the surge of need that she brought forth in him. He tried to be gentle as he took her into his arms and finally reached down to lift her gently in his arms and then strode to the center of the room and placed her gently on her bed. Maria was breathing in quick short breaths and was clearly frightened. Choundry calmed his passion and slowly kissed her face and then her neck, gently caressing her back until he felt her relax into his arms, then she began to voice a gentle moaning sound. Maria's passion burst forth unexpectedly and she grabbed him to her.

They shared a night of such passion that Choundry felt might have made a slave of most men. Maria's pent-up need from seven years without her husband lent an almost demanding nature to her lovemaking. Choundry tried his best to be the kind of lover that Maria needed; strong one moment and tender and gentle the next. By the first rays of the morning, neither had slept at all and they lay spent in each other's arms. Maria whispered that Choundry must be gone before sunrise when the servants would be about the villa. He dressed and with a last embrace they made their way to a door that was partly hidden in the corner of one of the rooms in Maria's suite. Before he left, Maria told him that he could return to her the next night if he wished but to wait until two hours after dark and to only knock at the hidden door if he saw a candle in her bedroom window. Choundry made his way silently into the darkness just as the sky was growing light in the east. He walked through a still town at a time when all respectable folks were still abed. His heart was singing and he felt as if he could take on the world.

When he reached his Inn, he stepped quietly up the stairs and entered his room. Lying down on the bed, he found it hard to find sleep as he could still smell the scent of Maria on his clothing and his hands. He didn't want to go to sleep for fear that he would wake up and not be sure that what had happened had not been a dream. Eventually he stood for a moment and pulled pen and paper from his bag; and writing a single word: "Maria" on a piece of paper, he then placed it on his nightstand and then he lay back in the bed to finally fall asleep just as the sun came up above the horizon.

The next day, or rather later the same day, Choundry awoke at eleven. He lay there quietly remembering all that had happened and finally looked to his nightstand to find the note with the single word written on it. It had happened! He jumped from the bed and, donning his clothing, he realized that he had a ravenous appetite. Jumping down the steps two at a time he entered the common room with a smile on his lips. Andy was seated at a bench facing toward the steps so that he would be able to see Choundry when he finally came down from his room. Andy looked at the smile on Choundry's face and, with a twinkle in his eye said, "It seems that the dance lessons were worth every penny spent!"

Over the next several days, Choundry went about purchasing what he would need for his upcoming trip. At night he walked to the outskirts of town and look to see if the candle had been left burning in Maria's window. On all but one night the candle was there. Choundry would walk quietly to the door and rap gently on it and Maria would open the door and allow him into her home. He would stay for several hours but would leave well before dawn. Their passion remained strong but Maria had resisted his attempts to make their relationship public. Finally, she sat on the edge of the bed and told Choundry, "I am not ever going to allow another man control over me again. If you cannot accept me and my love without declaring ownership to the world, then we must part."

Choundry dropped the subject and never referred to it again. He knew that the age difference was an issue and the fact that he was a foreigner didn't help either. He had to accept Maria on her terms.

As the days came and went and the time for his departure drew near, the candle showed less frequently until one evening when he visited Maria's home after an absence of several days he asked her if she regretted their relationship. She held him close and shook her head, "No, I adore you and I treasure the time that we have together, I know that you are leaving and may never return so I must ensure that I survive your leaving. If and when you do return you are welcome here in my arms but I must retain the strength that I've gained since my husband's death."

Finally, when the ship was set to leave the next day, Choundry received a message from William asking him to come to his office. When Choundry arrived, William came to the front of the office and grabbed Choundry's arm and led him down the street and onto the wharf. Pacing forward to the first set of piers, William stopped and pointed to a large ship with greyish sails. "There she is," he said excitedly. "Our venture to the Indies has returned with a fortune in spices! It made it through pirates and terrible storms but it did make it! My competitors all said that it couldn't be done but, with the right crew and a fast ship, we prevailed. Our fortunes are set! You own a goodly portion of what is in her holds and I've already most of it sold even before the ship was even tied to pier."

Chapter 15
A New Adventure Begins

They returned to William's office and had a celebratory drink. Choundry assured William that he was ready to take ship the following day and that he would be taking a small portion of his wares as trading merchandise. He would be forced to leave the majority with William and asked that all but the silver ware be sent on to distant ports and sold for what it could fetch. Willam agreed and they shook hands and parted with William wishing him Godspeed.

The next day Choundry and Andy boarded the *Fair Wind*, a slender schooner with two masts and a smaller crew than Choundry had been used to. The ship was clean and well worked. The Captain's name was Wilbur Barth and he was originally from Liverpool. He had been working for William's shipping company for many years, having worked his way up from a deck hand to eventually the Captain's place on the ship. He was unaware that Choundry was in a partnership with William but he had been entrusted with the knowledge that Choundry was on board on a special mission for the owner of the ship. Choundry and Andy settled in and Andy made his way forward to check and make sure that their merchandise was stored appropriately.

The *Fair Wind* left the harbor later that morning and sailed south. The first half of the cruise was almost uneventful with the exception of a storm that brewed up and brought with it a cloud of sand that descended on the deck and left it gritty and the sails a grimy grey color. The ship was washed clean later the same day when a squall came up from the south and blasted through only minutes after the Captain had reduced sails. Captain Barth had called the timing of the storm almost to the minute; it was obvious that he had years of experience at sea and that he knew these waters well.

They continued their cruise until one day Choundry and Andy were looking toward the coast and saw the familiar outline of the entrance to the harbor that held Banti-town. Captain Barth said that he'd sailed these waters for years but had no knowledge of any port or town along this stretch of coast. Choundry warned him never to enter that particular port even to verify its existence as he might never have the opportunity to leave once he'd entered.

They sailed several days further and finally Captain Barth told them that they would be sighting the port that Choundry had been asked to assess. He told them the man who declared himself the governor of the site had named the port "San Pedro." The last time that Captain Barth had been through, he had seen only one small ship tied up at the wharf and he had sailed past, on to the next much larger port down the coast. Captain Barth told Choundry that he would be putting in to San Pedro this time but was not happy about it.

"I like this place not at all," he said bluntly. "The people are not happy and the men who serve the Governor are some of the worst scum that I've seen in my days."

With a shake of his head, he called to the helm and ordered his crew to make ready to enter the small harbor.

Once they'd tied up to the single pier, they walked into the small town of mostly mud-walled buildings. There were a few people walking around the town. Choundry was mildly surprised to note that most of the individuals he encountered appeared to be of Middle Eastern descent. He and the Captain, along with the first mate from the ship all walked through the town looking for any building that looked substantial enough to house someone who called himself the "Governor'.

They finally found the only wooden-walled building close to the end of town. They walked to the entrance and tried to decide if they should knock, or even how they could knock, as there was no front door, only a curtain made of what appeared to be bamboo strips. A smallish man poked his head through the curtain, looked at the three men and said, "Ah, kind sirs, please say who is to be announced to the Governor?" When the Captain replied, and said who they were, the little man disappeared into the building. After several minutes, the man reappeared to hold the curtain aside and wave them in through the doorway.

The room they stepped into appeared to be the building's main room though it had a dirt floor. A small pig could be seen and heard rooting in a pile of old rags in the far corner. The oddest part of the room was the ornate chandelier that was suspended from the log-and-thatch roof. Chairs were situated around the outer perimeter of the room and a table was turned on its side in the corner. It appeared that the room had been cleared quickly in order to make room for the single piece of furniture that dominated the middle of the room; an over-large straight back chair that was intricately carved and then gilt covered. Directly in front of the chair was a small footstool that was covered with what appeared to be the spotted hide of a wild animal. The small man who greeted them told them to wait in the middle of the room while he went through another curtain at the rear of the room. He could be heard talking to someone out of sight.

A minute later, the man reappeared to tell them that the Governor would see them in a few moments. An uncomfortable hush fell over the room as the three men stood and waited, looking at each other occasionally and smiling at the absurdity of their situation. Eventually a small gong sounded in the adjoining room and the small man stood at what he obviously believed to be "Attention" and stated loudly, "All bow for his excellency, Governor Don Alphonso Martinez." He then bowed deeply forward as there emerged from the curtain a man of medium height but with an enormous belly that seemed oddly balanced atop a pair of thin legs.

Choundry and his companions had forgotten to bow as ordered as they stood, mouths agape, staring at this odd man. The small attendant glared at them as he returned upright from his bowed position. Don Martinez came around the chair and, stepping on the stool, climbed up onto the absurdly decorated chair. He carried a bored expression on his face as he looked to his attendant and asked, "And who is it that comes to my door unannounced?"

The Captain stepped forward and introduced himself and his first mate as being from the ship in the harbor that was part of the fleet belonging to William Thompson from Lisbon. Choundry then stepped forward and introduced himself and told the Don that he was "a merchant traveling down the coast in the hopes of selling his wares and finding new markets."

The Don totally ignored Choundry, but seemed to brighten as he smiled to the Captain "Ah, Mr. Thompson has finally seen fit to send me the ship that I ordered. Did you bring the funds as well?"

Captain Barth bowed slightly and said, "Forgive me but the ship that you have requested may well have been delayed. I am merely on my usual cruise along this coast making my way to the Cape and then back carrying supplies to the settlements. I have stopped at Mr. Thompson's order to ask you for a bit more time to consider your request."

At this the Don's face took on a mottled red appearance and he said, "How dare that merchant make me wait. I have wasted too much time already, greatness awaits, and it is time that I seized the moment."

As he said this, he looked to his left with his head tilted slightly back and his eyes held as if gazing at a distant horizon that only he could see.

After sitting for a moment, he looked to Captain Barth and his eyes took on a shrewd gleam. "What of the ship that you now sail? I have need of a fast ship and that may do nicely. If, as you say, it is only a matter of time before Mr. Thompson sends me a ship, you can wait here, or I will have someone take you to a nearby port and I can use this ship. As you say, you will most likely have to wait only a brief period. Whatever supplies that you carry I will purchase with the immense wealth that my ventures will produce, it will be as nothing to the barrels of coins that will be mine."

Captain Barth replied, "I am sorry, Don, but that I may not do. Mr. Thompson was clear in his orders to bring this cargo to the Cape and return to him as quickly as possible. I will leave at once that I may complete my cruise and bring word to Mr. Thompson."

The Don hurried to answer: "You must not leave so quickly, I must first give you dinner and show you some of the riches that I have gleaned from this pagan land. You will be amazed at the elephant tusks and rich animal furs that I plan to take to the Americas. Why, the ostrich feathers that I have alone would make enough to warrant the trip in themselves! You must stay, I forbid you to leave until I have had a chance to treat you as the guest of a Governor should be welcomed. Return to me this evening when the bell rings and bring as many of your men as you'd like, the feast will be mighty!"

With that Choundry and the other two men turned and left the Governors Palace, having to step quickly to avoid the pig droppings that now littered the entryway.

Striding back to the ship, Choundry said in a subdued tone to the Captain,"I like this naught. That man appears mad, and I think that we should cast off as soon as we reach the ship."

Captain Barth shrugged and said, "I dare not enrage the man if he is to possibly be in business with Mr. Thompson. What would I say when we returned; that I decided to run when he invited me to dinner? No, I must go but I will leave most of my crew aboard and we will make this quick. I like it not either but there is not much that I can do just yet.."

The more that Choundry thought of the prospect of going back ashore as the guest of the Don the more worried he became. He pulled Andy aside and told him of his concerns. They talked at length regarding what might occur and if there was anything that they could do to prepare for whatever might happen. Choundry told his old friend to gather packs for the two of them and place supplies in one of the smaller ship's boats just in case they needed to flee. He also asked that his weapons be brought out and held ready.

As the dinner hour was approaching, Choundry made some last minute preparations with Andy. They agreed to various courses of action should the need arise and also ways that Choundry could warn Andy if something were to go awry. As he prepared to leave the ship, he told Andy to stay sharp. Choundry wore a light coat despite the heat as he wanted to mask the presence of the pistol that he had placed in his belt at the hollow of his back. He also took a small dirk that he hid in one of the deeper pockets of his trousers. Choundry met Captain Barth on the deck of the ship as they prepared to go ashore. He looked to the Captain. "I wish that you would heed my warning, Captain. I fear nothing good will come of this evening, I would be happy to tell William that it was my decision to leave."

Captain Barth said with a smile, "I am the Captain and I'll not hide behind another man when I make decisions, I'll agree that I like this man not at all but we'll get this dinner out of the way, I shall promise to stay until the morrow and then we will leave as soon as we get back aboard. That way if he has anything untoward planned, we will slip and be gone before he can act. Now let's get this unpleasantness out of the way."

The Captain, again accompanied by his first mate and Choundry, left the ship and walked back into town. Arriving at the "Governors House," they went through the routine of being announced and shown in. This time the table was back in the middle of the room and the chairs were positioned around it, each with a bearded and turbaned man seated. There were no other chairs available for the three of them, so they stood at the foot of the table awaiting the Don. As they waited, Choundry took the opportunity to study the seated occupants of the room. Each appeared to be of similar ethnic background, with a swarthy skin coloring, long beards, several had sharp downturned noses, and each wore a small sword belted at his waist on his left side. These men studied Choundry and his two companions as well. No one spoke.

After a few minutes, the Don appeared as before from behind the curtains to the rear of the room. He walked quickly in a strutting manner and went directly to his seat.

After clambering again into his chair, he puffed his chest and, looking to Captain Barth he blustered, "Mr. Thompson does not know the man of destiny with whom he is dealing. I have decided that I will seize the moment and take what is mine. You too will learn what it means to anger one such as I."

He said the last with a brief nod of his head apparently to someone to the rear of the building. Choundry looked to Captain Barth just in time to see a full foot of steel blade burst forth from his chest. Blood quickly welled to the Captain's mouth and his knees started to buckle. Choundry spun on his heel, seeing in his side vision a blade swinging down onto the neck of the first mate. As

Choundry spun, he twisted his body and flung himself downward. He heard a whistling sound as he heard, rather than saw, a blade swing right where his head had been. He continued on with his fall to the floor and turned it into a controlled roll that took him several steps from his attacker.

It had all happened so fast that his two companions had gone down without a noise, everything seemed surreal in that Choundry had the impression that everyone else was moving at half speed and that his awareness had elevated to the point where he could hear the tiniest of noises. He continued moving backwards to give himself some maneuvering room. As he did, he pulled the pistol from his waist band and fired into the chest of the nearest man as he rushed in with his wickedly curved blade held overhead. This gave Choundry just a moment as his attackers paused briefly following the discharge of the weapon. Choundry had the satisfaction that at least he had warned Andy with the sound of the pistol and that Andy would therefore have a chance to warn the crew.

As Choundry spun and lunged toward the door he could hear a series of noises all around him; the sound of the Don screaming to his men, "Kill him," Kill him," the sound of running feet and then several loud crashes coming from the outside of the building. Choundry sprinted out into the growing darkness and made a sharp right to avoid any shots being fired through the doorway. He weaved left and then right again and then started to run toward where the ship was moored. Although growing more difficult to see by the minute, Choundry could just make out a mass of men struggling at the end of the wharf, there seemed to be dozens of strange men fighting to break through onto the ship.

Choundry could not understand why the ship was still tied to the dock, his warning shot should have provided enough time for the crew to cast off and move away from this attacking crowd. He raced down to the end of the wharf, coming up on the backs of the men assaulting the ship. As he moved he grabbed a piece of lumber that was leaning against one of the posts. He raised the length of wood above his head and as he approached, he brought it down on the neck of one of the men struggling at the back of the mob. He felt a sickening crunch as the man seemed to melt down onto the wood of the wharf. He sought out the closest enemies and then brought the lumber back up and then down twice more with similar results before those at the rear of the mob turned and started yelling to alert the others. Choundry swung the lumber piece up to block a sword stroke and then reversed it to send the tip slamming into the man's stomach. At least four men, each with a curved sword, started to move toward Choundry. At that time, he also heard a yell of triumph as the mob surged over the remaining defenders onto the ship's deck. Choundry knew that all was lost and that if he stayed any longer his death would be assured. With a mighty swing he threw the blood-coated piece of lumber at the men who were approaching and then ran to the end of the wharf and dove deeply into the waters of the harbor.

Choundry had always been a strong swimmer and he had enjoyed many a carefree day with his friends diving and swimming from the rocks of his native coast; this at a time when it was not uncommon for even veteran sailors to not be able to even tread water. He swam deeper and headed down under the ship's keel, eventually surfacing on the other side of the ship and out of the view of the men on the wharf. The attackers on the boat were not aware that anyone was in the water and if they did it would not have mattered as they were intent on killing the last of the crew and then moving on to start their looting of the ship. Choundry dove again and swam underneath the water, away from the ship, and then came up for a gasp of air and dove again and then again, swimming deeper into the gathering darkness.

He had a vague notion of where he was going but hoped that all of his efforts wouldn't be for naught. It would have been a close-run thing but he was hoping Andy might have had sufficient time to get away before the ship fell. He knew that he had only minutes before the search would be on for him in earnest and his only hope was to be in some place that they wouldn't expect. He started swimming in strong steady strokes moving northward up the coast. He stayed far enough from the shore that any splashes he might make wouldn't betray his presence. He continued on making steady progress. His aim was to make it around the headland and into the area where the whitecaps from the ocean met the calmer, protected waters of the harbor. It was there that he had arranged with Andy to meet should the worst happen.

Choundry swam with a steady rhythm, stopping every few minutes so as to not become too tired should he meet some unexpected obstacle. He tried not to think of the giant maneaters that had been spotted in these very waters when they had sailed in. Eventually, during one of his rest periods, Choundry thought that he could hear the sound of waves cresting. He swam on and then finally he began to feel that he was swimming into the area where the waters mixed. He stopped swimming and treaded water. Looking towards shore, he realized that he may have swum further out than he'd anticipated.

Swimming quietly on his side, he started to work his way closer to the shore and within minutes, felt a wave of relief as he could make out the silhouette of a man crouched in a small boat. Although he knew it could only be Andy, Choundry felt that he should continue to move quietly as he wasn't sure if others might be about. Swimming close to the small boat and seeing that the figure crouched in the boat was indeed Andy but that he was staring fixedly ahead toward the shore. Choundry was going to call out to his friend but didn't want to frighten him. Andy would be fearing all manner of attack, and he might react without thinking to an unexpected voice from the ocean at his back.

Choundry softly whistled the first bars to a familiar sea chanty. He saw the shadow stiffen and turn slowly to gaze out to sea. Choundry slowly swam into view and stopped with his hand on the gunwale of the boat. Andy grasped his hand and blurted, "Thank the Lord, I thought you gone fer sure."

Andy reached down and helped pull Choundry further into the boat until he was seated in the boat dripping and shuddering in the cool night air.

Choundry looked to his friend and said, "Let's be quick about it, mate, we have to be well away before mornings light and we have to be further then they could imagine that we'd be or we'll find them waiting on the shore when the sun comes up." With that, each man took an oar and started to row as vigorously as they could northwards up the coast.

Chapter 16
Flight Through the Wilds

As the night went on, the two spelled each other by shifting from one oar to the other so that each man rowed on the left side of the boat and then took a spell on the right side. They made good time once they were far enough out from the shore and beyond where the waves were forming. As they rowed, they talked of what they would need to do. They could not return to the San Pedro harbor; it was clear that the ship had fallen and from what they'd seen there would be no survivors allowed so that no one could bear witness to the foul deed. It was for that same reason that they could expect an unrelenting search for them as Don Martinez would be ruined and made a hunted criminal should the theft and murders ever be discovered.

Choundry and Andy knew little of this portion of the coast but had a general understanding of the distances they would have to travel. The reality was that the challenges would be mighty and, even if they found a small port to stay in, the Don could apparently muster sufficient men to overwhelm any puny defenses that these outposts might muster. They must plan for a lengthy journey and they could expect to be hunted on the sea as well as the land. Being sailors they were loath to leave the sea but they soon realized that they would be very visible, and vulnerable, on the water. The Don had several smaller vessels, as well as his newly captured ship, with which to put on a search. If they were ever discovered at sea they would have only one recourse and that would be to make for the shore. In the event that any of the Don's men would be along that section of coast as well, they would be easy targets as they attempted to make a landing. Considering this, they soon realized they must quit the sea and move inland. As neither man had much experience at living off the land, it was with a heavy heart that they committed themselves to sinking the boat, when the time came, and then heading inland.

They continued rowing on through the night and then started moving in toward the shore. As they neared the breakers they could see that there were a number of small rocky outcrops with waves crashing against them. Choundry felt that it was important that they not leave any tracks when they went ashore as they could expect their hunters to have at least one party walking the beach. Running the small boat up behind a large formation of rocks, Choundry held the vessel steady while Andy climbed up onto the rocks. Once Andy had reached a secure position, Choundry handed up all of the supplies and belongings until the boat was emptied. Choundry asked Andy if he could heft some of the rocks that were wedged between the larger boulders. Andy was able to pull several free and then handed these down to Choundry who set them in the bottom of the boat. Choundry then rowed the boat out into deeper water and then, standing in the heaving boat, he grabbed one of the rocks and raised it above his head. He brought it down swiftly and released the rock, allowing it to crash into the boards at the bottom of the boat. There was an immediate snapping noise as two of the boards fractured and water began to gush upwards from the bottom of the boat.

Choundry had planned to sink the boat in deeper waters so that their pursuers would not be able to discover where they had gone ashore. His plan had gone a little too well as the boat quickly took on water while Choudry tried to maneuver it closer to shore so that he could avoid the possibility of any hazardous tides as he swam the remaining distance. He finally gave up trying to row the boat when his strokes no longer produced any visible forward motion as the weight of the water made the boat almost immoveable. He wedged the oars into the body of the boat so that they would not float free when the boat went under. As the water started to slosh over the sides of the boat, Choundry slipped over the side and made his way toward the rocks on which Andy awaited.

Much to his relief, the tides and currents were not too severe in this area so he was able to make his way to the rocks with little difficulty. He climbed up on one of the lower rocks, keeping clear of the ragged edges that were encrusted with barnacles and seaweed. Clambering atop the rocks, he sat down next to Andy and looked toward the shore to plan out their next moves. Their supplies were their greatest asset but also their greatest liability; moving what they had would take two trips up from the beach and would therefore double their chances of leaving any signs of their presence. It was already becoming full light so they needed to move swiftly. If they were discovered, their pursuers would make a quick end to the chase. Moving quickly they stepped from rock to rock until they had made their way well off of the beach. They dropped their goods and then turned to make the journey back again for what remained of their supplies.

Once they were off the beach and settled, Choundry stood for a moment scanning the sands and rocks to see if they'd left any sign of their passing this way. He then looked down the beach as far as he could, to see if he could spy any sign of pursuit. Seeing nothing moving along the length of the visible coastline, he ducked back into the foliage.

After Choundry and Andy had rested, Choundry said, "We have a few choices. Either we find a place to hide and wait for the pursuit to pass us by or we move now while we can in the hope of staying ahead of our pursuers."

They both preferred to keep moving because they knew that once their hunt had overreached them, they would be forced to watch both their rear as well as to their front. Neither knew exactly how far they would have to travel but they decided they would stay as close to the shore as they possibly could during their journey.

Although it had taken two trips to bring their supplies up from the shore, they felt that if they organized everything into two large packs that would only leave the small keg of water to carry between them. It took them the better part of an hour to get everything stowed in their packs and to work two sets of straps on each pack so that it could be worn on the shoulders. They worked spare shirts in such a manner that each pack was provided a degree of padding to the straps so that they wouldn't bite too deep. The keg of water took a bit longer as they finally decided to cut a sturdy pole and bind the keg to the pole. Clean water would be almost impossible to find in this wilderness and neither man could afford to develop a debilitating disease.

Choundry and Andy figured that they had enough food and water for about six days of heavy traveling. That would not be nearly enough to get them to where they needed to go. For weapons, they had two cutlasses, and Choundry's small dagger. Andy had not had an opportunity to grab Choundry's musket but that was just as well as the extra weight would have been too much, and they'd have had to leave something behind. Before they started out, they talked about how they should proceed; walking game trails would be permitted but anything larger that looked as if it was used by man was to be avoided; they could not leave signs of their passing anywhere that their pursuers could discover. Both men knew that the Don could not allow them to survive so there would not be any lessening or dropping of the pursuit; the men following them would know that they had to kill the two of them or they would be facing an even more relentless hunt themselves that would eventually end in the gallows.

Both men had limited experience with surviving in the wild. Andy shared that he would often sleep outside under the stars with his boyhood friends but that he'd always taken a loaden picnic hamper with them. Choundry had experienced mostly day trips and hikes but nothing even close to the scale of their looming trek.

Choundry and Andy stood and hefted their packs, knowing that, although the weight of the packs was rather daunting, they soon would have much less to carry as they went through the supplies they had. When that happened, they would be wishing for a return of that weight and the security that it signified. They started walking northward and tried to stay out of sight of the beach but still within earshot of the crashing waves. They did well the first day and managed what they thought to be several miles. The areas near the ocean had a sandy soil and the trees were stunted. Rocks were everywhere so they were careful where they placed their feet, especially after seeing several evil-looking serpents lying atop some rocks basking in the heat from the sun.

Choosing a place to sleep took them longer than they expected. Once they had decided to find a spot to bed down, they went quite a way without seeing anything that might give them a degree of protection from the weather. They kept moving, hoping to find something defensible should wild animals search them out. It was obvious that they could not use fire as the smell of the smoke would give them away from even a great distance and the light from the fire would be a veritable beacon to draw their pursuers to them. They made their way toward the shore in an attempt to search out a slightly rockier terrain, thinking that they might find a place where a cave could be found. As it started to get difficult to see, they finally had to settle on two rocks that formed an angle, allowing them to have some degree of protection at least at their backs. They used their cutlasses to sever several small branches, low down on some of the nearby trees. They stacked these to allow them a cushion on which to sit as well as place something between themselves and any of the numerous bugs and serpents they'd seen during their days progress. They also cut several small bushes that could be piled to their front to hide them from any casual onlookers.

Andy and Choundry sat side by side as night fell. They ate sparingly of the supplies that Andy had hurriedly been able to pack just before he was forced to flee. Choundry asked him several questions about what had happened but was most interested as to why the crew had failed to move the ship away from the dock even a short distance, as this would have made a significant difference in the course of the attack and might have given the crew at least a chance to beat back the assault. Andy paused for a moment and finally said, "It must have been swivel guns that were mounted somewhere on the dock. I'm not sure how they got them there without us seeing em but they had several of their men just sitting around the wharf just looking like they were bored and wanted to watch what was happening on the ship. When the yelling started and then we heard what must have been yer shot, I yelled to the crew to beware and gather to fend off an attack. I'll say that those lads sure were game for a fight as they lay forward and each one of them was ready with a weapon; the crew must have sensed something was amiss because each man was ready and armed."

"They gathered to the front of the ship and it was just then that thems on the dock must have touched off their swivel guns. It swept a good many of those lads aside like a broom, and many of them were turned to a pulp. The rest stayed their posts but, as ye saw, the wave of attackers that came down the wharf caught us before we could cast off. I could see it was going to go bad for us so I stayed and helped until I knew that I needed to do as ye ordered and make ready our escape. I had placed everything in the ship's boat that we kept tied to the back of the ship so all that I had to do was skinny down the rope and make my way far enough from the ship before those on board could see what direction that I went. I do have to say that they will surely miss the boat and are certain to know that we escaped. There's no use hoping that they'll think us lost as from what you told me earlier, your escape was sure to be remembered."

They sat in the dark and at first Choundry doubted that either one of them would sleep but they finally decided to take watches. It was the hard-learned life of a sailor that eventually came to their aid as sailors learn to sleep wherever and whenever they have a chance. Choundry chose first, watch and then two hours later woke Andy and then he laid down to take his turn at catching some sleep. They did this on and off throughout the night until finally the skies started to brighten. Again, eating sparingly of their stores and drinking several gulps each from the water cask, they tried to set their hiding place to rights so that to anyone following them might pass without noticing that the area had been disturbed. There was nothing for the trees where they had cut the branches except to rub a mud mixture on the stub of the branch so that it wouldn't stand out quite as much.

They started out much as they had the previous day. Much of the land ahead was similar to what they had passed through the previous day. They were gradually forced to move further inland from the coast, and the thinning of the scrub trees was no longer providing adequate cover. They found that the surrounding jungle was more difficult to traverse but certainly provided cover so dense that there was little chance of being seen from any distance. By mid-afternoon, they came to a clearing where there were several mud huts that were in various states of disrepair. Not a soul could be seen throughout the village. No movement, no noise, it appeared that the place was devoid of life entirely.

They decided to risk entering the village in the hope that, if the people were truly away, they might find supplies or articles that would prove useful in their trek. Choundry and Andy left their packs and supplies hidden in the trees after they had skirted around the village as they wanted to be able to leave in the direction that they needed to travel if they were discovered and had to flee in a hurry.

Walking across the central area of the little village, they could see various articles broken and thrown about. On entering the first hut they found the desiccated corpse of a person huddled in a corner. Much of the flesh had long gone from the body leaving near-skeletal remains that were held together by tough bits of sinew and ligaments. The individual who had died here had met a violent end as their skull showed signs of being crushed.

Looking about the hut, they found a simple gourd that had been hollowed out to use as a bowl or scoop, they gathered this as well as some leather straps that they cut from a series of poles gathered together over the fire pit in the middle of the room. They went to the next huts and in three they found bodies that also showed signs of violence; one body showed where the rib cage was cut nearly through by what must have been a sharp bladed instrument. In the last hut, they found the bodies of two infants, both of whom had been ravaged by some animals but one of the pitifully small bodies also clearly showed damage to the skull.

They were finally able to find two large hides that were partially hidden under the crushed corner of one of the huts. They saved these in hopes that the hides could be used to shield their bodies at night. The pottery that remained unbroken was all too large to be practical to carry with them. They did find a couple handfuls of dried seeds in the bottom of one of the pots. They decided to take the seeds, even though they were unfamiliar to both men, reasoning that eventually they would reach the end of their supplies and at some point, would need to start learning what might prove edible from the resources at hand.

There didn't appear to be any fresh water source nearby although they knew that there had to be some source of drinking water close by or the village would not have been located there in the first place. Although puzzled by the empty village, they were cheered somewhat by their finds. As they left the village behind, they decided to chance walking one of the paths that led in the direction they were traveling simply because they had already left tracks in the village. If they were to be discovered, then the best thing would be to put as much distance as they could between them and the village as quickly as possible. They walked rapidly for what must have been the better part of a mile, all the while peering ahead and listening to make sure they did not run into anyone coming down the path from the opposite direction.

At one point, they decided that they should step away into the brush and resume their journey as they had been doing previously. They continued on for two more days. Their stores were dwindling at an alarming rate and their keg of water was sloshing as they walked. The packs were easy to carry now and their progress was slightly better than when they had initially set out as both men were becoming hardened by the demands of the journey. Wild animals were surprisingly scarce with any creatures that they had seen being frightened by the contact and disappearing quickly into the nearby jungle. The vegetation was starting to thin a bit. Occasionally they found the carcass of an animal that had long before been killed, some bearing the signs of a predator while others appeared to have been killed by man. One such carcass was of a creature that must have been the size of two of the largest horses that Choundry had ever seen. It was on its side, partway into a small scum-covered pond. Whoever killed the creature had sawed off something from its nose. Andy and Choundry could not conceive of what such an animal would look like if alive and what had been removed. Whatever had been removed must have been of some great value to the hunter as it was the only thing missing and no flesh seemed to have been removed from the carcass.

Several times during their last day of travel they had come to trails that were obviously cut by man. There were plenty of tracks in the deepest mud but nothing that showed recent use. It seemed by the increasing frequency of these trails that they must be approaching or nearing a larger settlement. The very next day they came to a series of clearings that must have been some type of tilled land. Whatever had been grown here had gone unharvested and now lay in ragged piles. Upon closer inspection the vegetables ended up being some type of tuber that when tasted seemed to be very starchy but might be edible if they had no other options. Since it was cultivated by men, it was a safe bet that it could be eaten by Choundry and Andy; a much less dangerous choice then chancing something unknown that they might find in the jungle. The two men quickly gathered small piles of the roots and placed them into their half-empty packs. The additional weight when they donned the packs seemed somehow reassuring. At least they wouldn't starve in the near future.

They continued on, walking in the fields rather than on the main track. As they moved forward, they saw that they were again coming to another settlement, but this one was much larger and the buildings were in relatively good repair. Here again, as they neared the village, they could not see any movement or activity. After studying the village for an hour, they felt sure of what they would find when they entered. They had some food now, but their concern had now turned to finding a source to replenish their drinking water.

As they walked across the field, again to prevent leaving easily identifiable traces of their presence, they came across the bodies of several people; two men and one elderly woman who lay amongst the ruined crop. Each showed either a bullet hole or signs of having been cut down with what could only have been some type of bladed weapon. They appeared to have been killed within the last several days as the scavenging and desiccation of the corpses had not progressed as far as the victims in the other village.

They decided to chance stepping into the nearest huts and were rewarded with the finding of a large water-filled gourd suspended above the floor of the hut using some twisted smaller vines in place of ropes. They stepped from that hut to the two adjoining structures and in each they found the same suspended water-filled gourds. Having replenished much of their water cask they decided that it would not be a good idea to explore further. As they backed away from the village, they could see a central open area that was clotted with the bodies of numerous villagers.

Here and there they found other bodies, each either an elderly person or a very small child. Even the dogs had all been killed. In looking through the bodies strewn about they noticed that these individuals had not died as quickly as the others they'd found. Many showed the signs of torture and some of the others were killed in especially vicious manners. Some were missing limbs or showed multiple deep cuts that were designed to cripple, not kill. Whoever had performed these terrible acts had actually enjoyed what they were doing and killed everything that they could in as many different ways as could be imagined.

The scenes in the village deeply disturbed Choundry and Andy. Choundry looked to his companion and said, "I would have never dreamed that one person could visit such devastation on another, let alone enjoy the performing of the deed. These people had been trying to raise families, work their fields, and live a good life. These people could just as easily have been my family or yours back home."

They tried to erase any signs of their passing but knew that it would not stand up to close inspection.

They left the village, following what appeared to be a large game trail. They did notice some footprints in the dust, but these did not seem to be newly made. After walking the better part of an hour on the track, they stopped next to a dense brush to catch their breath. As they stood staring ahead to see what might be waiting for them in the next 100 yards of visible trail, they heard a low moan coming from the brush immediately to their right. Both men froze in shocked surprise. They looked to each other and then again tried to peer deep into the briars.

Circling the brush quietly, Choundry eventually came to a track in the dirt that looked as if something had been dragged back through a small opening. One of the larger pieces of brush had a dark smear at its base that looked suspiciously like dried blood.

Choundry stepped back from the brush and Andy came over to him. They talked briefly in whispers regarding whether they should just ignore whatever was in the brush and move on or whether they should attempt to see what they could do for whatever poor soul had crawled into this hiding place. Both men knew that it would be exceedingly dangerous to crawl back through the brush, approaching whatever wounded person lay in the center of the brush without having any way of knowing whether whoever was injured would deem them to be a friend or foe.

As they debated what they should do, they heard a faint shot to their rear. At first it seemed that they might have been mistaken at the cause of the noise until they heard another gunshot straight ahead in the direction they had been walking. A signal? Someone hunting game or others like the hidden individual in the brush? Or could it be hunting groups of the Don's men seeking to encircle their prey and signaling to make sure that each party was in their appointed place? It really didn't matter. The reality was that they could not go forward or return the way they had come.

At a loss momentarily, they again heard the moaning coming from the dense brush. Choundry looked to Andy, "It looks as if we best find a place to wait out those who are hunting us or whoever may have escaped the pillaging of yonder village. It seems to me that whoever is hiding in this briar patch has escaped their notice at least once already so maybe we should see if there is enough room for us as well."

With that, Choundry doffed his pack and moved to the small opening. Going onto his belly, he wriggled his way back through the brush following the slight trail that he could see from whatever person had already found refuge here. He had to crawl his way back a further twenty feet until he could see what appeared to be the center of the thicket. There was a small hollowed out area of about eight feet in the center and Choundry could see the form of a man curled into a ball on the far side of the small clearing. He called back to Andy that he should hand in the packs. Once he had them in hand, he pushed them ahead of him into the thicket. He told Andy to use some brush and wipe out any trace of their passing and then to back into the small entranceway and to continue to brush out their tracks as he backed into the pile of brush.

Once the two of them had successfully made their way to the center of the brush they sat quietly for a moment staring at the back of what appeared to be an elderly tribesman.

Choundry said, "Andy, look to the man here and see what you can do for him, I am going to crawl back through our little passage and see if I can make the entrance a bit more difficult to see."

Choundry took his knife and chopped a small briar bush down and, crawling face forward into the small entranceway, he pushed the briar bush ahead of him until he had it positioned close to, and blocking, the small path. To a casual observer looking in the hole they would see it ending in a seemingly impassable wall of thorns. Choundry then backed up, again removing any traces of his passing.

When he came back into the small clearing, he saw that Andy had the elderly African sitting up and was giving him a cup of their precious water. The elderly man barely had his eyes slitted open and much of the water was dribbling down his bearded chin to fall onto his frail thin chest. Andy looked to Choundry and said, "He said a few words in what seemed to be Spanish but then he just faded out."

Choundry replied, "We'll leave him be for a bit to rest and then give him some more water. Hopefully we won't have to stay here very long but if we do, we'll have to make sure that he doesn't moan like he did before, or we'll be easy pickings if we're discovered. All they'd have to do is put a match to this tinder pile and there is little we could do to stop them."

The briar thicket gave them the advantage of being impossible to see from the outside. On the other hand, it also meant that they too could not see if someone were approaching. That meant that silence was absolutely critical. The three of them sat quietly through the rest of the day and periodically they tried to give the elderly man some additional water. During the second attempt, the man drank the liquid without spilling any. As the cup emptied, the old man opened his eyes briefly and Choundry quietly whispered in his ear in Spanish, "Friend, we are friend, you must be very quiet as the bad ones are near." The old man looked into Choundry's face and wearily nodded his head to show that he understood.

As night fell, they sat close together for warmth, spreading the two hides that they'd gathered to provide them a degree of cover from the evening cool as well as any possible morning dew. It seemed that they would be safe from predators while in this thicket but they decided, as they talked in whispers, that they would follow their usual routine of standing watch and watch to be sure that they did not inadvertently give away their positions should anyone come near. As they lay there, Andy on first watch and Choundry lying down to sleep they could hear faintly, far in the distance, the sounds of laughter and then occasionally what sounded like the frightened screams of a woman. After whispering to one another about what the noises meant, the old man could be heard to voice in a ragged whisper, "It is the slavers. They have stolen my people and are killing all the ones too old or young to make the journey up the coast."

He sighed at hearing the distant screams, "This is the second village that I have been in that was so destroyed. The young men of the village did not heed my warnings and bragged of what they would do to the men with the fire weapons. Little did they know that they and their families would be as weeds before the mighty grey giant. They did not listen to what I had to say, they felt that I was just an old man telling them stories to frighten the little ones at night. Now they know."

The old man's name turned out to be "Mumba" and he had spent his early years among a people who used to live right along the coast. A Portuguese monk had come to live with them and Mumba had learned to speak a version of Spanish from the man. He had been a chief in a small village several days walk inland when one day raiders had descended on the hapless village, killing some and gathering all who remained into the central area of the village. They proceeded to pull out all of the young and healthy villagers and then placed heavy ropes that would not break on their hands and ankles. Those who resisted were beaten mercilessly or killed outright. The rest of the villagers were pushed into the nearby river, forcing old and young into the waters regardless of their pitiful screams. The old man had managed to grab a small piece of floating debris and let it carry him down river, hiding amidst the bodies floating along with the current. He had walked from the town where he had been a respected elder to eventually reach the village of a distant relative; to be taken in to live off the charity of the village.

Checking the old man for injuries, they found a long shallow cut that went from his right shoulder blade up through to the side of his neck. The old man said he had received the injury as he had fled the slaughter. With his past experience he had known what was to come so he had run just as the men with the long blades started in to killing those they could not take with them. This time he was struck by a spear that glanced off his right shoulder blade to skid across his upper back and to eventually pass on over his right shoulder as his upper body was torqued downward by the force of the thrown spear.

The old man was definitely a survivor and made of strong stuff. By the morning light he was sitting up and gnawing on one of the tubers they had brought from the village. He seemed in good spirits and was happy to have found someone who he could stay with until he found his new home. He saw their small pile of remaining supplies and, when Choundry asked him if he knew how to find drinkable water the old man chuckled and said, "You seem as ignorant as a new born, I will show you how my people live in the brush, there is plenty to eat and water everywhere; even right under your feet!."

He laughed as if it were hard to believe that someone could not know how to harvest the bounty that he seemed to think surrounded them on every side. When he had finished his breakfast, he gathered a nearby twig and broke that in half, handing one piece to Choundry. He then used the piece that he still held and, crushing the end, proceeded to use the twig to scour his teeth clean. Choundry did as he was shown only to find that the twig had a pleasant flavor and it served main well to scrub his teeth. The old man laughed and said, "Use as you like but do now swallow the juice or you will be making water from your bottom."

At this, Choundry threw down the twig as the last thing that he needed was loose bowels during a time when they needed to remain in hiding.

They stayed in the thicket for that day and well into the next. Toward the end of the second day they heard a group approaching from the track that they had been following. Words could be made out as they passed, the language unknown to Choundry or Andy. They could clearly hear the clanking of iron shackles being dragged through the brush. Choundry realized that this was what the old man meant when he had mentioned earlier the "heavy ropes that would not break." Finally, the sounds faded down the track and nothing more was heard that day. Later that evening they again heard the noises from the village. The screams were even more disturbing now that they knew what they meant.

At midday of the third day hidden in the brush, they decided that they had best move along as their supplies were getting dangerously low. Once they had made it out of their hiding place, Mumba took them north along the track for about a hundred yards and then he stepped off the track and onto a path that was hidden behind a screening bush. The track was a footpath but thin enough that it must have been seldom used. It seemed a reasonable risk to take this footpath especially as they now had a local guide. Mumba walked quickly with a strong stride as if he had not been suffering greatly just days earlier.

They made their way quickly along the path and, coming to a large grove of trees with an open area to their left, Choundry took the lead momentarily as Mumba stopped to smell the air. Just as Choundry began to step around the nearest tree a man wearing a turban and holding a musket in his hands turned to stare at Choundry with eyes wide in alarm. Obviously, the man was just as startled as Choundry by the unexpected meeting. Choundry knew that he only had moments before the man yelled an alarm. He thrust out quickly in a fighting technique that he had learned when working with Dan but thought that he would never need. A killing blow designed to bring a man down quickly by crushing his throat. The blow landed cleanly, and the crunching sound of the man's throat being crushed was the loudest noise that came from the conflict as the man slowly toppled to the ground to lie still. The entire struggle had taken less than two minutes. It was hard to believe that a man's life could be end so quickly but after having seen the evil that these men were capable of, Choundry didn't think twice about removing one of these men from further sins against the people who inhabited this land.

Now they were faced with a dilemma; what to do with the body and which way should they go as the chase would surely be on now that they had revealed themselves. Mumba stepped forward and took the knife from the dead man's belt and proceeded to hack at various parts of the still switching body. Choundry was going to stop Mumba but then thought that maybe the old man needed to do this for some type of revenge; he also had to admit that he didn't care what was done to any man who could do what this man must have participated in.

They left the body where it lay after removing the man's sword, musket and taking up a small bag of supplies that had been partly hidden at the base of the tree. Adding the supplies to their packs, Choundry took the musket and ammunition and handed the sword to the old man whose eyes gleamed at this great gift. Choundry allowed Mumba to retain the small dagger that he had used just minutes before as Choundry already had a small blade of his own and he'd rather not handle the blood-covered blade after he'd seen what acts it had recently been used to perform.

They might only have moments before the alarm was sounded but the man could have been an outward scout whose absence might not be noticed for hours. Choundry and his companions moved quickly forward, looking for an area where the undergrowth was thicker and where they could lose themselves in the jungle. Choundry set a blistering pace that soon had Andy struggling to keep up. Mumba seemed to have the ability to walk at whatever pace was set without any outward signs of tiring. He seemed cheerful and showed no ill effects from his ordeal or his wound. They pushed on for several hours without hearing any alarm being raised to their rear. As it grew into evening, they slowed their pace and started looking for a place to hide and sleep for the night.

Mumba motioned for them to continue marching forward and eventually, after stopping and searching the ground closely, he must have found what he was looking for as he led directly into the dense growth that lined the path. He'd gone only twenty yards when he stepped into a culvert and seemed to disappear.

As Choundry followed close behind, he could see the corner of the old man's robe as it merged with what appeared to be solid stone. As he ventured closer, he saw that there was actually a hidden entrance to a small cave. Choundry had to duck his head and step over a small boulder to enter. The entrance was hidden from the top of the culvert by the presence of a pile of stones that lay in front of the opening and obscured the view of the small cave in such a manner that it blended in with the surroundings. Choundry stepped deeper into the cave and then stopped to allow his eyes a chance to adapt to the dark. Mumba had stepped ahead and it became apparent that he was familiar with the cave's layout. He walked to the far corner and removed a small stone from a deep cleft in the rock revealing a small hole through which dim evening light streamed into the cave.

Once the three men had entered, there was still ample room to lay down and stretch out. Since they were so close to the trail, they were unable once again to make any kind of fire. It would be another cold camp this night although they wouldn't have to worry about night chills or morning dew wetting their clothing. They were now down to their last rations. The water keg was nearly empty, but they had not needed to tap into it this past day as Mumba had discovered many different spots where water could be found. At one tree there had been a hidden cleft between two large branches where rainwater had collected as it ran down the bark of the tree and became trapped in a pocket. At another spot, Mumba had stopped them as they were walking through a particularly rough stretch of ground. He had started to sniff the air and then walk around in circles sniffing and poking the ground with a stick. After a few minutes of this, he bent down and started digging into the loose soil. By the time he had gotten down approximately eight inches it became obvious what he was doing when the hole started to fill with water. Mumba looked to Choundry and said, "Water found in this manner is cleaned by the soil and good to drink, you can drink this water and not have the ache here," as he rubbed his stomach.

Mumba seemed to possess a wealth of knowledge regarding survival in the bush and once he found that Choundry was an eager pupil, he went out of his way to show specific plants that could be eaten. He pulled open rotted logs to show the massive grey slugs that he said were delicious, proving his point as he swallowed several without even chewing them. Mumba had shown Choundry a plant that, when cut with a sharp knife, produced a quick spurt of water that if he was quick enough to catch it in his mouth tasted palatable but slightly starchy.

Choundry asked Mumba how he had found the cave. The old man smiled and said that he had passed this way many times before, and that he had found the cave during one of his trips when he had left the trail looking for what he called a "dream plant."

Choundry paused and looked to Andy to make sure that his friend was tolerating the trek well so far. Andy had started the trip with a slight belly from the relatively easy living they had enjoyed since leaving the *Merlin*. He was now back to his slim self and seemed to be growing stronger every day. When they had first met, Andy had been a meek sort of character who had stayed in the background for fear of calling attention to himself. The past several months had made a different man of him. Choundry thought with a grin of the changes that they both had gone through in such a short timeframe. Some men were worn down by adversity, but Andy seemed to grow in strength and confidence with each ordeal that they faced and conquered. Even Andy's stride was different and he carried himself with a certain confidence now that Choundry found admirable. Choundry promised himself that once they found the time that he would teach Andy some of his fighting techniques.

They continued their practice of setting watch on watch and as usual they excluded Mumba from the practice as he had no use for the concept of time, and he saw no reason for anyone to remain awake. Halfway through the night, Choundry thought that he heard a distant noise but as he sat in the dark at the entrance to the cave, he couldn't hear anything further. He woke Andy at the appointed time and went to lie down for his turn at getting some sleep. As he lay there awaiting sleep, Mumba sat up and told Choundry, "In the morning we must start to watch for animals that are dangerous, we are leaving the area where my people and the hunters usually venture and the animals will not be as frightened of man as those found close to our homes. We also come to some waters soon and we must watch for the water pigs."

Chapter 17
New Adversaries

In the morning, they stepped out on the track and resumed their journey, entering a region where the vegetation was becoming sparse and they were forced to walk in the open for dozens of yards at a time. Mumba stepped to the front of the group and led the way. They no longer needed to stay with the track as they were able to make good time now that they did not have to fight their way through undergrowth. They started to hear occasional sounds of animals as they gave trumpeting noises or guttural growls or coughs. At one point, Mumba motioned for them to stand still as he crouched and moved forward. He stalked up to a low brush and stood slowly to gaze over the top. He motioned with his hand to Choundry and Andy to move slowly forward. They imitated Mumba's crouching manner and stepped up to the thick brush. Upon peering over, they were able to make out in the distance several giant grey forms. Choundry couldn't believe what he was seeing. The grey beasts seemed as large as houses. He realized that these must be elephants and, when he saw one giant sporting a pair of immense tusks, he thought him to be the male of the group.

Mumba motioned them forward and they continued on, skirting wide around these beasts. By midday they were approaching a wide stretch of open land that was covered with low grass and only dotted with an occasional small tree. Choundry was reluctant to walk across such an open area as they could easily be spied by anyone in the vicinity. He still feared pursuit, especially with the death of one of their pursuers. He also felt that there might be a chance that the Don could have sent men around in front of them by boat or overland to prevent them from reaching any outposts of civilization that might be found along the route they were traveling.

Choundry decided to wait until evening and make their journey across this open land during the nighttime. "I've no wish to brave the night and the predators that we might find but I think we've little choice, it's either chance the killers that could be in the night or be found by the ones that are following us."

As they sat quietly waiting for nightfall, Mumba tilted his head as if listening to something. He moved quietly to his feet and, grabbing the sword that was given to him, he treaded softly into the nearby low brush. They could see his head and shoulders as he moved through the grass, he suddenly paused a moment and then he could be seen to raise the sword above his head and then bring it down in one swift stroke. A few minutes later, he came trotting back to them holding the wriggling headless body of a massive snake. Mumba was grinning widely as he held the dripping snake in front of him and he said proudly "We eat well today!'

He then sat down and proceeded to skin the snake and slice off long slivers of flesh that he placed on a nearby rock, he continued to slice and carve until he had reduced the snake to a pile of skin and chunks of boney matter. He then sat and watched the pieces of meat as they lay on the rock, all the time using a piece of brush to wave the flies away. Choundry and Andy looked to each other. Neither wanted to voice what they were thinking but each knew that they needed food and especially food that would give them the energy needed to sustain them on the lengthy trek that remained ahead of them. As the sun finally started to wane, Mumba lifted a slice of meat and placed it in his mouth to chew with obvious relish. He finished and swallowed the meat. He held up a slice of meat in each hand and thrust them towards his two companions. Choundry had already decided not to show his reluctance so he reached out to take the sliver of meat in hand and then brought it to his lips. He placed it quickly in his mouth and started chewing. He was pleasantly surprised to realize that the heat of the sun had cooked the meat nearly as well as a frying pan would have. The meat was tough and had a gamey flavor but it was actually quite good. He looked to Andy and they both smiled in surprise. Reaching out they began to take more of the strips and continued with their meal until it had all been consumed. Even though the snake had been very large, the meat that it produced had not been enough to adequately feed three men, so they were still hungry when the meat was gone, but they decided to conserve the last of the remaining tubers and the small amount of provisions that they had remaining.

They drank deeply from the half-filled cask, anticipating a long dry walk across the open land during the night with little chance to stop for rest. They needed to be across into the low hills they had seen in the distance before morning's light. If there were hunters ahead of them, they would surely be posted atop one of the hills in the distance and if the three of them were anywhere in the open when the sun came up, they would surely be seen.

They stood and started their walk into the descending darkness. They made good time for the first few hours but then they started to encounter an area with deep gullies and washes that required utmost care in feeling their way down the steep sides and then choosing a safe route to climb up the other side. In one such gully they found a small, slightly stagnant pool of water and stopped to wash some of the grime from their bodies before they resumed their journey. The gullies became more numerous as they continued, and the time that they had to spend traversing these obstacles began to mount. It gradually became apparent as they made their way through several time-consuming obstacles and eventually entered an area of low sand dunes, that they would not make the other side of the open areas before dawn. They picked up the pace but even without the presence of the gullies, the distance seemed to not lessen and the low hills still remained in the distance as the moon went down and a faint light could be seen in the distance. They pushed on but were at least a mile from the hills as the sun started above the horizon. They found a small inundation between two sand dunes where they could crouch down and study the terrain ahead.

As they sat quietly, after taking draughts from the keg, they tried to trace out the route that they should follow in order to reach the hills as quickly as they could. As they sat looking ahead, Andy grabbed Choundry's arm and pointed to the top of one of the nearby hills. Near the peak of the hill Choundry could make out a glint flashing periodically. He knew what that must be and quickly called to the others "Down."

"That must be someone glassing the desert to see if anyone comes," he said. "It could be one of the Don's man hunters waiting for us to walk into the sights of his gun."

When Choundry mentioned that they had limited choices since they couldn't wait out in the sun or they'd surely be baked alive, Mumba shook his head and said "Come, I show how my people travel the sands and how we sleep through the heat of the day when we must."

He then went to one of the dunes and started to dig into the shifting sands. The surface sands moved as he dug but the ground underneath had been baked to a dense consistency. As Mumba continued to dig, he hollowed out a portion of the hill. Once he had made a shallow bowl-shaped depression, he brought Andy over and motioned for him to lay in the hole that he'd made. Once Andy had laid in the hole, Mumba placed the hide blanket over him and then reached up to cascade the sand down onto Andy's body covering him to a depth of over a foot but leaving his head uncovered by all except the corner of the hide. The only thing showing was Andy's face. He coughed several times but called out to Choundry that the sand had a coolness to it and as long as his face was covered, he had a degree of relief from the pounding sun. Mumba prepared the same type of depression in the sand for Choundry and then buried him as well. Choundry could then see Mumba as he scooped out a spot for himself and then lay down with a cover and pulled the sands down upon himself, he then finished his cover by laying one of the packs loosely over his head. There was no need to set a watch and they couldn't see anything even if they did so all three fell asleep the best they could and stayed where they were throughout the heat of the day.

Choundry awoke as the sun was starting down and he rolled out of his cover, staying low as to not be seen by the lookout on the hill. He shook out the blanket and rolled it again to place it in his pack. Andy joined him in a few minutes, followed by Mumba. Choundry looked to the others; "We should be able to start soon but I see one big problem; with there being no wind and our tracks standing out as they do in the sand, we may be able to pass unnoticed tonight, but our passing will surely be noticed in the morning."

Andy took a moment and then spoke up; "We may have little choice but to face them directly and eliminate them as a threat if we can, I for one am tired of running from these scoundrels and after what we've seen they are capable of, I'd rather rid this land of their curse if we could."

Choundry translated what Andy had said for Mumba's sake. The three of them sat quietly and finally Choundry said, "I have to agree with you, Andy. We are about out of supplies and the way that the land lies, we can't be sure what type of terrain we'll find ahead. We've been told that there are rivers ahead and that should mean cover from the surrounding trees but it does look as if we are expected. It seems that we have little choice. What say we travel ahead and go as close as we dare to see if the odds be such that we could dare an attack?"

The three men agreed and then stood to make the last leg of their journey across the sands.

The journey to the low hills took the better part of half the night. They moved slowly as they approached the foot of the hill where the watcher had been perched during the day. Although there would have been little for the man to see if he had stayed on the hill during the night, Choundry still maintained a peak alertness as he crept up the side of the hill. He felt strongly that they needed to make sure that they not leave a potential enemy in their rear.

Reaching the top and looking across the flattened lookout point, he was able to determine that the hill was unoccupied. Looking ahead, he was afforded an unobstructed view of the valley that lay beyond. Approximately a half mile from where he was standing, Choundry could see several fires burning. It was difficult to see what was happening around the camp that was located in the valley but there was activity, and he could just make out some muffled sounds drifting up to where he stood.

Retracing his path down the hill he located his two companions and told them of what he had discovered. "Let's make our way to this camp. If we are lucky, they will be limited in their night vision with the large campfires that they have lit and we will be able to see what we are up against and then we can make a decision as to what to do."

The valley that they entered showed signs of increasing vegetation and they crossed several small gullies that appeared as if they had recently had some type of water flow. They made their way closer to the now easily seen fires. As they drew close enough to hear the murmur of words being spoken, they could just make out the forms of a large number of local villagers sitting huddled together, their skins gleaming in the firelight. Walking amongst them and going about various tasks, they could see several of the familiar cloth-wrapped figures with their customary headdresses and wearing the curved swords belted to their waists. Each of the men carried a gun with them wherever they walked. Choundry and Andy watched for a while and counted only five of the enemy walking about the camp. They knew that there must be more of the men acting as guards. As they were in no hurry, they would wait for a while to see if the guards were changed and thus find out where they were located and how many were posted.

After approximately an hour of waiting, they were rewarded by seeing three of the men each grab a plate and walk out into the darkness. One of the men walked towards where Choundry and his companions were waiting but then turned and started up a path that led to a small grouping of trees to their right. After a few minutes one of the men returned back down the path to resume his work around the fire. All the while the three of them lay in the darkness listening and watching the activity below, they could hear a low undulating moan coming from the huddle of villagers. The slavers within the camp were moving about in random patterns but, since they were so heavily outnumbered by the huddled villagers, they appeared to be very aware of what was happening throughout the camp and their attention seemed to be focused inward at the huddled mass of villagers.

"I make it five in the camp and three watchers," said Choundry. "That would be a difficult number to overcome, especially as they each have muskets and we have only one musket that we aren't even sure works." Mumba smiled in the dark and pulled his newly acquired sword from his belt and made a dramatic chopping motion with the blade and then pointed to where the hidden guard must be located within the group of trees. He said, "I can move quieter than these men can hear, if we rid ourselves of the ones in the dark then we have only to deal with the ones down there." He pointed to the camp.

Choundry and Andy talked for a moment and then Choundry pulled the three close "As I see it, we've little choice," he said. We must eliminate these men and do it as quietly as we can, there are three guards so we must make our way to each guard in turn and look for an opportunity to bring them down without alerting those in the camp."

Mumba stated that he could bring down the one guard to the right, so Choundry and Andy decided to make their way to their left, behind a combination of low rocks and low growing brush until they could approach one of the guards on the other side of the camp. The three split up and Choundry led the way down and away from the camp in a wide circle that would bring them up again as they neared their quarry. As Choundry was making his way, he repeatedly glanced toward the camp to make sure that the men there showed no signs of alarm. He noticed that one of the men was much larger than the others and that he wore a much better set of clothes wrapped about his body as well as those swathing his head. He also carried an odd-looking musket that was slender but much longer than the ones carried by his companions.

As they neared where the other guard must be, they finally spotted a figure outlined against the firelight and standing with his back to the night. He was looking intently down into the camp as if he were looking for something in particular. In a moment it became clear what he was waiting for as one of the men by the fire walked over to a small group of villagers and reached down to seize the wrist of one of the cringing women. With a heave he lifted her to her feet and started dragging her into the waiting darkness despite her struggles and pitiful moans. Choundry felt a wave of rage course through him and he took the opportunity of the guard's distraction to step as close as he dared and then, bringing his cutlass high, he brought it down on the head of the unsuspecting man with a solid "thunk" that split his head down to his chin. The man fell and lay without even a twitch. That would leave seven enemies remaining and if Mumba were able to dispatch his man that would leave six; four walking the camp, one remaining guard, and one man somewhere in the bushes. Knowing that each of these men carried a musket did not overly concern Choundry as muskets were notoriously inaccurate at long distances. That is why they were used by armies in massed volleys so that they had some hope of bringing down enemy soldiers since some of the bullets were bound to find a target even if by sheer chance. Muskets were most dangerous at a close range so as long as they had the element of surprise and could get in close before the muskets could be put into play, they had a real chance of success. The real weapons that they needed to beware of were the curved swords that these men carried. The men before them appeared to go nowhere without their weapons and they seemed to move as if swords were just familiar parts of their body; they must be very practiced with their weapons if they were such an obvious ingrained part of their lives. Surprise would have to be almost total in order to allow them even a chance of success. Even with surprise, Choundry knew that their chances of coming through this without losses or grievous wounds was very small.

They waited a moment more hoping to see if Mumba joined them and then they started to make their way down to the edge of the camp. They expected to see Mumba emerge from the dark on their right side but instead they were startled to see him emerge from their left side. The old man was wearing a wide smile as he held up his grisly trophies; the heads of two men, each severed at the neck and held hanging down by their hair. Mumba had not only dispatched the guard that he had gone after but evidently, he had skirted the edge of the camp quite quickly and eliminated the other guard as well. Choundry smiled and then motioned for Mumba to place the severed heads down and come with them. He told the old man of the enemy who had dragged the young woman into the brush and asked him to find and eliminate that man so that Choundry and Andy could focus on the remaining men in the camp. Choundry had his cutlass and his small knife and Andy carried their one musket. Choundry pointed to a thick brush close to the camp and whispered to Andy to make his way as close to the camp as he could and draw a bead on one of the four men in the camp. Choundry would move as close as he could and, once Andy had fired, he would charge in and take out as many of the remaining enemies as he could before they realized that they were under attack.

Parting as planned, each made their way down closer to the camp. As Choundry edged as close as he could in the sparse vegetation on his side of the camp, he counted slowly to one hundred and felt that Andy must soon be in place. He had approximately twenty yards to cover to reach the nearest enemy, who was seated on a log watching the actions of the other men. Choundry was almost holding his breath in anticipation of Andy's shot when he heard a very distinct "thunk" noise coming from the darkness followed by the scream of a young woman. The man to Choundry's front jumped to his feet, while at the same time a roar erupted from the far side of the camp with the immediate effect of blasting one of the men back and into the fire. His screams added to the momentary chaos and Choundry chose that moment to rush forward. The man that was Choundry's target heard him coming and spun round, lifting his own blade swiftly from his belt and raising it high to block the downward swing of Choundry's cutlass. With a "clang" as the two swords met Choundry stepped in closer and, using his other hand, drove his short blade deep into the gut of the man and ripped upward to make the kill quick. The man fell with a groan and Choundry pulled his short knife free and continued on towards the remaining two men who had stepped close to their friend who was now smoldering in the flames.

These two men rapidly turned when they realized that they were in danger. The two remaining slavers included the very large man who seemed to be in charge. While Choundry was preparing to move forward to attack, he saw the giant man grab the other man by the shoulder and pushed him in Choundry's direction, all the while shouting curt words that obviously were meant to make the man move to the attack. The shorter man stopped and raised his musket to his shoulder and fired quickly, Choundry could feel the bullet as it passed close by his head, he made an involuntary flinch to the left and the man threw down his musket and rushed in with his sword raised high, screaming an odd phrase over and over. Choundry waited in a crouch, keeping his eye on the big man to make sure that he wouldn't make use of his musket while Choundry was distracted. As he turned back to his immediate threat, he saw the larger man turn and start to run into the surrounding gloom.

As Choundry adjusted his stance to take on the thrust from his attacker, he suddenly felt more than saw a blurred motion pass him to his right. In what seemed almost impossibly fast action he saw the man to his front double over and tumble to the ground no more than a yard from Choundry's feet. The man was doubled over as if hiding a terrible secret when Choudry saw that it had been Mumba who passed him as he stood awaiting the charge; Mumba had swept in and caught the man with a sweeping cut to his midsection before he could guard against it. The unfortunate man was almost cut in two and he died within seconds of hitting the ground but probably not before he saw the descending blade wielded by Mumba as it came down to sever his head.

Choundry wheeled and looked vainly for the remaining man that he had seen fleeing in the brush. Although the attack had seemed to take only a few moments, the sky was growing light and Choundry could begin to make out objects further out from the camp. He ran in the direction that the man had disappeared. Knowing that he had to catch the man, or he would surely find others to return in force to wreak their revenge. He had to bring the man down before he was lost or at least follow him until it was light enough to have a hope of bringing any long chase to a successful end. Choundry ran down the path that left the clearing; following in the direction the big man had fled. It was still too dark to make out any footprints so Choundry had to make his best guess as to what direction that the man would choose.

Choundy felt sure that the man would not run uphill as this would slow his progress and make him all the more visible as he would be exposed on the hillside. That left only a general direction that he could flee and Choundry chose the easiest route as he felt the man would choose speed over guile, at least at first. As he continued along the most logical path, the sky brightened further. Choundry stopped behind a small rock outcropping and peered around to see if he could spy the fleeing man. Suddenly, it seemed that the rock beside his head exploded! He felt a searing pain across his right cheek and up across his temple and into his scalp. He fell quickly, and as he regained cover he heard the distant report of gunfire. Chondry quickly clasped his hand to the side of his head to stem the flow of blood that he could feel trickling down the side of his face. All that he could think of was "What an incredible shot!

The man he was chasing must have been a hundred yards ahead of him and yet he was able to come within inches of hitting Choundry!"

Listening intently, he could hear the distant sound of his quarry climbing up through the hillside to his front. Choundry stood and started to run forward in a crouch. He still needed to catch the man before he got away, nothing had changed although the man had proven that he was dangerous and skilled. Choundry must now be doubly careful and find some way to get ahead of the man and stop him before he could get much further. Choundry stepped to the side and tried to find a quicker way up the hill. As he moved a little further, he stepped out onto a partially hidden well-beaten footpath. Although it presented the danger of being visible periodically, the path gave him at least a hope of being able to outpace the fleeing man and get into a position to ambush him.

Choundry set out on a run and started to work his way up the hill; hopefully the fleeing man wouldn't discover the path as then Choundry would find himself running directly into the man's sights. Even with a musket, he would have a fair chance of making a telling shot. As Choundry moved swiftly along the path his worst fears were realized when he saw off to his right, the figure of the large man jump atop a boulder projecting for the underbrush and take careful aim at him. It was at least fifty yards, so Choundry felt that he had a better than fair chance of evading injury as long as he kept moving. The man stood for a second and then a flash and bloom of smoke could be seen followed by an almost immediate jolting impact to Choundry's left thigh. He felt himself falling but managed to catch himself on a small tree long enough to ease himself to the ground.

Even though injured, Choundry could not help but be amazed at the man's marksmanship. The thought of being able to hit a running figure at that distance was totally unheard of! Looking up he saw that the man had taken the time to reload and was even now bringing the gun to his shoulder to make a killing shot. Choundry looked around and realized that he was in the open with no cover even close by. His only hope was that the marksman would miss and give him a chance to crawl to cover. Having seen the man's skills, Choundry knew that his luck had run out. Gritting his teeth in anticipation of the impact of the bullet, he watched in fascination as the man brought the gun up and tucked it almost gently against his cheek; his finger reached up to the side to grab ahold of the trigger mechanism but seemed to hover over the weapon as if its owner had become distracted for a moment. Choundry did see a sudden movement at the base of the boulder and then a flash as something swung out of the brush and came in contact with the back of the man's lower legs. With a scream, the man fell to the top of the boulder and then rolled off to the side into the brush. Further movements could be seen and then words were screamed out in a pleading manner that ended abruptly.

A few seconds later, Choundry was amazed to see Andy's smiling face popping up from behind the boulder; he was brandishing the man's gun and yelling down to Choundry. Andy then realized that Choundry had been wounded. He ran down the hill, jumping from rock to rock. He was holding the man's weapons, and he had a bag slung over one shoulder. As he approached Choundry, a look of worry showed on his face and when he saw the nature of Choundry's wounds he stopped in consternation. Choundry smiled and said, "I'm afraid my dancing days are over for a while, my old friend."

Chapter 18
Fewer Options

Andy roughly bound the wound in Choundry's leg, which was still bleeding steadily. He helped him regain his feet, and they hobbled together down the path until they reached the campsite where Mumba and the villagers awaited. Mumba came to Choundry immediately upon seeing that he was wounded. He smiled after a moment and said, "The bone is fine, and you do not spurt the blood, so you will live. Quick, we must find some things and make a binding to stop the bleeding and make it heal clean."

While they were gone, Mumba managed to free the villagers who had been chained together. The group looked to number approximately one hundred and fifty individuals, and they were all young, mostly between the ages of 15 and 30. Mumba called orders, and several young men came running to ease Choundry down onto the ground, and several ran to build the campfire up. Mumba found a small iron pot and sent two of the young women to fetch clean water from the nearby stream. Once it had been brought, he had it placed over the fire and then ran off into the brush, saying that he needed to find a special root. While they waited, Andy pulled one of their remaining extra shirts from their pack and ripped it into strips. The wound was clean in that it had entered in the front and slightly to the inside of his left thigh and then passed through to emerge on the outer portion. Luckily, the bullet had not hit a bone or blossomed when it hit, as the exit would not much larger in size than the small entry wound. It did not appear that any clothing had been pulled into the wound, so there was at least a small chance that infection might not set in. Choundry knew that if he were on board a ship right now, the most likely outcome would be that his leg would be severed to prevent corruption.

After a period of time, Mumba returned from the brush carrying several objects, at least one of which was a dirt-encrusted root. He wandered about the camp until he found a flat rock and another rock that was slightly larger than his closed fist. He brought the two to Choundry and set about making his poultice. He chewed off chunks of various plants and then placed each carefully atop the flat rock. After biting through one of the plants, he turned his head and spat repeatedly as if he needed to make sure that none of the juice remained. He then finally took the root that he had found and carefully cut and then peeled it until he held a white-colored piece about the size of a small potato. When he looked about, he saw the pile of bandages that Andy had produced. He grunted, nodding his head in satisfaction. He ground all of the plant and root ingredients carefully together until they formed a woody mash, and then he continued to work them until the mixture became an even finer blend. He then broke the pile into two roughly even sections and, took one of the piles, and placed it into the now boiling water. He came back to pick up the pile of bandages and took those back placing them into the boiling water. With a few curt words, he sent one of the young men to fetch a stick and then return to stir the contents of the pot.

Mumba then returned to Choundry and proceeded to tell him what he was doing: "The roots have a magical power that makes them poison to eat, but when handled in the right way and with respect, the plant heals those who know its ways. We make a healing soup now, and we must make sure that anything that touches your wound has been blessed by the holy soup."

With that, he cut away the leg of Choundry's pants well above the injury site. He then dipped a small bowl into the pot and brought it close to Choundry, setting it aside to cool. "Remember, the magic must not broken. Nothing can touch this wound without being blessed by the magic waters first.."

After a few minutes of waiting, the bowl of "magic soup" seemed to have cooled enough, and Mumba then ripped the dressing from Choundry's wound and proceeded to squeeze his leg until a fresh gush of blood appeared from each injury sight.

"We must give an offering of blood to the gods before we use their magics, Mumba proclaimed. With that, he took the bowl and started to pour the contents slowly over each wound site, making sure that the liquid had poured into the holes and washed the remaining clotted blood away.

Mumba looked to Choundry and Andy and said, "Now comes the difficult part. Again, you must always remember to not let anything touch the wound unless it has been blessed by the magic waters, or the spirits will become angry, and they will attack the leg, and you will die. Watch what I do carefully so you know that I show respect due to spirits of the root."

Mumba took the bowl back to the pot and dipped out another portion of the liquid. He took it and laid it aside but only waited a few minutes. He then placed his hands in the liquid and proceeded to wash them very carefully, all along talking to himself in a low voice. After he had washed his hands, he ordered one of the young men to dig a small hole nearby. He then drained the small bowl into the hole and kicked dirt atop until the hole was filled; "I give some of the roots back to the earth as a blessing."

He then went back to the remaining blend of root and plant mixture atop the stone and, scooped it up, and brought it to Choundry. He applied the mixture to each of the wounds and held them in place until he seemed sure they would not fall off. Mumba then went to the pot and, taking the stick that was used to stir the contents, pulled out several of the bandages that had been boiled in the mixture and lifted them up high to allow them to drip back into the pot.

When they stopped dripping, he then brought them to Choundry and proceeded to wrap the bandages around the injured thigh. As he finished, he stepped back and said, "There is but one more thing to do." He then took the bowl and scooped some of the liquid from the pot. "We have used the magic on the outside of the wound, but now we must use it on the inside as well. You must not worry about the root. I have prepared it as the spirits demand, so it should not kill you unless you are unworthy."

Choundry looked at Andy with obvious apprehension, but he could feel a warmth already spreading from the freshly applied bandages, and the pain from the wounds had begun to ease significantly. Choundry felt that he should trust Mumba, and, in truth, he had little choice; their chances of escaping the Don's men had been slim before, but with Choundry unable to walk, their discovery was all but a certainty. They needed to travel fast and get away from this site before anyone came looking.

Choundry was unsure how they would travel, but he asked Andy to prepare their belongings and see if he could find any provisions among the dead men's belongings.

Andy came back a while later and laid their packs and weapons together to the side. During that time, Choundry had several minutes alone to contemplate what they should do. He knew that Andy would argue the point, but he asked Andy to sit beside him as he told him, "My friend, we have traveled many miles together, and we may yet travel many more together, but you must now leave me to go and find your way to the coast and try to flag down a passing ship, I cannot travel right now so I must find a place to rest until my wounds have healed and then I can make my way to join you. There is no reason that the two of us should sit awaiting the hunters. One of us should return to tell the authorities what befell the ship and our friends."

Andy looked to Choundry and, with a steady gaze, said, "Aye, we've traveled many a mile together, but you've not known who I am yet. If ye think that I'll walk away from you like that, I'll have no more said of it, and that's a fact."

At that moment, Mumba returned and sat with the two of them. He said, "We must move on, but I do know not what to do with these children.," indicating the group of villagers standing nearby as if waiting to be told what to do. Choundry thought for a moment and then asked Mumba if any of the villagers understood any of the Spanish or Portuguese languages.

"Yes, there are several who know the words," Mumba said. Choundry asked that Mumba have the villagers called over to Choundry so that he could speak with them. Once the group had made their way over and encircled where Choundry sat, he asked that those who knew his words would translate for the others. He then called out in a strong voice, "Listen to me. We have saved you from the men who killed your families and destroyed your homes. Know this; it is now too dangerous to live in these lands, and you must now travel far to find a place where you will be safe from the slavers. All of your elders have been killed, so you do not have the wise council that they would have provided to you, and you no longer have a chief. My companions and I must leave quickly, and more of these bad men will come here soon. You all must leave as well. I say this to you all: You need a wise and brave man as your chief, and you need someone who can lead you to a safe place. You need one who can teach you how to defend yourselves and your families against the slavers."

Pointing to Mumba, Choundry continued, "You have seen this man kill many of these bad men, and he has shown me to be the wisest of men. We have saved you all, and we give you one more great gift: our great friend Mumba as your new chief. Know this: follow his words in all things. Your ancestors have given you the gift of a strong, steady, and wise man to lead you to a better home. My friend and I owe Mumba a great debt: he is our brother. I have never met a better man or a braver warrior. Honor him and obey his word."

During this time, Mumba looked on with widening eyes and a somewhat frightened look on his face, but he remained silent. The crowd of men and women surged forward and clasped their hands on Mumba and caressed his head, all beseeching him to lead them.

Mumba stood, and pushing out his thin chest, he shook his head and shouted to the people, "Yes, yes, I will lead you, but you must obey in all things as we have a dangerous path to follow. My people…..", here he stumbled and then coughed, "My people, gather the things that the evil men had with them and gather any foods that you can find. We must leave quickly and be away from here before our enemy knows what has happened, shoo shoo," he motioned, and the crowd dispersed to do as commanded. Mumba called to several men standing nearby, and they stepped forward, bearing what looked to be a stretcher cunningly made from cut poles and vines intertwined together. Mumba motioned to Choundry, "Get up and get on this," indicating the stretcher, "Your leg must rest and we have much need to hurry." Thankful that Mumba had thought of his needs and that help was at hand, Choundry stood and hobbled over to sit and then recline. The leg didn't hurt as much as it had earlier, and Choundry gave a silent thanks to Mumba again for the healing powers of the poultice. Mumba called two other young men and ordered them to carry the pot along with them as they would need the healing soup again.

The group headed out and moved at a rapid pace. Mumba's people were all young and healthy, and there were no elderly or young children to slow them down, so they proceeded at a rapid pace along a large path through the ever-thickening undergrowth. Whenever they stopped for a rest, the men assigned to carry

Choundry were switched out, and the women stepped quickly into the surrounding woods to gather what food they could find. Even though they did encounter some game as they traveled, they could not use the muskets for fear of attracting the attention of their hunters. Choundry began to worry about the fact that there were two types of hunters in the surrounding area: those seeking additional slaves and those hunting for Choundry and Andy. He was concerned that, with the huge number of people now in their group, hiding their passage was no longer an option and that he and Andy were now making the danger to these young people all the greater merely by their presence. The sooner that Mumba and his people could break away from Choundry and Andy, the safer they would be. In addition, they would be even more rapid in their journey if they did not have to care for him. He made up his mind that the first chance that he had to set the group free from his burden, he would take it.

They set out on the trail again and traveled this way for several days. Each evening, they would find a campsite, and Mumba would send out guards to warn them of any enemies approaching. They would quickly make a fire and then heat the pot's contents. Mumba would unwrap Choundry's wounds, place the bandages in the pot to boil, and then repeat the process that he had shown on the first application. By the end of the third day, Choundry was able to hobble about the camp and take care of his own needs. Mumba deemed that Choundry's wounds were healing and that he no longer needed the magic from the root. He ordered a deep hole to be dug, and then he poured the remaining "healing soup" into the hole and ordered it covered. The wound was no longer oozing, and it had healed and scabbed.

On the morning of the fourth day since his injury, they started out making a rapid passage but quickly came to a large river. They had two choices: take the left direction that would lead them towards the coast, or take a right, and that direction would lead them further inland. They stopped to discuss their best course of action, and Mumba ordered his people to disperse into the undergrowth and rest while he talked with Choundry and Andy.

Choundry summarized what he was thinking: "Mumba, you are a man now with great responsibilities. You know that you must take your people to safety, and if we turn toward the sea, you will be trapping your people between the river on one side and the slavers on the other with the ocean blocking your way, you must turn at the river and take your people on the paths you know that will take you deeper into the jungle; you must leave us here and go your own way now. Andy and I have enemies who search for us, and every day that your people stay with us, they are in a greater danger than they need be. You must take your people and go."

Mumba sat silently, obviously trying to find some way to honor these friends who saved him in his time of need and who were responsible for finding him a new life of great deeds. The silence continued as each man thought quietly of what this decision would mean.

Their thoughts were interrupted by one of Mumba's men creeping back quietly along the trail that led ahead. He talked quietly with Mumba and the older man said several words and then sent the young man back along the trail towards the large group waiting along the trail. Mumba moved closer to Choundry and Andy and told them, "My young man tells of a place along the river ahead where a small hut sits. He tells me that he can hear several voices arguing, but he was too afraid to go forward for fear of alerting them to our presence." Choundry fretted at his inability to go forward and see for himself, so he asked Andy if he and Mumba would go forward to scout ahead. Choundry sat alone after the others had left, and he tried not to worry about his friends while he waited. He thought that he heard something in the distance, but after listening intently for several minutes, he heard nothing further.

After what must have been at least two hours, one of Mumba's men returned and gave word to Choundry and the others to proceed ahead. Choundry was still being carried on the stretcher, but he couldn't help but sit up to try and see what was waiting ahead. They eventually emerged into a small clearing where a hut was located approximately twenty feet from the bank of a large river. Andy, Mumba, and several others were standing in the open. At their feet, there appeared to be the bodies of several men who resembled the slavers they'd previously encountered.

Choundry stepped off of the stretcher and hobbled over to where the others were standing. Andy reported that they had found these men engaged in some form of argument and close to blows. They seemed so distracted that it was obvious that they had been given an opportunity to get close and spring a trap with virtually total surprise. Andy was happy to report that they were able to bring down what turned out to be four of the slavers without injuries to any of Mumba's men. It was at this point that Choundry looked over to see the smiling Mumba showing off three of the severed heads of the slavers. Andy continued, "Our luck has not run out as yet, my friend. There are two things that you need to see.." With that, he walked to the hut and inside found stacks of hides and tusks in one corner, but in the other, there were piles of food supplies and a rack that held several muskets and at least a dozen of the curved swords. Andy then turned and led Choundry down towards the river and pointed out a small rowboat that was partly hidden by some reeds. "Weapons, food, and a way to the sea if we'd like. What more could you ask for?"

Choundry laughed and said, "Well, we already have enough weapons for our needs, but these will be welcome to Mumba and his people, and they may give them a chance to fight back should they encounter slavers again. We can take a small amount of food, but Mumba's people will need this much more than we will, so we'll take what we need and give the rest to them. This appears to be the chance that we'd hoped for to lessen the danger to our friends by making our own way."

They quickly sorted out what they were going to take; Mumba's people used the hides to make packs of food, and others were given weapons and formed into small fighting groups. Mumba stood on the riverbank, clearly torn by his desire to stay with his friends and by his responsibility to get his people on their way. Choundry and Andy shook his hand and wished him and his people a good future. Choundry thanked Mumba for healing his leg and for guiding them through the jungles. With tears freely flowing, Mumba turned and waved his people into motion, disappearing quietly into the jungle.

Chapter 19
A Return to the Sea

Choundry and Andy decided that they, too, should leave this place as quickly as they could, even if it meant finding a spot to hide in the boat for the rest of the day. Earlier, Andy had already worked out what they were planning to take, and Mumba had several of his men place the goods in the boat. It was only left for the two of them to work their way down to the boat step in. Choundry's leg was still very painful, and he was using utmost care not to break open the wounds again. Once he had positioned himself in the boat, Andy shoved off, and they started gently floating down with the current.

Choundry experienced an odd feeling of returning home as he felt the first rockings of the boat. He had almost forgotten how much a part of his life being on the water had become. The river was about fifty yards wide at the point, with thick vegetation bordering each side. Choundry was concerned about their drifting down the river and meeting someone coming up or being seen from any other possible groups of slavers located along the banks. He suggested to Andy that they cross over the river and find a small inlet in which to hide the boat until the end of the day and then see whether proceeding downstream under the cover of the night might be manageable. After rowing across, they decided to risk traveling at least a mile before they chose a spot to hide. Once in place, they arranged the packs so as to allow them an opportunity to ease themselves into a position of comfort, and they could then do their usual watch-and-watch arrangement.

The afternoon passed quietly except for an incident toward evening when their inlet was visited by a large reptile of some sort that sported a massive array of gleaming white teeth in a mouth that seemed a yard long. The creature eyed them for a while and then slowly drifted toward them but must have evidently changed its mind and decided to leave these visitors alone. After a few anxious moments, the creature floated off slowly downriver. After seeing this colossus only an arm's length away, both men had difficulty relaxing enough to sleep again.

As night fell, they were blessed with a clear sky and a nearly full moon. They pushed off from shore, and each man took hold of an oar and held it in both hands to guide the boat away from any obstacles hidden by the current, as well as push them away from any overhanging branches that might hook the boat and capsize it in the current. Neither of them saw any reason to actually row the little craft as the current was carrying them at a reasonable pace, and they had no idea where the river would take them anyway. They decided that stealth was more important than speed, so they sat quietly in the boat, straining their eyes to see what might be ahead as well as keeping a watch for more of the serpents that seemed to inhabit these waters. In addition to the dangers presented by the river itself, they also had to look for signs of any pursuit.

Both Choundry and Andy felt it unlikely that they would encounter anyone afloat who would not have some sort of light affixed or that they would pass any type of settlement that would not be betrayed by lights or noises. As they floated further down the river, they noticed the waters were moving a bit slower and that the channel seemed to be narrowing, with small bogs and marshes forming to the sides. As the sky began to brighten, they decided to tie up again to stay hidden for the rest of that day. In the evening, they started out again and made way for several hours down river without see any signs of men along either shore.

They did, however, chance upon another example of this continent's bizarre creatures; as they continued their slow drift downstream, their boat drifted lazily towards a series of small, brown- colored islands. Drawing close to these odd shapes, both men were surprised to see a small spray of water pushed into the air next to one of the mounds, which was soon followed by a massive head rising from the water. With an explosion of water, the mound nearest the immense head burst forward. This cascaded into each of the other mounds, in turn, exploding into its own fury of brown river water and white froth. The creatures were bigger than their boat! To have them turn from quiet docile lumps in the river to awe-inspiring behemoths with maws that gaped wide enough to take both Choundry and Andy in one bite left both men terrified and frozen in place as they continued their drift downstream.

Later, once they had had a chance to calm down, they continued their close study of the river ahead, and at one bend of the river, they noticed where someone had once gone ashore and made a camp. Though it appeared long deserted, the campsite showed that they might be approaching a more traveled part of the river. As they continued on, they noticed other signs of the area being inhabited at some point; a section of one riverbank had been cleared, and the stumps looked to have been sawn or chopped recently. A short time later, they found a small snag in the river that showed above the water. Some of the logs that were partially submerged showed where they had been lashed together at some point with small vines.

Choundry and Andy finally decided to put into the riverbank and hide for the day. They had plenty of supplies, although not many of them were very appetizing. In one pack, they had a rough grain that could be eaten but required much chewing and needed to be taken with large amounts of water. In another pack, they had several of the starchy roots that Mumba had found so appealing. In Andy's earlier search of the slaver's hut, he had found pieces of dried meat that had appeared inedible; he had left these behind but was now wishing he'd brought along a few, if for no other reason than to offer an alternative their bland diet. During his search of the hut, Andy had also found another small container in which to carry drinking water. Their diet was much less enticing than when they had the skills of Mumba to find edible roots and even some berries. Both men knew that they could not dare to trust their own limited knowledge enough to eat from the bushes that lined the river even though they were probably sitting amongst a veritable feast of food had they known what was safe to eat.

Again, at nightfall, they set out. As it turned out, they had made a wise choice to stop as they had. They had traveled no more than a half hour before they saw lights clustered along the opposite bank. They gently paddled the boat in order to stay close to the far side of the river as they drifted quietly past the settlement. At one point, a small dog could be heard barking, but this faded into the distance as they continued downstream. Eventually, they decided to place the oars in the oarlocks so that they could row the boat should they need to maneuver quickly to avoid any further dangers. They would need to be even more careful the further they proceeded. They seemed to be getting close to the coast, and that would mean they would soon be leaving the sheltering safety of the jungle. When they left the river and set out upon the sea, they would be bringing their journey to an end one way or another. Once exposed to searching eyes along the coast, they would be gambling that they would chance upon a friend before they were discovered and run down by their enemies.

Choundry knew that they must have traveled several hundred miles since they'd escaped the slaughter brought on by the Don's men. The distance that they'd traveled was nothing compared to that required for them to travel anywhere, even close to civilization. Had Choundry not sustained his injuries, they might have been able to eventually out-walk the Don's men, but they were now limited in their choices and must now hope for something close to divine intervention. Once they reached the sea, they would surely be seen, and at some point, the chase would be brought to an end.

Choundry and Andy drifted quietly for several miles, seeing little but sensing a subtle change in the wind. Around midnight, they slowly drifted around another bend in the river when they noticed two things almost at the same time; the distant sounds of ocean waves breaking against a nearby coast, and then they saw a series of fires located on either side of the channel close to what must be the mouth of the river.

The Don's men had guessed that should Choundry and his companion choose to return to the sea, their most likely course would be to come down one of the major rivers that drained the inland. The two friends sat quietly, knowing that the inevitable alarm would soon be raised as the firelight started to reflect off the side of their vessel. They drifted on until they were even with the fires. Sharing a tense stillness, the two men began to think that they might make it through the watchers when their hopes were dashed as a voice was raised on one shore and a pistol was discharged. Alarms were being raised all along both sides of the river as Choundry, and Andy sat up to each grab an oar. Moving to the center bench, they started to pull on the oars in hopes of moving past the firelight and into the dark beyond before those on shore could bring their weapons to bear. Several shots burst out on the shore to their left, and these were followed shortly by a volley from their right.

Splashes leapt into the air all around the boat, and it sounded as if they had been attacked by an angry swarm of bees as bullets swept past close at hand. One shot skipped several yards out to their side and then thunked into the side of the boat. Both men leaned into the oars and pulled harder to gain a few yards further into the darkness. Their little craft started to buck as the onrushing waves started crashing into the front of the boat, sending droplets of salty water spraying over the faces of the two men. In minutes, they were far enough out that the random shots that continued from the shore had little chance of finding a mark. Choundry knew that those on shore would be running for their own boats, and it was only a matter of minutes until they would be taking up the chase. He asked Andy to take a moment and charge both muskets in preparation for repelling a chase.

Andy fumbled in the dark and, after a few minutes, returned to his seat and took up his oar. He started rowing again and, between pulls, he told Choundry "I charged both guns but the one that we took from the giant was odd and more difficult to load. I thought that I noticed a difference before, but I am no judge of firearms as I've only used them seldom. I'd rather not even own one as I don't trust them, the only reason that I care for one now is to keep these pirates at bay."

They still had two or three hours of darkness in which to travel before their pursuers would be able to see them and close in. Their only real option was to continue north, as going down the coast to the south would just be taking them further into their enemy's territory. Choundry angled the small boat out further into the ocean, he felt that men accustomed to life ashore would be somewhat reluctant to go far asea unless they had good reason. The strategy, even if it worked, wouldn't gain them much, but any advantage was worth pursuing. During one of the infrequent rests, Choundry told Andy, "I am truly sorry, my friend. I had hoped that we might have a good bit more time upon the sea before the chase was afoot. It seems that the luck that we enjoyed in our journey is now exhausted."

Both he and Andy pulled well and hard for the next hour. They then took another break to rest themselves and listen for pursuit. Hearing nothing, they laid the guns close at hand and then took long drinks as they could most likely expect a long run of rowing once they had been spotted. As the sun started to rise, Choundry and Andy strained their eyes, looking landward, and were disappointed to see their pursuers much closer than they'd hoped.

The lead boats of three small craft were less than a hundred yards away. Shots rang out, and yells erupted as those on the lead-chasing boats spotted their prey. Choundry and Andy lay into their oars, but after a brief burst of energy, the events of the last several weeks started to show as both men started to lag and then slow their efforts at rowing. Eventually, Andy stopped and crawled down to the bottom of the boat, where he grabbed one of the muskets and then raised it to take aim at the lead boat. With a snap, bang, and flash of powder, Andy took his first shot. Unfortunately, there didn't seem to be any effect on any of the boats, and neither of them could spot any telltale spouting of water to indicate a miss.

Choundry knew that he would barely have time to get a shot off before they would b overrun by the attackers, but he quickly took up the unfamiliar weapon and raised it to his cheek. Taking aim at a man standing in the front of the lead boat, he held his breath and squeezed the trigger. To his surprise, the man jerked back immediately and was thrown bodily into those behind him; obviously, a solid body shot. No sooner had Choundry time to register surprise at the hit when the lead ship erupted in a massive cascade of broken timber, water, and red carnage.

The two friends had only a moment to wonder at what had happened when they heard several booms erupting behind them and further to sea. Turning quickly, they beheld the sight of a large ship bearing down on them at an angle. The ship turned slightly to bring its guns to bear and roared out another salvo of shots that swept overhead and landed amidst the two remaining chase boats. The men in those boats were frantically trying to turn their crafts and flee the terrifying apparition that had just emerged from the gloom to wreak havoc upon their fellows. Each boat was destroyed in turn as the ship showed that her gunners were no slackers; the spouts from the plunging cannon balls showed an admirably tight pattern as they shredded the boats. Within minutes, the waters shoreward were littered with wreckage and no signs of any survivors could be seen among the debris.

213

Chapter 20
A Reckoning

Choundry held his hand to his brow to shade his eyes from the glare of the rising sun as he tried to see who he could thank for their rescue or curse as just another enemy. The sight that greeted his eyes was a welcome one as he recognized the size and shape of the ship as a frigate and was elated to see the Union Jack drifting lazily from the staff. Within a few minutes, the big ship was hove alongside. Seeing Choundry was wounded, they lowered a chair that he was able to clamber into and be raised up and onto the ship's deck. He was quickly followed by Andy while several sailors were sent down to fetch their belongings.

Choundry stood stiffly as a man approached who was walking in a dignified fashion. He wore a reddish coat and had a worn, gilt-trimmed hat. He paced to within several feet of the two men and, bowed slightly, and then introduced himself as "First Lieutenant Masters of his Royal Highnesses frigate *Swiftsure.*" He paused a moment and asked, "And to whom do I have the pleasure to be speaking?"

Choundry smiled with relief and said, "My name is Choundry Anders, and this is Andy Somers. We are partners with the British shipping firm William Thompson, which is based in Lisbon. We were late of the schooner *Fair Wind,* which several weeks ago put into the Port of San Pedro. The so-called Governor there killed the Captain of the ship and all of the crew, and we were hard-pressed to escape and then make our way this long distance in an attempt to find someone in authority who could avenge the evil deeds wrought on His Majestie's subjects. I am mainly pleased that you and your ship happened along when you did, as I fear that our journey was about to end in another manner."

The Lieutenant stood with his mouth slightly agape in awe until he said, "My, what an amazing story! You must come to meet with Captain Steward, as I am sure that he will want to hear what you have to say. Please follow me."

Choundry and Andy followed the officer forward, but Choundry had a great deal of difficulty climbing the ladder, so the Captain called down and told the Lieutenant to take the guests to his cabin and that he would be down straight away. After making their way below, Choundry and Andy were seated in the Captain's cabin, where a few moments later, the Captain joined them and ordered a bracing drink.

Choundry recounted their tale to the Captain from the point where he had received instructions from William through all that had happened. He found upon recollection that it was difficult to tell of the death of Captain Barth and of his men, but he left nothing out. Once he had finished, Andy filled in a few other facts that Choundry had omitted, but when silence fell in the cabin, the Captain sat for a moment and said, "You gentleman have been sorely tested to come through such as this and work your way through hundreds of miles of wilderness, I would find it difficult to give credit to your story if your very appearance did not amply support your claims. You say the pirating and murder occurred in the port of San Pedro?"

When Choundry confirmed this, the Captain said, "We will travel to this port and meet this so-called Governor for ourselves, and if he can be captured, he will face a swift justice. For now, please allow me to offer you two gentlemen a cabin to rest and restore yourselves. I will have our ship's surgeon come to you to see any of the wounds that you have suffered. I assure you that a travesty such as this being wrought on British subjects will be dealt with most severely."

Choundry and Andy thanked the captain and his Lieutenant and then went to the assigned cabin. It seemed only minutes before they heard a knock on their door, and a diminutive but well-built man entered carrying a small bag. He went to Choundry and introduced himself as Dr. Chamberlain. He said that he had been ordered by the captain to look into Choundry's wounds. Realizing that he had to be careful or he would sound as if he'd suffered sunstroke as well as his other injuries, Choundry looked to the doctor and said, "I would appreciate it if you could clean the wound to my face and scalp, but please leave the wound on my leg be. It was treated by a very renowned medical man on shore, and I have been told that no one is to touch it further. I trust him implicitly, as he truly seemed to work magic."

Several days later, found them rounding the part of the coast that Choundry remembered as being just short of San Pedro. He informed the Captain, who ordered the ship to move to and await darkness. He brought his lieutenant of Marines to a meeting with Choundry and Andy to discuss the layout of the port and where they could anticipate finding the Don. The Marine Lieutenant asked several questions regarding the number of men in Don's service and the types of weapons that they could bring to bear. Choundry was sure to warn the man of the hidden swivel guns located at the end of the wharf. He made a sketch of the small town and drew in what he could remember of the mud huts and the central building.

Around midnight the *Swiftsure* put on some canvas and started to slowly work further down the coast; within two hours, they could make out some dim lights from the port. The Marine Lieutenant and his men entered the ship's boats and, accompanied by Andy, rowed quietly ashore. Just as dawn was touching the sky, those aboard the *Swiftsure* heard several shots fired in the town and then silence. After a period of approximately a quarter-hour, they could see a fire being built in the center of the town. The Captain snapped shut his night telescope and said, "That's the signal; have the ship underway and prepare to receive boats'.

The *Swiftsure* glided forward until it was directly out from the small wharf but still in sufficiently deep water that she could turn and move readily should an enemy appear. After approximately an hour, they could see several of the ship's boats making their way back toward the *Swiftsure* through the still waters of the bay. The marines returned on deck with several prisoners. The Lieutenant of Marines came to the Captain and reported that the town had been successfully captured with no marines injured. He said that his men had been forced to kill several of the Don's men before the rest fled, leaving the Don to be captured. He went on to add that there appeared to be a large number of individuals chained and held in pens at the far end of the town. Captain Steward told the Marine Lieutenant to return to his men ashore and free the captives.

Turning to the prisoners huddled amidships, he asked Choundry and Andy to identify any of those present who had participated in the massacre. As they approached the small group, a man strutted forward and stated in what he must have believed to be a voice of authority, "How dare you come into my home and take me from my bed! I am the legal Governor of this Port and a confidant of many important people in Lisbon. I am here with legal authority and merely going about my duty to secure this land from the savages who infest it. I demand to know by whose authority you have disturbed my sleep and murdered some of my employees."

When Choundry stepped from behind the Captain and the Don was able to see who was among his accusers, he seemed to deflate into himself and started to stutter…."This man is a liar. I don't know what he has told you, but I bought the ship with gold coins and sent his captain and men to the Cape in another one of my many ships."

Choundry started to say something and then stopped as he recognized the man standing to Don's rear as the man who had escorted them into the building. He noticed something familiar about the clothes that the man was wearing when he realized he had on the same coat Captain Barth had been wearing when he had been murdered. Choundry hobbled forward until he stood in front of the Don. He said, "Just in case the good Captain was to be tempted to believe any of your stories, I would like to point out that your assistant is wearing the coat that Captain Barth had been wearing at the time that you had him killed. If the Captain inspects that coat, I am sure that he will find a tear in the back of the coat and a tear to the front where the sword tore through after your men had struck Captain Barth in the back like the cowards they are."

Captain Edwards had his Lieutenant make the necessary inspections and was able to find the tears and even remnants of the bloodstains in the areas as predicted. The assistant stepped forward, and, taking the coat off, he hurried to say, "The Don made me wear this foul clothing. I had nothing to do with the crimes committed by his excellency, but I will do my duty to tell you all about what the Don has done and where he had the bodies of the slain seamen thrown. I can tell you too of the whereabouts of the stolen ship, and when it is scheduled to return, all I ask is my life, your majesty."

The next several days passed quickly, and the Captain rendered verdicts on the Don and all of his men except the assistant. A gibbet was raised in the middle of the town, and the prisoners were marched one at a time to the gallows and hung until dead. The Don had tried to present a manly front all the while but eventually broke down into a sobbing and pleading wreck as he was brought forward to have the noose draped around his neck. The Captain ordered their bodies thrown to the village hogs as the Don had ordered the bodies of Captain Barth and his men to be disposed of. The assistant was taken aboard the ship and sworn in as a landsman on his Majesty's ship, the *Swiftsure*.

There was little in the manner of trade goods still at the Don's warehouses so it would seem that the *Fair Wind's* cargo had been sent to the Americas along with whatever human cargo that had been crammed in for the voyage; Choundry realized that the Don's request for a "fast ship" had been prompted by his hopes to minimize the inevitable deaths of the slaves packed like cordwood into the hold of the ship.

As it happened, the stolen ship was not expected back for several weeks so the Captain decided to leave one of his officers ashore with a contingent of marines and seaman to await the return of the stolen ship and affect its recapture if at all possible.

Chapter 21
Recovering

Choundry and Andy stayed with the *Swiftsure* as it continued its cruise further down the coast, but they left the ship with their belongings when they put in at the Cape. Choundry found the local merchant house for the Thompson shipping company and told them who he and Andy were. The local man was at first somewhat unbelieving, but he had to give credence to the tale as Captain Barth and the *Fair Wind* were long overdue. He provided them with sufficient funds for local accommodations and set up a credit line that they could draw upon for their other expenses. They were told that a Thompson ship was expected within the next fortnight and that they could arrange passage back to Lisbon with the ship when it arrived.

After finding suitable quarters and taking the longest and hottest bath of their lives, the two men started to make their way through town, purchasing items of clothing to replace those lost or left behind during the attack on the *Fair Wind*. Each man ordered two sets of clothing and a new pair of shoes to replace the ragged specimens that barely held together on their feet. Both men had retained the weapons they'd captured, but Choundry was not pleased with the feel of the curved blades that the slavers had carried, so he found a sword that seemed extremely well-made and balanced. It cost a small fortune, but Choundry had learned many times over that there are times when the only investment that you had made that had any value was the quality of the weapon in your hand. He still lacked the true skill that he needed to wield such a weapon, but he hoped to remedy that as soon as possible.

Packing their belongings, they settled in for the remaining days to enjoy the sights and people of the Cape towns. Choundry's wounds were healing well. The scar across his cheek and temple was still pink and raw, but much of the scar could be hidden by merely letting his hair grow a bit longer. The leg wound remained painful, and he still retained a heavy limp when he walked, especially when he became over-tired. Choundry thought to take advantage of their remaining time to strengthen his leg and regain the stamina that he'd lost with the wound.

He set about progressively longer and longer walks through the town and then into the surrounding countryside. As the days flew by, he eventually chose a two-day route of travel and started out, with a much-complaining Andy, to walk the two days through, stopping at an inn during the evening and starting out again in the early dawn.

"You don't have the slightest idea of what it means to be a gentleman of ease," decried Andy as they crested yet another hill to see only several others ranging in front of them. "It's just my luck to find a friend with a fire in his britches and an itch on his feet." Choundry stopped and turned to his friend and, with a smile, said, "Aye, Andy, I couldn't have ever wished for a truer friend or a stouter back to share my adventures. I never did thank you for saving me when that giant was marking me for his shot. You are a true friend, and I owe you much."

Andy looked sheepish for a moment and then brightened as he peered ahead. "We'll mark the debt paid if we stop at the tavern that I see yonder, and you give me at least an hour to down a few ales and rest my tired feet."

By the time the Thompson ship showed in port, Choundry was almost back to his original strength, and he had only a slight limp. He met with the ship's captain and booked passage to Lisbon. As the ship was scheduled to sail the very next day, Choundry sent for their belongings, and the two friends stayed that night in the ship's cabin assigned to them. The journey took slightly longer than they could have wished as they hit a strong storm right after they'd left the Cape and had been driven for miles until the storm abated, and they could resume their cruise.

Upon hearing that Choundry was a partner to Mr. Thompson, the Captain of the ship took pains to offer the freedom of the ship to Choundry and Andy. Choundry asked if the Captain would be kind enough to allow him to practice his fledgling navigation skills and assist with the noon sightings each day. In addition, he asked if he could be allowed to stand watch with either the Captain or one of his officers. He found the opportunity to learn more about the handling of a ship to be an exciting distraction from the boredom of a lengthy journey. The Captain and his officers seemed genuinely pleased to share their shifts with someone so obviously eager to learn and who had such astounding adventures to relate. Choundry also took the opportunity to study the charts that were on board; he knew that he had a great deal to learn, and with his love of travel and adventure, he would never know what bit of knowledge might be crucial at a later time. He also worked with the sailors in the topmost portions of the web of rigging and sails. He'd never had the opportunity to learn the life of a topman as he'd promised himself when he first boarded the *Merlin*; his energies had been focused on learning how to merely survive. Andy chose to enjoy the rather extensive selection found in the Captain's personal library. He would occasionally come on deck to find Choundry covered in tar and descending from the rigging, only to shake his head. When Choundry eventually came down to the cabin that they shared, he would tell him, "With all of the things that you are learning, you still hadn't the foggiest idea of how to sit still and relax."

Chapter 22
Candles

The rest of the journey was relatively uneventful, and the day finally came when the two men found themselves walking down the walkway from the ship onto the familiar boards of the wharf in the port at Lisbon. As was William's preference, his ship had tied up as close as possible to the Thompson Merchant house, so they had only a short walk to their friend's shop. Upon entering the store, they started back through the aisles, only to hear a loud cry from ahead.

"Praise the Lord! I can't believe my own eyes, and we had feared you both dead and gone. Welcome home, gentlemen…I must fetch Mr. Thompson; he will be elated to hear the news!" With that, Edward spun on his heel and ran into the back of the store, yelling for his master.

Moments later, William came running back through the door. Upon seeing the two of them, he broke into a broad smile and rushed to grab Choundry's hand. "It is truly a good day. I feared you were lost even after we heard that you'd been saved following your miraculous adventure." At Choundry's puzzled look, he went on: "You may not know, but the *Fair Wind* was recaptured by the men of the *Swiftsure*. Then, he sailed back up the coast and finally returned here. We had to pay a partial salvage fee as one of the crew members had been kept alive to navigate the ship, so the King's men could not claim that it had been abandoned. Please, please come inside and tell us what has happened."

After sitting down in William's office and having a large drink thrust into each of their hands, Choundry proceeded to tell the tale of all that had happened. William interrupted only once to say that it had come as terrible news to hear of the death of his friend Captain Barth, and it was one of the most difficult things that he'd ever done to tell the Captain's wife of the loss of such a treasured husband and father. William added that he had a matter of business to discuss with Choundry once he had finished his tale. Choundry then went on to tell of the various events and trials that had occurred on their journey, of the people that they'd met, and the battles fought. Edward fair swooned when he told of some of the more graphic portions of the tale, and William sat in stony silence as he heard of the killings of the young and the elders of the local tribes. When Choundry had finished his tale, silence settled in the room. William sighed and shook his head in dismay.

"It sounds like an adventure book dreamed up in the mind of some of the writers in London. I am glad that you have healed of your wounds and that the two of you were of such stout character that you were able to make it through such an incredible journey. I've always said that there is no stronger oak than an English oak, and the strongest men are bred on the same coasts."

William went on to add, "Just a word of warning. The Don was a scoundrel and virtually a pauper, but we must be careful about what is said in Lisbon. He was still part of the aristocracy here, and they would not take it kindly should we start making accusations. He received the justice that he richly deserved, so if you agree, we will keep this to ourselves for now."

Choundry could see that there was little to be gained by spreading the story and much goodwill that could be lost should certain people take umbrage. He readily agreed that they should keep the story to themselves if possible.

A little later, Andy and Edward went to move the two men's belongings from the ship they'd arrived on, and they had been able to secure their old lodgings in the Inn that was close by. Choundry and William sat enjoying a few quiet moments when William started in by saying, "As I mentioned earlier, there are a few business-related items to discuss. The first is that your investments continue to grow at an admirable rate. Both you and your brother are becoming very wealthy men. Another thing I think that we need to discuss and strategize on is that I fear that tensions between England and France are about to boil over again. I have pulled much of our shared funds from shipping and placed it into more secure investments until we discover whether we will see another war. If war does happen, it will ruin many merchants as ships are seized by the enemy or appropriated for the Crown's use. We have many investments now and many funds to put to use. I am afraid that I will be needing your services again to help decide where we should place our assets for the most good. For that, we must wait until you and Andy are much rested and you have a chance to renew acquaintances."

The last remark was said with a slight sparkle in William's eye.

He continued, "The other matter that I would like to discuss is one that I wish you not to feel compelled to agree to, as it is purely up to each man what charity they give to others. I am speaking of the goods that were brought back on the *Fair Wind*. The original goods shipped with Captain Barth were no longer there, of course, but the ship returned with a hold bursting with valuable cargo from America, including bales of tobacco and cotton, along with an American whiskey that is much sought after back home. I would like to propose that the cargo be sold and that the profits from the journey be given to the widows and families of the men who were slain. I'd not see any family thrown into poverty while I profit from their loss." Choundry agreed immediately and thanked his friend for the gesture, as Captain Barth's loss had been weighing heavily on him as well.

Once they'd made this agreement and set a time to get together later to discuss the future, they started to both stand in preparation for parting. At that point, Edward and Andy came into the office, and Andy was carrying the unusual gun that had been taken from the giant slaver. William took one look at the gun and asked where in the world they had come across such a prize. Choundry told of how the man had shot him twice with the weapon at an amazing range and that he'd nearly done for him until Andy showed up to hamstring the man and then finish him off.

William caressed the stock of the gun and told Choundry, "This is what is called a long rifle by the Americans. I have only seen two of its like. It is said to be unequaled in accuracy due to the rifling and the unusual length of the barrel. Keep this with you, my friend. With the adventures that you get into, I can't imagine anyone who could use this weapon more."

With that, Choundry gave his leave and started toward the front of the store. As he passed the front desk, Edward called to him, "Before I forget, there has been one of your customers who has stopped here several times while you were gone. She keeps asking for some type of special candle that are well suited for a sconce in her window. She tells me that you had been able to order her just the right type but that she has used them all up and is in need of more. She left me a note and asked if it would be given to you upon your return. Choundry took the note and tried not to notice the smile on Edward's face.

Choundry and Andy went to their lodgings and rested through the remainder of the day, supping as the evening grew dark. Choundry told Andy that he would be back later but that he wished to take a walk in the evening. Making his way up the road, he eventually found himself outside of a familiar building. As hoped, there was a small light glowing in a certain window, and when Choundry lightly rapped on the window pane, he heard movement inside. A moment later, the door creaked open, and Maria's lovely face looked out to quickly become wreathed in a smile. She motioned him in, and when he stood in her room, she held him close, tilting her head back, and then they kissed with great passion.

Once Maria had a moment to catch her breath, she reached up to tenderly touch the new scar on Choundry cheek and forehead, "Ah, my brave adventurer, what have you been up to? I must hear it all after we've had a chance to get to know each other again."

With that, Choundry bent down to resume another passionate kiss, but Maria broke free for a moment, "But first, I must extinguish that candle. Since you left, I have used all of the candles in the house, and my servants have purchased most of those available in town. Until I can find more to purchase, you will have to stay here with me, at least until we get to know each other again...."